PRAISE FOR ROBERT AIELLO's WORK

SHADOW IN THE MIRROR:

"Robert Aiello's second novel of suspense is as sleek and mesmerizing a thriller as you are likely to read this year. An uncompromising page-turner, SHADOW IN THE MIRROR revisits the intriguing world of magic and mentalism with Mr. Aiello's principled, engaging hero Grant Montgomery. ...Deft misdirection, clever sleight of pen and a heart-pounding flourish make this a compelling read that will keep you up well past midnight. Robert Aiello's talent is no illusion. I was hooked from the very first page."

Richard Montanari, bestselling author of THE VIOLET HOUR and KISS OF EVIL

"...Robert Aiello spins a compelling yarn starring an attractive celebrity mentalist as the good guy and a luscious evil twin as the bad girl. Add in a sadistic gangster with an ice pick, several dashes of poison, and a macabre buried clue, and you have a fine read in a classic mode. I can't wait to see the movie!"

Christine Andreae, bestselling author of SMOKE EATERS and GRIZZLY

"You'll like SHADOW IN THE MIRROR, its suspense and complex plot. Grant Montgomery is a great character—empathetic, smart, and fun to read about..."

Barbara D'Amato, bestselling author of GOOD COP, BAD COP and past president, Mystery Writers of America

"...his second book featuring retired mentalist and entertainer Grant Montgomery is a solid followup to his debut (THE DECEIVERS)...Aiello's plot is compelling."

Pittsburgh Tribune-Review

"Aiello keeps things engrossing and moving at a fast pace...you'll find an interesting hero (in Grant Montgomery)..."

Pittsburgh Post-Gazette

"Robert Aiello takes a plot and characters that are very real and creates a story that keeps us in suspense. Just when I thought I had it figured out and began guessing what was going to happen next, he fooled me. ...Grant Montgomery is fast becoming one of my favorite fictional characters and I can see him right up there with Dirk Pitt. ...Needless to say, I can't wait for the next one."

Diane Morgan, Editor, New Book Reviews.com

"Extremely evil antagonists provide plenty of suspense throughout the book. The killer is revealed half way through the story, which creates some intense moments...if you have not read Aiello's first book (THE DECEIVERS), don't despair. SHADOW IN THE MIRROR works well as a stand-alone. However, you may wind up craving the first book in the series anyway!"

The Romance Reader's Connection

"This is a fast-moving story; well-written with excellent characterizations; full of suspense and intrigue."

MyShelf.Com

"...the book provides a very good read and some true suspense. ...real chills along the way...SHADOW IN THE MIRROR is an enjoyable nail-biter of a book. Rating: Very Good."

Curled Up with a Good Book

THE DECEIVERS:

"The Deceivers is a strong suspense drama that never eases off the throttle until the climax is completed. ...Robert Aiello shows he has the right stuff to become a major player in the suspense genre."

The Midwest Book Review

"...readers will find themselves thrilled with who gets their just deserts...for author Aiello has done justice to developing Montgomery and the rest of the cast of players in this first, and most interesting, tale of suspense."

ForeWord Magazine

"In...this fast-paced suspense novel—the author's debut as a fiction writer—Aiello's succinct, page-turner style features cliff-hangar chapter conclusions...Grant Montgomery is destined for a long shelf life...Aiello wields words with power, and the descriptive narrative surrounding murders is unsettling."

Pittsburgh Tribune-Review

"The story line is fast paced and exciting...Grant is a great character deserving of future starring roles..."

Harriet Klausner, top reviewer for Amazon.com

THE DESPERATE HOURS

by Robert Aiello

The Desperate Hours

Published by Hats Off Books™
610 East Delano Street, Suite 104, Tucson, Arizona 85705 U.S.A.
www.hatsoffbooks.com

Publisher's Cataloging-in-Publication
(Provided by Quality Books, Inc.)

Aiello, Robert.
The desperate hours / by Robert Aiello.
p. cm.
LCCN 2005920717
ISBN 1587364484

1. Magicians--Fiction. 2. Suspense fiction.
I. Title.

PS3551.I334D47 2005 813'.54
QBI05-800210

In memory of Terry, whose Irish heart is still smiling.

CHAPTER ONE

The man with thick eyeglasses had been stalking her for nine days. He had to be certain of her daily routine, so that when the time came, he would make no mistakes. He stationed himself in front of her apartment building hour after hour, trailing her day and night whenever she left the building. Staying as connected as her shadow, yet invisible.

Friday, 7:30 A.M. This was the tenth day. He had been waiting for an hour in a rented car parked a half block from The Halifax apartment building, where she lived and worked in Pittsburgh's Golden Triangle, the nucleus of the city.

Suddenly he spotted her.

Colette Hershfield greeted the doorman and walked out of the building.

His heart began to race. He was aware that his heart pumped like a piston when he saw her for the first time each morning. He quivered as if he had been exposed to a sudden chill. The mere sight of her could do that to him. A sweet excitement that came from tracking her while she remained unaware of her pursuer. He watched her, observing the outline of her legs against her skirt as she walked, the movement of her breasts as she breathed. He smiled. But his smile was rooted in years of nurturing his smoldering hatred, years of anticipating how he would get even. Now his heart hammered with the realization that soon his revenge would come to fruition.

Her auburn hair at shoulder length swayed in rhythm to her stride as she strolled through the plaza adjacent to The Halifax. She wore dark chocolate-brown pants and a teal turtleneck sweater that caressed her body as she moved, leaving no doubt about her physical attributes. Colette was going for her usual morning walk.

When she was about fifty feet in front of him, he got out of the car and started to follow her. He strolled along the street, wearing a smile, as if he were enjoying the clear morning. His lenses magnified his eyes to the size of eggs, out of proportion with his lean face. But behind the glasses and the deceptive smile, his eyes were cold, and he never took them off the woman he was following.

She walked alone, always in the morning. If only she had walked at night, he thought, taken a different route, somewhere remote, rather than the city streets, then he would have a better opportunity. But it couldn't be done in broad daylight in the heart of the city. Even so, he knew he was close to making a decision.

With each day, he grew more confident of her routine. He estimated that in forty or forty-five minutes, she would return to her apartment building where she worked as a public relations consultant who owned her own business.

The stalker followed her on Liberty Avenue past the Gateway Center office buildings to Smithfield Street. He watched her as she stopped occasionally to review some of the fall fashions displayed by chic mannequins in department store windows. When she lingered at one of the windows admiring an ankle-length silk robe, he knew she was envisioning herself wearing it. And he began to tremble slightly when he also imagined the sleek fabric enveloping her body, as if he were sharing an intimate moment with her.

She aroused him, but Colette Hershfield was not his ultimate prey. She was merely a means to an end. The real target was her lover, Grant Montgomery, the man who had fired him more than fifteen years ago when he still had a career as the agent of the world's leading mentalist. When he still had a family, still had a future. Now all of that was gone. It was Montgomery's fault, and the mentalist was going to pay dearly for it. The stalker was going to see that Montgomery lost the one person he loved most in this world. Just like he had lost everything.

Colette ambled on to Grant Street, then over to Fort Pitt Boulevard, where she met a frail, silver-haired woman she obviously knew, chatted briefly with her, then headed back toward the Point, the tip of Pittsburgh where three rivers merged. With every step she took, he remained a half block behind. He adjusted his heavy glasses, but he had no difficulty seeing her.

She finally reached the Point and walked leisurely through Point State Park, inhaling deeply, drinking in the rich morning air. She stopped for a minute to admire the flashing play of sun on the blended rivers of the Monongahela, the Allegheny, and the Ohio, then continued toward the Gateway Center office complex. He sensed that the morning was warm and comforting to her. Finally, she returned to The Halifax forty minutes after she began her walk, just as he expected. Colette Hershfield stopped to talk for a minute with the elderly doorman as she did most mornings, then went into the building to begin her day's work.

He knew that most days she worked alone in her apartment. Clients rarely met with her there. She usually had meetings with them at their places of business. However, artists, printing representatives, and other suppliers she worked with did meet with her in the building, but only occasionally. He also knew that most of her evenings were spent with Grant Montgomery, either in her apartment or in his Mount Washington home.

He decided to stake out The Halifax for the rest of the day, then sat in his car, watching the window of her apartment on the fifth floor. For hours. And after observing her all this time, as sure as he could ever be of her behavior pattern, the stalker confirmed his decision. He would have preferred to do it late at night, outdoors in a secluded area where a scream couldn't be heard. But after ten days of dogged tracking, he knew he would not have such an opportunity. So the man with heavy glasses and cold eyes would have to seize the one chance he did have.

He would act when she was most vulnerable. When she was in her apartment alone.

Grant Montgomery smiled at the woman he had been dating for more than a year. "Do you think you'll ever finish decorating your office, or are you always going to find something to change?" He eased his six-foot-four-inch frame into one of the country-style wicker chairs surrounding her kitchen table. Grant had dark brown hair, a touch of gray at the temples, and heavy eyebrows that seemed to intensify his gaze. He was in his mid-forties, and kept his slender body in good shape. He unconsciously traced with his thumb the one-inch scar on the left side of his chin, where he had been hit by a piece of shrapnel when he served in Vietnam.

Colette Hershfield laughed. "Just like a man, expects everything to be done overnight. I'm just tired of that lighting fixture. Ever since I converted the room into my office, that overhead light seemed to be out of place. I want something more stylish to fit in with the rest of the furniture." When her mother, a prominent Pittsburgh socialite, had died more than a year ago, Colette decided to have her mother's bedroom converted to an office where she could run her own public relations consulting practice. Being the sole heir of a family fortune, Colette didn't need to work, but she was only in her mid-thirties and wanted to keep active.

She had the room completely redecorated by an interior decorator who, after completing the job, had become one of her clients. The office was furnished in cherrywood furniture, including its enormous desk, L-shaped computer station, bookcase, and file cabinet. A round glass conference table with four deep green upholstered chairs were in one corner of the room. Specially made wood blinds matched the furniture, which was enhanced by a light gold carpet. She was pleased with all of it, except the hanging pendant light, which the decorator referred to as an accent piece. Colette didn't think it fit with the new decor of the room. She was now having it replaced with a more modern fixture.

"I made the decision to do it a few days ago when I was taking my morning walk," she said, "and I'm glad I did. The maintenance man will be through installing it in a few minutes, so just cool your heels."

Grant laughed. He had dated her ever since he retired from show business as a mentalist and returned to Pittsburgh two years ago. At the time, Grant worked with his old friend, Tom Santucci, assistant chief in charge of investigations for the Pittsburgh Detective Bureau, in cracking a phony psychic scam in which Colette's mother had been a victim. That's how he had met Colette. And he was instantly attracted to her.

He observed her now as if he were seeing her for the first time. She was five-foot ten, slender with hazel eyes. She usually wore her hair at shoulder length or in a braid, but lately she was experimenting with different hairstyles. Today it was pulled back into a bun. She had eyes that could penetrate your soul, but she often attributed that quality to Grant, saying, "You have eyes that make a person's life an open book."

He smiled, thinking of all they had in common. Their love of jazz and classical music. Their preferences in art and literature. Their ability to still enjoy the old-fashioned pleasure of a sunset or to wake naked in each other's arms in the middle of the night, listening to the steady drumbeat of a rainfall. Together, they enjoyed a wide range of interests, but there was one subject they didn't discuss. Her divorce. Colette had been hurt deeply by a husband who had cheated on her when they lived in San Francisco. The memories were still painful for her, and Grant had never pressed her to reveal any of the details, confident that Colette would tell him about it when she was ready.

Even though more than three years had passed since her divorce, she still needed time to distance herself from the experience. When Colette loved, she loved totally, unconditionally. And when that love was betrayed, it wounded her as gravely as if she had been felled by gunfire. Perhaps worse, because her trauma was slower to heal than a bullet wound. She had not dated for a year following her divorce, then began dating several men, but no one steady until she met Grant.

Colette poured coffee for both of them, and they sat at her kitchen table with the morning sun filtering through the sheer curtains, glazing the room in a honey-gold hue. "You know, I think it's great that you consented to do the benefit performance for Children's Hospital. I know it wasn't an easy decision for you."

"I promised myself I'd never perform again," he said. "Too many people take it seriously, and are more than willing to believe I'm psychic. That's one of the reasons I got out of the business in the first place. But since I'm not doing this for money, I haven't broken my promise to myself."

"I'm glad you decided to do it," she said. "What changed your mind?"

Grant took a sip of coffee and leaned forward on the table. "Oh, primarily because it's for a great cause. The money we raise will go toward helping a lot of kids who, God only knows, need help. That, plus the fact that I guess this is my way of giving something back to the city where I grew up." *Or trying to make amends for a highly lucrative career based on deception,* he thought.

He lowered his eyes and remained silent for a moment, toying with the coffee cup.

"What time did you say your performance starts?" she asked.

He was aware that she knew the answer. "Eight, Wednesday at the Benedum Center," he answered. "The show should be over by nine-thirty. Then they're having the buffet and cocktail reception at ten at the Hilton. Most of Pittsburgh's elite will be on hand. That's where we'll raise most of the money. Incidentally, I have a front-row seat for you. Why don't I pick you up at seven-thirty?"

Colette shook her head. "No, Grant. I remember you telling me that you used to mentally prepare yourself for an hour or so before each performance, and I don't think you should change that just to pick me up. It's sweet of you to ask, but I'm a big girl and I can get to the theater by myself."

That was another quality about her he loved—her consideration. "No problem," he said. "I really don't need much preparation time."

She shot him a sideways glance. "Yes, you do. You haven't performed in about two years, and although I know you'll be sensational as always, I don't want you to change your routine for me."

"Okay, if you insist," he said. "But remember that the show is only two days away and, as busy as you are, I'll still expect you to be on time—even without my chariot."

"Are you kidding?" she said. "The world's leading mentalist comes out of retirement for a special performance, and I wouldn't miss a minute of it. Do you realize that other than seeing you on TV regularly, this will be the first time I've seen you do a live performance? I never thought I'd have the opportunity."

Grant smiled. "After the performance, you might wish you never had the opportunity."

"Baloney. Don't give me this false modesty stuff. I've read your reviews, remember? Not to mention the fact that I think all show business people, retired or not, must be real egomaniacs at heart," she said, smirking.

Grant feigned a hurt look, trying to suppress a smile. "Well, if that's the way you're going to be, then I'll just leave and sulk all day." He couldn't contain the smile any longer. "I'd best be on my way so we can both get some work done."

They rose from the kitchen table. "What are you up to today, mister retired person?"

Grant smoothed his tie. "Working out a few remaining details for the show. Good performances require a lot of advance planning."

"I'm sure." She accompanied him to the front door. "How are the ticket sales doing?"

"The Benedum is sold out as of yesterday."

She arched her eyebrows. "That's terrific. Retired or not, you still have a lot of fans out there. I know you're going to be a knockout."

He reached out and ran his hands lightly up and down the sides of her arms. "Why don't I pick you up tonight about seven? I thought we'd do Chinese, if you're in the mood. Jimmy Tsang's, okay?"

"Sounds wonderful."

He placed his arms around her and drew her closer. Her warmth seemed to engulf him as their bodies pressed against each other. They kissed, and his thoughts flashed back to a night not long ago when he was lying next to her, hearing her soft moans as she responded to his touch. "Tonight at seven," he said.

Grant left her apartment, and took the elevator to the underground garage of The Halifax, where the management allowed him to park at Colette's request. As he drove out, he appreciated that Colette didn't expect him to escort her to his benefit performance. He actually could use the time to mentally prepare himself, regardless of what he told her. In fact, he needed it now more than ever.

He hadn't performed in more than two years. Another performance was the last thing he ever expected to do. But when he received the letter from Children's Hospital asking for his help, he didn't have the heart to refuse. To give another performance—for a good cause or not—he would have to reach into that part of his psyche that he had sealed off more than a year ago, wanting to forget the memories associated with it. Now he had to open that door again and reenter a world of deception that had fooled so many people who thought him psychic in spite of his denials. A world of fame that two years ago drew him into a tragic police case, ending in the death of a kidnapped ten-year-old boy whose mother thought Grant's psychic powers could divine the boy's whereabouts and save her son. But Grant had failed, unable to convince the mother that he had no such powers.

When her son was found murdered, Grant had blamed himself for the boy's tragic death, fearing that the police's theory was true, that the boy's abductors had panicked and killed him when they learned that the man billed as the world's greatest mentalist was brought into the case. He had retired from show business then, vowing never to do another performance. Now—for a good cause, he told himself—he had agreed to go back to the stage, to that world of deception he had relinquished, wondering if the end really justified the means.

Grant's hands felt clammy on the steering wheel of the Lamborghini. He glanced into the rear-view mirror, but he was oblivious to the traffic behind him. All Grant Montgomery saw were the beads of perspiration on his forehead.

After Grant left, Colette went into her office, where Frank, the maintenance man, was stepping down from his ladder. He had completed his work in replacing the pendant with recessed lighting.

"That looks a lot better," she said. "Even gives better light."

"I think so, too," he said. "I checked everything out for you. No problem with voltage. Everything's copasetic."

"Thanks, Frank."

The maintenance man folded his stepladder. "If you don't mind my asking, Miss Hershfield, that was Grant Montgomery in here, wasn't it?"

Colette smiled. "One and the same."

"I don't want to sound star-struck," he said, "but do you think you could get his autograph for me one of these days and have him sign it 'To Frank'? My family would get a kick out if it." He dropped his gaze, appearing embarrassed. "I would've asked earlier, but I really wasn't sure it was him. I didn't want to interrupt you." He picked up his toolbox and smiled.

"I'd be happy to do that for you," she said, suspecting that he really wanted the autograph for himself. "And you shouldn't have hesitated to ask him."

He lifted his ladder, and walked with her to the front door. "Well, sometimes those stars don't like to be bothered," he said. "I've read where some of them even get nasty with their fans."

"Grant isn't that type of person, Frank. He's a fine man who's very accommodating. He hasn't forgotten his roots.

That's why he's living here now, rather than in Hollywood. Pittsburgh's his home town, you know."

"I know. Thanks, again," he said. "Let me know if you have any problem with the light."

Colette opened the door and smiled as he left the apartment, his thin frame weighted down by his toolbox in one hand and his ladder in the other. Frank was always pleasant, and she was often amused by his shyness. That was just part of his charm. But she wondered how he could work with electrical equipment and function as a general fix-up man when he obviously had poor eyesight. He wore such thick glasses.

CHAPTER TWO

For the past half-hour, Sam Kassler had sat in his office, debating with himself whether or not to make the phone call. If he called her again, she might refuse him just as she had done each time he called during the past two months. But if he didn't call, he would have no opportunity with her at all. He looked at the phone on his desk as if it were an instrument of defiance. Then his eyes seemed to be drawn past the phone, past the two red leather chairs in front of his desk to the silver-framed photograph of his wife and daughter on the credenza against the wall.

What would they think of him now if they knew what he was planning? The only person he really cared about was his nine-year-old daughter. Emily was everything in life he ever wanted, everything he now lived for, everything good that came or ever would come from his relationship with his wife, Blanche. That ungrateful, nagging bitch who was never satisfied, always driving him to make more money, to buy a better house in a better neighborhood. Always pushing him to associate with more influential people, to obtain a higher position with Marshall, Sterns and Nobel, Inc., the stock brokerage firm where he'd worked for the past seven years—day and night—and where he had risen to his current position as executive vice president. And still it wasn't enough for her. Nothing was ever enough for her. Everything he did, he did for Emily, or so he told himself. Yet he knew that was only partially true. It was Blanche's constant nagging that drove him to his limit, beyond which, he told himself, he could take no more. But he always did. Somehow she continually managed to stretch his endurance to new limits, unexplored regions of his psyche where he treaded on ground that was mined with danger. For his wife, he had nothing but contempt that eventually converted to hatred. She wasn't even attractive to him anymore. Blanche had let herself go with too much liquor and too much food. She indulged herself with every pleasure, every whim. He had even suspected that she was unfaithful to him. But he couldn't prove it. If he ever caught her with anyone...but she was too clever for that.

At fifty-one, Sam Kassler looked older than his years with hair almost totally gray, sagging dark skin under his eyes, and thirty extra pounds of weight he had put on his five-foot, seven-inch frame during the past five years. He attributed his aging appearance to the grueling, unwanted lifestyle his wife imposed on him. At first, he would lie awake at night, thinking about divorcing her. And when he finally summoned the courage to ask her for a divorce, she didn't even seem hurt.

She merely laughed in his face.

She would never give him a divorce, and it was useless for him to try to reason with her. That's when his contempt for her flamed into hatred. That's when he began to lie awake at night, listening to her alcohol-labored breathing, no longer thinking about divorce, but about killing her. And the only reason he didn't go through with it was his daughter. His precious Emily. He couldn't bear to have his daughter hate him for killing her mother. And he could end up behind bars, perhaps never to see her again. So he gave up his thoughts of murder. He would go on living with his wife and daughter, go on being hounded by Blanche from whom there seemed to be no escape.

But he needed something more in his life. A way to release his frustration and anger. To get even with the shrew he was forced to live with. To experience again the soft touch of a woman.

But not just any woman.

It had to be the woman who came to dominate his thoughts until he was now totally captivated by her, the woman he had met six months ago at a cocktail party and later decided to hire as a consultant to his firm.

The phone, sitting there on his desk, seemed to loom twice its size. *God help me,* he thought, *I have to try again.* He picked up the receiver and punched in the numbers.

His heart quickened when he heard her soft voice. "Hershfield Public Relations. May I help you?"

"Colette, this is Sam Kassler."

"Hello, Sam. How are you?"

He noticed the sudden restraint in her voice. He feared she was going to refuse him again. He couldn't let that happen. Not this time.

"I'm fine," he said. "I've been on vacation for two weeks. That's why I haven't responded to your recommendations on the marketing plan. I still need a little time to review them."

"That's no problem. Did you go anywhere interesting on your vacation?"

He hesitated. "No, actually my wife and I just decided to relax at home."

She knows how hard I work, he thought. *She might think it strange that I didn't have the time to review her recommendations over the last two weeks.*

"Colette, I was wondering if you and I could get together to review your ideas on the program? If we met at your place, we could work uninterrupted." His own words sounded hollow and insincere, even to him.

"Well, I think it would be more productive if we waited until you reviewed the proposal first," she said, her tone polite, but with an unmistakable professional distance. "That way, you can formulate some questions and have an opportunity to show it to others to get their input as well, particularly your communications man. I think the rest of your management should feel they have some ownership in this. That way, they're less likely to throw up roadblocks when we're half way into the program."

She was right, but he knew that it was a stall, that she didn't want to be alone with him in her apartment. "I understand, but too many fingers in the soup at this stage wouldn't be wise," he said. "Too many people involved now would only confuse the issue. We can get everyone's input after you and I agree on the right approach."

"If that's how you want to proceed, that's fine with me," she said, "but I think it would be best if I met in your office. I'm undergoing some remodeling now and my place is a complete mess."

Another stall. He could feel his stomach begin to churn. "You know, Colette, we're going to put a lot of money into this program, including twenty-five thousand for your fee, so I want to make certain that we spend the money wisely." He let it sit at that for a moment. Her one-year contract with Marshall, Sterns and Nobel called for a total public relations budget of two hundred and fifty thousand dollars. But the thinly veiled threat was a desperate, useless attempt. He was well aware that Colette was independently wealthy, and didn't need the stock brokerage firm as a client.

"That's my objective, too," she said. "But I don't see why meeting at your office would cause us to spend the money unwisely."

"No, of course not," he said. "If you feel more comfortable, we can meet in my office. Colette, I ..." His hand began to tremble. "Well, I wonder if you and I could get together at your place for a drink? I don't care what your apartment looks like, but there are a few things that I'd like to discuss with you in private." He knew he sounded desperate. He held his breath, waiting for her answer.

"Sam, look, I don't want to insult you, but we've been all through this several times. I've told you that there's another man in my life, and I have a serious relationship with him. I'm not about to see anyone else, particularly a married man. I thought I made myself clear by now."

"Colette...I'd just like to be with you for a little while—"

"Sam, if this doesn't concern your business, I don't think it would be a wise move for either one of us."

He broke a pencil with his right hand, unaware that he was pressing the jagged edge of the wood into his palm. "I was instrumental in your getting my company as a client. Is this the thanks I get?"

"I'm sorry, Sam, but your company hired me for my professional counsel, and for nothing else. Marshall, Sterns and Nobel is a good account and I enjoy working on it, but if you and I are going to continue like this, it's not worth the hassle."

For the next few seconds, he heard only silence. A deafening, unbearable silence that made him want to put his hands over his ears, to crawl into a hole and never come out. But he couldn't let it go.

"Colette, listen to me—"

"Sam, please stop it, for your sake and mine."

He took a deep breath. "Am I that repulsive to you?" he asked.

"You're not repulsive, Sam, you're just too persistent. Perhaps that accounts for your success in business, but it's not going to bring you success with me. Now, we can forget about this conversation, and I'm perfectly willing to do that. But if you keep this up, you're going to force me to resign this account, and if your president wants to know why, I'll tell him the truth."

"Are you threatening me?"

"Absolutely not," she said. "I'm only telling you the way it is. You're a married man with a family. My interest in you is only professional, and that's the way it should be with you, too. Somehow you've lost sight of that, Sam, and I'm trying to give you a wake-up call."

"I've never been spoken to like that by any woman," he snapped.

"I'm sorry to be the one to break that record," she said, her tone still modulated, but firm. "I think it's best that we put this behind us and not pursue it any further." She paused for a few seconds. "Let's just forget about it and get back to business. What do you want to do about the marketing plan?"

He hung up without answering her.

Kassler sat at his desk humiliated, burning with anger, hating himself for having begged her, hating her more at the moment for having rejected him again. He put a quarter-of-amillion-dollar account in her pocket, and she had just treated him like he was some flunky. Like his wife treated him. But he still wanted Colette so desperately, he ached for her. He had fantasized so often about being with her, speaking softly to her, touching her, their bodies in union with each other as she accepted him passionately, wanting no other man except him. An adolescent fantasy, to be sure, but one that haunted him.

He slammed his fist on top of his desk so hard a sharp pain shot up to his shoulder.

Suddenly Sam Kassler began to shake, unaware that his passion for Colette Hershfield had become an obsession that was careening out of control.

Colette stepped out of the shower, dried herself and put on her terrycloth bathrobe. She felt fresh and alive, looking forward to her date that evening with Grant. She worked her hair with a blow drier for several minutes as the waves sprang back into place with each stroke of her brush.

With her hair dried, she walked into her bedroom and went directly to her walk-in closet. She wanted something special to wear. It wasn't a special occasion, but Grant was a special person. His homecoming took place with hardly any fanfare. But when she met him, she felt a flourish in her heart that might as well have been the heralding of a trumpet. Now she was finally with a man she could trust. He had made a difference in her life, and he did so with ease. He was sincere, unpretentious. Grant Montgomery was the kind of man who was at home dining with royalty at L'Arpege in Paris or eating a hot dog at Heinz Field, rooting for the Pittsburgh Steelers.

And yet Colette knew there was a part of Grant that he didn't share with anyone. A dark place where he fought his own demons in a private war. It had to do with his misgivings about his former profession as a world-renowned mentalist and with his experience in Vietnam. In the year they had been dating, he didn't talk much about those vestiges of his life, only making an occasional reference that indicated painful memories. But just as he didn't press her for all the details of her aborted marriage, she would not prompt him to fully open the door to that secluded corner of his psyche that seemed off-limits to her. There was still a little part of themselves they held back from each other.

She believed that someday they both would find that extra reserve of strength to share all their secrets. Until then, she didn't want to lose what she had in this man. Not ever.

Colette reached for the knee-length black dress with thin straps, flipped off the robe and stood naked, holding the dress against her body, admiring it in the full-length mirror framed inside the closet door. A little dressy, perhaps, but they might stop at a cocktail lounge later. She smiled. Grant will like this one.

Jimmy Tsang's Restaurant on Center Avenue in Shadyside was one of Grant's favorites. The atmosphere was strictly oriental, from the waiters and waitresses to the sculptures of Chinese dragons, demons and symbols decorating the walls. A little garish for some tastes, Grant had conceded, but the food was exceptional. The restaurant was packed with diners.

Grant studied the woman sitting next to him. The flickering light of the small glass-enclosed candle on the table highlighted the luster of her hair, which she wore at shoulder length. Her black dress with thin straps enhanced her creamy smooth shoulders and revealed the beginning of her cleavage, just enough to be enticing. Colette was gifted with a rare combination of sophistication and innocence that could bewitch him. She smiled and he was lost.

"A penny for your thoughts," she said.

"They're worth much more."

"What makes you think so?"

He returned her smile. "Because they're of you."

She cocked her head slightly. "Are they good thoughts?"

"What do you think?" he said.

The waiter came to their table and served the Chardonnay they had ordered.

Colette lifted her glass. "I have a toast." Her hazel eyes held his for a moment. "To the success of your performance at the Benedum. I can hardly wait the forty-eight hours to see you on stage."

Grant lifted his glass to meet hers. They both took a sip of wine and placed their glasses on the table. "To tell you the truth, I'm really not looking forward to it."

She nodded. "I know you're not, Grant. But I love you for putting your personal feelings aside, because you'll raise a lot of money for Children's Hospital. And that's what's important." She paused and smiled. "I really am excited to see you perform in person."

"I'm excited to see you anytime," he said. "You know, we could have a lot more time together if you and I decided to play house." It wasn't the first time he had suggested they live together, but he knew Colette still was being cautious. She shook her head. "Oh Grant, I know, but I just don't think that now is the time."

He took another sip of wine. No point in pressing her. Living together became a commitment she wasn't ready to make. Not yet. "I understand. There's no rush."

She looked at him for several seconds. "I hope you don't take my reluctance as a rejection. You know it isn't."

He reached out and placed his hand on top of hers. "I know. And I hope you know something, as well."

She smiled with the confidence of a woman who knew she was deeply loved. "I do, but I like to hear it anyway."

"Not unless you promise to make it up to me," Grant said, feigning a hurt expression. "If you're going to torture me so wantonly by refusing to live with me, then you have to do something to ease the pain." He looked at her with playful eyes. "And I get to select what that something is."

She had that impish look, the one he knew so well. "I hesitate to ask what you have in mind, but I think I know," she said. "When do you demand payment?"

"No time like the present."

She snickered. "Right here in the restaurant in front of everyone?"

Grant shrugged, pretending to be indifferent. "What's so terrible about that?" He smiled. "No one is going to hear you say 'I'm sorry.'"

She leaned her head back and laughed. "You got me that time."

He laughed with her. A second later, he saw the smile melt from her lips, and she looked at him for a long moment, her eyes misting.

"I *am* sorry," she said, "and I love you."

The maintenance man, who had assumed the name of Frank Hutchinson, sat at a corner table in Jimmy Tsang's Restaurant, observing Grant and Colette. The two of them seemed so preoccupied with each other that he was sure he wouldn't be spotted. Even if Colette did see him, it made no difference. He could make the excuse that his wife was visiting a relative, and he decided to eat out, rather than face his own cooking. And Montgomery would never recognize him. It had been more than fifteen years since Montgomery had seen him and, during that period, his appearance had changed totally. Now he was bald and wore thick glasses and was twenty-five or so pounds lighter. He wasn't even the same man, anymore. He had lost his wife, his family, his career. He couldn't get a job as an agent after Montgomery fired him for stealing money from him. After that, his soiled reputation spread throughout the entertainment industry, and he was ruined. So he started to drink heavily, and went from one menial job to the other until he finally realized that if he didn't stop drinking, he would kill himself. He did stop, and decided that rather than kill himself with alcohol, he would pull himself together long enough to kill Grant Montgomery, the man he held responsible for his misfortune.

But later he realized there was a punishment better than death, much better—take from Montgomery what he loves most, his girl. Just as he had lost his wife and son, neither of whom could take the shame he'd brought on them and eventually left him, he would make Montgomery lose someone close to him. He'd made that decision two years ago, and it had taken him a year to track down Montgomery and to get a maintenance job in The Halifax, where he'd worked for the past seven months. His two-week vacation had ended last Friday, but it had given him sufficient time to learn Colette's daily routine.

He continued to observe Grant and Colette, occasionally dropping his gaze and glancing around the restaurant, careful not to get caught staring at them.

The two of you seem so nice and cozy, he thought. *Montgomery, you son of a bitch. I'll make you know what it feels like to lose everything. I have a real treat in store for you.*

The waiter came to his table, and he gave his order. Then he adjusted his heavy, dark-framed glasses, and looked at Colette. He remembered what he had overheard in Colette's apartment when he was installing the light fixture. Montgomery wouldn't be picking her up Wednesday night. The mentalist would be out of the way, getting ready for his performance, and she would be alone. That was perfect. Having access to her apartment as a maintenance man had its advantages.

"Do you want a nightcap?" she said. They were in her apartment, and she had just turned the light on in the living room. They had decided to forgo the cocktail lounge.

Grant sat on the sofa, facing the fireplace. "Why don't you come over here and leave the light off?" he said.

"Chinese food must be an aphrodisiac to you," Colette said. She kicked her shoes off, went to the sofa and sat next to him.

He put his arm around her. "If that was a real fireplace, we could start a fire. And if you had a bear-skin rug in front of it, we could really have some fun. But you don't have either of those things."

She smiled. "You're so denied and abused. I wonder how you can get through the next day."

"I couldn't get through it without you." He drew her closer. The phone rang.

"Damn," she said. She got up and went to the phone in the kitchen. "Hello...hello. Who's calling, please?" She waited a few seconds, then hung up and walked back into the living room.

"Wrong number?" Grant asked.

Colette furrowed her brow. "I don't know. This is the fifth or sixth time that's happened, and I always get the call at night." She sat next to him. "I can hear someone breathing on the other end of the line." She shivered, nestling close to him, and he felt the warmth of her body. He inhaled deeply and her scent of lilac flooded his brain.

Grant took her hand in his. "I wouldn't worry about it. If it continues, we can report it to the phone company."

She stared into space for several seconds, still frowning. "Grant, there's something I haven't told you. I didn't think it was important...but now I'm not sure."

"What?"

She sat up and turned to him. "One of my clients has been trying to date me. I've refused him several times over the last couple months, but he's very persistent. Says he just wants to go out with me. To make matters worse, he's married. I told him at least a half dozen times that I don't date married men and that I'm keeping steady company with someone, although I didn't mention your name. But I can't get him to take no for an answer."

Grant unconsciously ran his thumb over the scar on his chin. "Who is this Don Juan?"

"Sam Kassler. He's executive vice president of Marshall, Sterns and Nobel. That's the stock brokerage firm I picked up six months ago."

"You think this is the same guy who's making the phone calls?"

"I don't know. I don't want to let my imagination run away with me, but I'm beginning to suspect that maybe it is him. Maybe he's checking up on me."

He patted her hand. "It could also be a prank, some kid who thinks it's fun to annoy or scare people."

She seemed preoccupied. "Maybe, but I'm starting to worry about it."

"Look, I don't want to interfere with any of your clients," Grant said, "but if this SOB is bothering you, I can have a nice little talk with him. And I'll guarantee you, he'll get the picture."

Colette shook her head. "No, I appreciate the offer, but I don't think that would help the situation. I've threatened to report him to his management if he keeps this up, so I'm hoping he'll stop. But now, with these calls late at night...well, I just don't know."

"If they continue, you let me know," he said. "I can arrange through Tom Santucci to have them traced."

"Thanks, I will."

Grant studied her for a moment. "I will have that nightcap. I think one would do you some good, too." He went into the kitchen and a minute later returned with two snifters of brandy. He handed her one. "Drink this. It'll steady your nerves."

She took a sip. "Mmm, this is just what I needed."

He sat next to her and, with his thumb and forefinger on her chin, turned her head toward him. Then he kissed her gently. "And that's just what I needed."

They sat in silence for several minutes, sipping their brandy. Finally he said, "I'm sorry you have to put up with that jerk and this business of the mysterious phone calls. I don't know if the two are related, but don't let it get you down. If this Kassler character continues to bother you, don't hesitate to report him to his company. You gave him fair warning. They'll deal with him, believe me. They don't want a sexual harassment suit on their hands. Companies rarely win those."

"I know. But if Kassler's getting weird and not thinking straight, I don't know if my threat will stop him."

"If it doesn't, I will." He placed his brandy snifter on the coffee table in front of the sofa. He lifted her hand and kissed it. He wanted to stay with her, but he knew she was still upset by the phone call and might not be in the mood. "It's getting late," he said, "and I think you could use a good night's sleep. I'll call you tomorrow."

He rose and watched her turn out the lamp on one side of the sofa, then the one on the other side. They faced each other in semidarkness, bathed in the pale moonglow that sifted through the sheer curtains of the living-room window.

"Don't leave me tonight," she said softly.

The faint beam from the window draped the contours of her statuesque body in soft light and deep shadows.

"I'm not going anywhere," he said.

A lone figure sat in a car parked across the street from The Halifax, squinting through his thick glasses, looking at the living-room window of a certain apartment on the fifth floor. He knew that Grant Montgomery was there with Colette.

Then he saw two lights go out, one a few seconds after the other. He gritted his teeth, then smiled. He knew he wouldn't have to wait much longer. Wednesday night was less than forty-eight hours away.

CHAPTER THREE

"To what do we owe the honor?" Tom Santucci, assistant chief in charge of investigations for the Pittsburgh Detective Bureau, sat behind his oversized mahogany desk with his suit coat buttoned to hide his expanding waistline. He winked at Sergeant Emilio Vasquez, who was sitting in front of him. Santucci was in his mid forties and had a receding hairline, which left him with a exaggerated widow's peak.

"Don't act like you haven't seen me in a year," Grant said. He nodded to Vasquez. "How are you, Emilio?"

"Fine, Grant. How's the Lamborghini?"

"Tip-top," Grant said. "You can take it for a spin any time you want." Grant knew the sergeant admired the Lamborghini, so he let him drive it as often as he could spare the car. He looked at Santucci with the assurance of old friends who could walk in on each other without an appointment. "Am I interrupting anything?"

Santucci shook his head. "No, we were just finishing up. Bullshit paperwork. Have a seat." He rose from his chair and went to the makeshift kitchen in back of his desk. He poured a cup of coffee and handed it to Grant, then filled his own cup and one for Vasquez. "What's on your mind?"

Grant sat next to Vasquez, facing Santucci. "I need some advice, Tom. One of Colette's clients, some guy who's married, has been bothering her and he won't take no for an answer. He says he just wants to go out with her."

Santucci took a sip of his coffee. "Yeah, I'll bet."

Grant gave Santucci a knowing look. "She's not naive. She knows what's on the bastard's mind. The problem here is that she's also been receiving phone calls at night from someone who doesn't answer. That frightens her. She got one the other night when I was there. She's not sure, but thinks it might be him. She can hear whoever it is breathing."

Santucci nodded. "One of those. He's never said anything that was threatening or even suggestive?"

"No, he doesn't say a word."

Vasquez turned to Grant. "You said this guy who wants to date her is one of her clients. You know his name and where he works?" The Hispanic sergeant, who'd become a U.S. citizen about eight years ago, had a dark complexion, black wavy hair and a mole on his right cheek where he claimed that, as a little boy, he had been kissed by an angel when he was asleep. Vasquez loved to tell such stories. When any of the other detectives had asked him what made him so special to be kissed by an angel, Vasquez told them that the angel knew he was blessed at birth to live his life with a pure heart. When one detective asked him how he knew an angel kissed him if he had been asleep, Vasquez told him to go fuck himself. He was outspoken that way, but Santucci considered him to be one of the finest detectives in the bureau. Vasquez had once saved Grant's life, and all he ever wanted in return was a chance to drive Grant's Lamborghini.

"Sam Kassler," Grant said. "He's an executive vice president with a large brokerage firm in town."

"God," Vasquez said, "he sounds like someone who should know better. A big shot like that can buy all the screwing he wants."

Santucci shot a glance at Vasquez and cleared his throat.

Vasquez looked at Grant. "Oh, I'm sorry. I didn't mean anything by that."

"No offense taken," Grant said with a half smile.

Santucci ran his fingers through his thinning hair. "You want to know if there's anything we can do, right?"

"I know it's a little premature now," Grant said, "but if he continues to harass her and she continues to get these calls, I'd like to know if you can do anything about it."

Santucci scratched the back of his neck. "Frankly, not a hell of a lot. Not unless he's threatened her. There's an old saying that you can't blame a guy for trying, and that's basically all you've got here. As far as the phone calls are concerned, she can't prove it's him. It would be her word against his."

Grant leaned forward in his chair. "Can't you trace her calls?"

"Sure," Santucci said, "but weirdos like that are usually smart enough to call from a pay phone, or they don't stay on the line long enough to allow us to trace them." He paused for a second. "Before we initiate an actual trace, we can put a beep tone on her line so the caller thinks she's taping her calls. Sometimes that scares them off. I'm sure she has an answering machine, right?"

"Sure. Why?"

"Well, she could use the answering machine to screen her calls," Santucci said, "and record a bluff message on it that says her calls are being taped and monitored. That's an effective way to discourage a phone harasser." He locked his jaw for a second. "Of course, there are some legal ramifications to taping phone conversations, so she'd have to be careful about that. But usually, the law is lenient about it if a person is being harassed."

Grant shook his head. "I don't think she'd go for it, Tom. That type of message wouldn't be appropriate for someone who operates a business out of her home. It would generate a lot of questions from other clients who call her."

"Unfortunately true," Tom said. "Does she always get these phone calls around the same time?"

"Always late at night," Grant said. "This is about the fifth or sixth time it's happened."

Santucci sighed. "That indicates it's not just someone dialing the wrong number, but even that doesn't prove anything."

Grant took a sip of his coffee and grimaced. Santucci liked to make it strong. "She's already threatened to tell his employer, but if he's the guy making the phone calls, that hasn't stopped him."

Vasquez's eyes flashed. "Why don't you have your woman threaten to tell his wife? That might work. He might be a big shot at work, but I'll bet he's afraid his wife would cut his nuts off if she found out. Most Latin wives would."

Santucci looked at Vasquez. "Emilio, not every woman has hot Latin blood in her veins. She could be one of those tolerant, submissive wives, who looks the other way and pretends everything's wonderful."

"I don't know women like that," Vasquez said with a puzzled expression. "I only know women who love passionately and will kill you for infidelity."

Santucci and Grant exchanged glances, and Grant tried not to grin. "Well," Santucci said, "if threatening to tell his wife doesn't work, we could arrange to talk to him. We'd have to be careful not to accuse him of anything, but we could tell him we're investigating these phone calls and that Colette gave us his name, said that he was forcing his attention on her."

Grant folded his hands, tapping them to his lips. "He could always deny that, even claim she came on to him, and say that he knows nothing about the phone calls."

"True," Santucci said, "but you never know—a visit from the police just might scare him off. On the other hand, sometimes it provokes them, particularly if they don't have their head screwed on straight." He shrugged. "It's hard to tell, but this guy has a responsible job, and I doubt that he'd want to jeopardize his career. He'll probably get the message and stop bothering her, that is, if he's the one making the calls. We could check out his background to see if he has any prior arrest for this sort of thing, but I doubt it. He wouldn't have that kind of a job if he did."

"You're probably right," Grant said, "but it wouldn't hurt to check him out, anyway." He carefully placed his coffee mug on a coaster on the polished mahogany desk that Santucci treasured, a birthday gift from his family more than a decade ago. "I wonder, Tom." Grant looked off into space. "If Kassler's head is left of center where Colette is concerned, I wonder if *anything* will stop him."

Santucci leaned back in his chair and placed his hands on back of his head. "Well, if push comes to shove, Colette can always issue a complaint against him for harassment, and we can get a restraining order against him. But by then, things'll have gone a little too far with this guy."

Grant didn't respond. He was still staring into space, preoccupied.

"Did you hear what I said, Grant?"

Grant shifted his gaze to Santucci. "I heard you, but I'm not going to allow things to reach that point."

Santucci leaned forward and spread his fingers with his palms facing Grant. "Now hold on, fella. Don't let your imagination run away with you. Just because I said there isn't much we can do now, doesn't mean that our hands are completely tied. If things get worse, you come to me. Don't take matters into your own hands."

Grant picked up his coffee mug, took another sip and replaced the mug on Santucci's desk. "I will," he said.

Santucci looked at him. "You will what? Come to me or take matters into your own hands?"

Grant stood, about to leave, and winked at Vasquez. "Why don't you teach this guy how to make a decent cup of coffee."

Sam Kassler sat in silence at the dinner table, toying with the rare cut of roast beef on his plate. At the other end of the rectangular table, his wife, Blanche, relished each forkful of beef, and was working on her second helping of mashed potatoes made with extra butter by the young maid they employed, who also served as their cook. Their social calendar didn't allow them to eat at home often, but on those occasions when they did, they usually had little or nothing to say to each other.

Kassler looked up from his plate at the woman absorbed with her dinner. Blanche was in her early forties, but looked ten years older. Her body seemed to be forming small fat folds with increasing regularity over the last few years. Her face was fuller than it had ever been, and the mudpacks and expensive pampering treatments couldn't hide a double chin that was beginning to form. Her waist, once svelte, was now competing with the width of her hips. She was a brunette, who had her hairdresser dye her hair once a month, religiously, to hide the premature gray streaks growing from her temples. Her eyes were puffed, frequently bloodshot, but she compensated with expertly applied makeup. Struggling to retain her once youthful glamour, her beauty was now more of a memory than a reality. But a trace of it still remained.

Blanche kept a bottle of Merlot wine at her end of the table, and poured the remains of it into her Waterford glass. "You're being very quiet tonight," she said as if their silence was unusual.

"What's there to talk about?"

"Oh, lots of things," she said as she lifted the glass to her lips. "Like why you haven't received a promotion in a long time, particularly with younger men in your firm moving up the ladder." She took a sip of wine. "Do you often feel like you have to look over your shoulder? If you do, I can understand how someone your age would feel that way."

Her tongue was particularly sharp this evening. He didn't know why. He felt a familiar burning sensation rising from the pit of his stomach. "Looking over my shoulder isn't one of my concerns. It's looking in front of me at the dinner table that sickens me."

"Ah, the inevitable insult," she said, smiling. "The last refuge of the loser. Poor Sam. Tell me, how would you feel about reporting to a much younger man? With your career at a standstill, surely you must've thought about that."

He narrowed his eyes. Why was she goading him now? They had been all through this a hundred times. "I'm in no mood for your insults. If you've got something on your mind, spill it."

She took another sip of wine. "Well, it's just getting a little embarrassing at the ladies auxiliary when they ask about you, and I have to lie and tell them how well you're doing. I think they're beginning to realize that you're not going to be president of the firm, that it's over for you." She looked at him, raising her false eyelashes as if in wonderment. "Is it over for you, Sam?"

His hands beneath the table grabbed the napkin from his lap. He began to twist it.

She looked at him pouring venom from her eyes. "I asked you a question, Sam."

He twisted the napkin harder.

"With all your other failings, don't tell me you're becoming hard of hearing, as well." Blanche frowned, obviously faking concern. "That's a sign of old age, you know. I hope they haven't noticed that at the office."

Sam Kassler could no longer stand it. He jumped up and slapped the napkin on the table. "You bitch. You've been hounding me to get the presidency of my company for years, so that you can prance around in your social circles with a new air of superiority. You arrogant, egotistical bitch. I've given you everything, including the very food you're now stuffing your face with, and still you're not satisfied."

Blanche was smiling. "Really, Sam, to get this upset over your failings won't solve anything."

His face flushed. "Shut your goddamn mouth. Our marriage has been over with for a long time, and you know it. I want a divorce."

Blanche casually looked into her salad plate, removed a green olive with her thumb and forefinger and plucked it into her mouth. She pursed her lips as she chewed it. "Oh, we're going to start that again, are we? You already know the answer to that, and I'll thank you to keep your voice down so the maid doesn't hear you make a fool of yourself."

"The maid?" He stabbed the air with his finger, pointing at Blanche. "You don't give a goddamn what our daughter thinks of us, but you're worried about the maid."

Blanche took her napkin and dabbed the sides of her mouth. "Thank God Emily's at a pajama party tonight and can't hear your ranting and raving." She placed the napkin on the table and looked at him, her smile beginning to form again. "You'll really have to try much harder to improve yourself so that some day, your daughter can be proud of you. At nine years old, she shouldn't have to feel that her father is a loser."

Kassler stepped away from the table and started toward her. He opened and closed his right hand several times, forming a fist. He had never struck her before.

Dolores, the maid/cook, who overheard the argument, entered the room. She looked sheepishly at both of them, showing her youth and inexperience. "I'll clear the table if you're ready for dessert."

Kassler stopped, still staring at his wife, then glanced at Dolores. "Give her my portion," he said and stormed out of the room. He walked into the den next to the dining room and closed the sliding doors with the jarring impact of wood slamming against wood.

Sam Kassler's hands began to quiver. In a few seconds, he felt his entire body shaking, just like he did when Colette refused him.

There was only one way out. He knew what he had to do.

Frank Hutchinson lay awake most of the night, too excited to sleep. Now, at daybreak, his eyelids were heavy as he watched in a mental fog the start of sunrise from his bed that directly faced the window of his two-room flat in Brookline, where he'd lived for the past seven months. The sky was streaked with ribbons of crimson that began to melt with the first blush of light. For several minutes, he drifted in and out of a scarlet dream world, where the difference between twilight and dawn was indiscernible. Suddenly his eyes opened wide and he was fully awake again, energized. He felt his heart racing. He was exhilarated by the anticipation of what lay ahead. He rose from his bed, put on his glasses, and went to the window. The salmon-pink sky seemed like a huge dome that slowly opened to reveal ivory clouds against a low horizon. The sun had risen on a new day. But not just any day. This one was special.

It was Wednesday.

Hutchinson began to pace his bedroom in his briefs and the undershirt that was ripped under his left armpit. He wanted a cigarette. He went to the night table next to his bed only to find a crushed, empty pack by the ashtray. He swore under his breath. He searched the ashtray for a butt, found one that was little more than half smoked, and lighted it. The stalker inhaled deeply, feeling the rush of nicotine in his lungs, a cathartic that soothed the raw edge of his nerves for a few seconds.

Tonight he would take the first step in his plan to get even with Montgomery, who would be preoccupied at the Benedum Center. Tonight Colette would be alone in her apartment, getting ready to attend Montgomery's performance. The show was scheduled to start at 8 P.M. At precisely 7:15 P.M. he would strike.

Hutchinson smiled, pleased with his meticulous attention to every detail of the plan. The waiting was finally over. It was time to act. And he knew that once he took that first step, there was no turning back.

CHAPTER FOUR

Grant Montgomery found it difficult to pinpoint what caused him to break the vow he'd made to himself more than two years ago. Was it the letter from Children's Hospital asking for his help through a benefit performance? Was it the faces of innocent children in need that he saw when he visited the hospital? Or was it his own need to make retribution somehow for a lucrative career that was founded on deception and ended in tragedy? He thought he had put that last question behind him. Thought he had buried forever the painful memories of thousands of trusting faces in audiences all over the world that now haunted him like ghosts from a recriminatory past. Thousands of faces that dissolved into one face, the face of a mother who looked at him for a miracle to divine the whereabouts of her kidnapped son, a miracle that was not forthcoming. But those memories that he thought were long buried, no longer able to torment him, were merely locked within his own psyche, waiting for the key that would release them.

Was he about to use that key tonight?

He had to put it out of his mind. He had a show to do tonight, his first one in more than two years. Nearly twenty-nine hundred patrons had bought tickets to a one-time-only performance. They were waiting to see the man billed as the world's greatest mentalist come out of retirement for a final performance and, regardless of his own personal demons, he must not disappoint. He had taken care of every last detail required to perform the miracles of mind he would demonstrate tonight. Nothing would go wrong because he was a perfectionist in planning and execution. And in the unlikely event that something did go awry, he could handle any eventuality with precise timing and skill honed by years of experience.

His only stipulation to stepping on stage one last time was that all the proceeds from the performance, including his fee, be donated to Children's Hospital without deducting a nickel's worth of expenses for advertising, theater profit, or union labor by the stagehands. Everyone agreed. Even the food and liquor to be served at the $250-a-head reception at the Hilton were donated by the hotel.

Grant thought about Colette and how eager she seemed to see him perform live for the first time. She said she had been fascinated by his performances on TV. Having her in the audience would be comforting. He could glance down at her in the front row occasionally to see her reaction.

He checked his watch. 3:20 P.M. Time to go to the Benedum to make one last check of all the details, and then he would come back to his Mount Washington home by 6 P.M. for a light snack, a mental preparation for his performance, and a half-hour's rest before the show. He would call Colette later this evening, before he left for the theater. He didn't particularly like the idea of her going to the theater alone, but later at the reception they would be together.

If it weren't for the cocktail reception, Colette would have selected something less formal, but she decided that the long green velvet dress was suitable for the evening at the Benedum and the follow-up black-tie reception. Standing in her slip and bra, she turned the neck of the hangar and hung the dress on one of the closet doors. Colette went into the entrance hallway and looked at the grandfather clock. 6:10 P.M. Almost two hours before showtime. She would call Grant, take a quick shower, brush her hair, and then get into the dress, which she hadn't worn in several months. She had plenty of time.

Colette sat on the edge of her bed, picked up the phone on the end table, and dialed Grant's number. He answered after the third ring.

"Grant, I just wanted to wish you the best of luck tonight."

She heard the familiar deep voice that had been trained for stage projection. "Thanks, baby. I have a front-row seat for you."

"After a two-year absence, you must be nervous."

"Not really. I've done it before, you know."

She wondered if he was putting on an act for her sake. "I see you're in good spirits," she said, "so I know you're going to be wonderful."

"It'll be great to have you in the audience where I can look down and flirt with you. After the show, I'll meet you backstage. We'll go to the Hilton together. So don't go picking up any strange men on the way to the theater."

She spoke in a low, seductive tone. "If I see someone I'm attracted to, I'll just raise my dress to show a little calf and give him a come-hither stare."

"Maybe I should've arranged to have you picked up by a tank and escorted by several armed guards," he said with a smile in his voice.

"Too late now," she said. "Well, sweetheart, I have to get ready for what I know is going to be a great evening. Break a leg."

Colette hung up, still wondering if Grant was fighting himself over giving another performance. But she knew he couldn't refuse this one, regardless of his innermost feelings about taking to the stage again. His unselfishness was one of the reasons she loved him.

She undressed, went into the bathroom and turned on the shower, letting the string-thin jets of water beat against her body. The water massage was so relaxing that she stayed in the shower longer than usual. No need to rush. Finally, she stepped out of the shower, her hair and body dripping water on the bathmat next to the tub. After she dried herself, she took a fresh towel and massaged her head, removing the excess water from her hair. Then she put on her terrycloth robe and walked out of the bathroom in her bare feet.

Colette went into the foyer and looked at the grandfather clock. Its face was crowned by a moon dial, and the pendulum swayed from side to side hypnotically. 6:35 P.M. She still had plenty of time. She went back into the bathroom and dried her hair with a blow drier, then began brushing it. There was magic in the way her auburn hair began to take shape as she handled with masterly ease the brush in one hand and the hair dryer in the other.

After the reception ended, probably at midnight, she and Grant would come back to her apartment and relive the evening over a nightcap. Then they would make love. She smiled, looking at herself in the bathroom mirror that covered the wall above the vanity. But her smile did not reflect an egotistical admiration of her beauty. Her smile was rooted in the deep love she felt for the showman who had taken center stage in her heart two years ago.

In the basement of The Halifax building, the stalker crouched in darkness in a corner next to a haphazard pile of empty cardboard boxes used for storage. Frank Hutchinson wanted to remain unseen by the other two maintenance men, who were working the night shift on different floors of the building.

With the sleeve of his gray work shirt, he wiped the perspiration from his forehead. He flicked on his flashlight to check his watch. 6:55 P.M. At precisely 7:15 P.M. he would strike. Only twenty short minutes away. There wasn't anything particularly significant about the exact time he selected, except that he had to act before Colette left her apartment. And years ago, when he was Grant Montgomery's agent, he had learned the value of perfect planning and precise timing, the hallmarks of a Montgomery performance. Now Hutchinson would put that lesson to good use.

He was more exhilarated than he thought possible. He knew Colette was in her apartment alone. He wondered how she would respond when the moment came. They would be in darkness so he wouldn't be able to see her face. But he would be able to feel her body stiffen to the sudden shock of his hands on her. He shivered at the thought of touching her body, the body he had followed for ten long days. Hutchinson wondered if she would try to resist, to fight her way out of danger. That would be a natural reaction. But it would be useless. She would know what hell was like by the time he was done with her. More importantly, Montgomery would know by the time he was done with her. He had waited so long for this day, planned so carefully. Now it was here and the moment would soon be his.

Crouched in the dark, he smiled, aware that with each passing second he was closer to his goal. The master fuse box that controlled the lights to each apartment in the building was several feet above him. Colette would not be able to activate any of the switches in the fuse box in her apartment. He had seen to that when he was installing her new ceiling light. All he had to do was disengage the master switch to apartment 522, and Colette would be in darkness. Then the first step of his plan would be initiated. He moistened his lips with his tongue.

The ticking of his wristwatch seemed to be getting louder with each minute, like a synchronized drumbeat, as if it were trying to sound an alarm, to betray his whereabouts.

He flashed the light on his watch. 7:01 P.M. His heart was pounding wildly.

Only fourteen minutes left.

Colette had just completed using a curling iron on her hair. Now all she had to do was get dressed. Still wearing her terrycloth robe, she went into her bedroom and sat at her dresser. She dabbed a touch of perfume in back of her ears and on the sides of her neck. It was a few minutes past seven. The taxi was scheduled to pick her up in front of the building at 7:45 P.M. so she still had plenty of time.

She took off the robe, casually tossed it on the bed, and put on pantyhose, then her bra. She went to the closet and was about to take the dress off the hangar when the phone rang. Maybe it was Grant.

"Hello," she said in a tone alive with anticipation. But there was no answer.

"This is Colette Hershfield. Who's calling?"

Still no answer. Then she recognized the heavy breathing.

"Look, I'm getting sick and tired of your foolishness," she snapped. "Sam, if it's you, then please answer. If not, stop calling this number or I'll report it to the police and have my calls traced." She slammed the receiver, and stood there for a moment. She made a mental note to tell Grant about it. When these calls occurred in the past, she was frightened. Now she was angry. Enough was enough.

Suddenly Colette was aware that she was standing by the phone in only her pantyhose and bra and felt strangely embarrassed, as if the caller could see her half-dressed. She shook her head. *Stop being ridiculous.* She was letting the caller unnerve her.

Colette went back to the closet and slipped into the long velvet dress. To zip up the dress, she had to stretch her arm behind her back, then over her shoulder. This is where a man would come in handy, she thought. If she could bring herself to think of Grant, she would forget about the caller, whoever the creep was.

She studied herself in the full-length mirror, pleased that the dress still fit perfectly and that she had made a good choice. She strapped on a gold wristwatch that Grant had given her for her birthday.

It was 7:15 P.M.

Colette was ready a full half-hour before her taxi would arrive, so she decided to catch the last half of the *CBS Evening News*. She picked up the TV remote control unit, about to press the power button.

Suddenly the lights in her apartment went out.

The dressing rooms backstage at the Benedum weren't exactly palatial, but then Grant had learned long ago that dressing rooms rarely were. Only in old movies were they spacious with huge back-lighted mirrors, had the star's name on the door in gold letters, and came equipped with myriad servants, who catered to the performer's every whim. This one was at least large enough to turn around in, and gave him sufficient quiet time to prepare himself mentally.

Grant checked his watch. 7:15 P.M., a full forty-five minutes before he would step back on stage, back into time to that world he knew so well and wanted to forget. But there was no point in worrying about that now. He had made a commitment to do this evening's performance. And, by God, it was going to be one of the best performances he ever gave.

He heard a knock on the door and opened it.

"Hope I'm not bothering you, Grant," the stage manager said.

"Not at all. Come on in." Grant held the door open for him.

"Just wanted to wish you the best of luck," he said as he entered the room. "Is there anything I can get you?"

"Not a thing, Joe. I'm as ready as I'll ever be."

Joe was beaming. "We have a sell-out audience tonight of twenty-nine hundred. I can't remember the last time we did that. Hell's fire, if this wasn't a benefit performance, we'd make a bundle."

Grant brushed a piece of lint from the lapel of his tuxedo. "If this wasn't a benefit performance, I wouldn't be here."

"Yeah, I know," Joe said. "Thank God, it's successful. We haven't tallied it all up yet, but I know we've raised a ton of money for the hospital. And, thanks to you, we're getting the kind of publicity out of this that money couldn't buy."

Grant smiled. "I'm glad it worked out well."

Joe opened the door, about to leave, then turned to Grant. "Oh hell, I almost forgot. Somebody called up a short while ago and left a message for you. Said Colette Hershfield would be a little late."

"Wasn't it Colette who called?" Grant asked.

"No, it was a man's voice."

Sam Kassler sat in his living room, drumming his fingers on the armrest of the chair, waiting for his wife to finish dressing. It seemed he spent his life waiting for her. Or listening to her complain. Lately she was getting worse in criticizing and hounding him. But last night he had made a decision, perhaps the biggest decision of his life. It wouldn't be long now.

They were going to the Benedum to see Grant Montgomery and then to the follow-up reception at the Hilton. Not that either one of them was particularly interested in seeing Grant Montgomery's performance. But Blanche Kassler wasn't about to miss any affair that would draw Pittsburgh's elite. The performance and reception would be covered on the TV news that night and in the *Pittsburgh Post-Gazette* and the *Pittsburgh Tribune-Review* the following morning. And Blanche would make sure that she and her husband were part of that coverage.

A ringing noise interrupted his thoughts, and Kassler reached for the phone on the end table next to his chair.

"Sam, this is Marty." Martin Lang was Kassler's real-estate agent. "I'm sorry I couldn't call earlier, but I took a chance on catching you at home."

"We're just about to leave. What's up?"

"We finally got a buyer for that hunting cabin in Tioga County." Kassler's father, in his will, had left him an old log cabin he'd built on a piece of wilderness land in the north central part of the state near Wellsboro. "A guy by the name of Frank Hutchinson who works at The Halifax saw it listed and called me. He's in maintenance. He said he was looking for something in that area as a hunting cabin. One of my people drove up there with him a couple weeks ago, and he fell in love with it. Can you imagine that? He goes big-game hunting every year with five or six of his buddies and said this was perfect for his needs."

Kassler laughed. "I didn't think we'd ever unload that place."

"He only wanted to rent it, but we told him no deal. It was listed for sale, not for rent. That's why I hadn't mentioned it to you. But he finally agreed today and put a thousand-dollar down payment on it. He'll finance the rest."

"How much did you sell it for?"

"Ten thousand."

Kassler laughed again. "Marty, you're a crook after my own heart. I didn't think we'd get even half that."

"I think we we're lucky to unload it at all. That cabin's in a pretty remote place and it needs a lot of work. But Hutchinson didn't seem to mind. You never know who wants what. Just goes to prove that there's a buyer for everything."

"Guess so. Thanks again, Marty." Kassler cradled the receiver, smiling.

He glanced at his watch. What the hell was keeping her? His wife could put on a pound-and-a-half of makeup and it wouldn't improve her face. He went to the bottom of the stairs and hollered. "Let's get moving or we're going to be late."

They had at least a thirty-minute drive into town from Fox Chapel, possibly longer, depending on traffic.

He looked at his watch. It was 7:15 P.M.

Colette was momentarily startled when the lights in her apartment went out. She was in darkness and wished she had a flashlight or candle nearby. She moved carefully into the foyer to where the fuse box was located. She managed to reach the fuse box, opened it, felt for the main switch, the one on the bottom, and tried to press it. She couldn't. It seemed to be jammed. She tried the other switches, one at a time, although she couldn't read them in the dark and didn't know which switch activated which light or which appliance. Same thing. They all seemed to be jammed. What the devil was the problem here? Of all the times for something like this to happen. And no flashlight in the apartment.

She worked her way through the foyer to the door, careful not to knock over the onyx statue of the discus thrower that was standing on a marble pillar. She didn't need to have a fourteen-thousand-dollar accident just because a fuse must have blown. She finally reached the door and opened it. The hallway was lighted. No problem there. Colette left the door unlocked and walked a few feet into the hallway. She could see the wafer-thin slivers of light threading through the doorjambs of several other apartments. Apparently, hers was the only one that had a problem.

She knocked on the door of apartment 520. A middle-aged woman with her hair in curlers cracked open the door, saw Colette, and removed the safety chain.

"Mrs. Marelli, I'm sorry to bother you, but all the lights went out in my apartment, and I was wondering if I could use your phone to call the maintenance office."

Mrs. Marelli ushered her in. "Of course, dear, please forgive my appearance. We were just getting ready to go out for dinner. You can use the phone in the kitchen."

Colette called building maintenance, explained her predicament, then hung up. She came out of the kitchen. "Thanks ever so much. They're sending someone right now to take care of it." She walked toward the door. "You and your husband have a nice evening."

"We will, dear." Mrs. Marelli admired Colette's velvet dress from top to bottom. "I hope this doesn't throw you late for whatever you had planned for the evening." Mrs. Marelli, who loved to gossip, was always a little nosy.

"No, I'll be fine," Colette said. "Thanks again."

Colette decided to wait in front of her door. She checked her watch: 7:25 P.M. Although the cab driver would wait, she didn't want to be late for Grant's performance. She still had time, if the maintenance man wasn't late in getting there. If he couldn't fix the problem before she had to leave, he could let himself out of her apartment.

Five or six minutes later, she heard the elevator door open, then saw him coming down the hallway, carrying his toolbox, smiling at her.

Colette breathed a sigh of relief. "Frank, am I glad to see you."

CHAPTER FIVE

The Benedum was starting to fill with coiffured women in ankle-length evening dresses and men in tuxes. Community leaders, including heads of corporations, educators, and politicians, exchanged pleasantries with one another as they were coming into the theater and as they were ushered to their seats. The women eyed the women, taking particular note of who was wearing what, and the men, for the most part, either chatted with one another or read the program with placid expressions. The buzz of anticipation among the women, with whom Grant had always been popular, began to spread on the main floor first, then throughout the balcony, and finally into the dress circle.

Grant was disappointed that Colette would not have a chance to see the beginning of his performance, but he was curious about who had called the theater to report that she would be late. Joe, the stage manager, had said it was a man's voice, but didn't know who, only that one of the ticket salesmen had taken the call and passed it on to him. Maybe it was a client, Grant thought. It would have to be some sort of crisis if it couldn't wait until morning. But if that were the case, the client wouldn't have called the theater. Colette would—and she would have talked to him, not left a message with a ticket salesman. So who was this man who left the message? His mind groped for an answer. If Colette had left the apartment in a hurry on her way to meet a client, with no time to call him, she might have asked the doorman to call the theater. That was probably it. But one hell of a client crisis must have demanded her immediate attention for her to miss part of the show. He remembered Colette often saying that, in public relations, you had to be flexible and remain on call twenty-four hours a day. And she was just that conscientious.

Grant was backstage with the stage manager and several stagehands. He looked through the curtain peephole and saw the theater filling up fast. He glanced at his watch. Twenty minutes before showtime. He should have felt that familiar surge of adrenaline that always preceded a performance. But he felt a sense of uneasiness instead. Maybe it had to do with Colette being late, or an unknown voice that left a message. Or maybe it was just a slight case of nerves, the result of forcing himself to appear again before an audience.

Grant took a deep breath, held it, then exhaled slowly. He repeated the exercise twice, an old ritual among show people to relax just before the curtain would rise. He recalled a similar evening, early in his career when he was trying to make a name for himself, before he was a headliner. He had been backstage waiting to be introduced to a New York supper club audience, arguably the most sophisticated, but unquestionably the toughest audience in the world. They had seen it all, and weren't easily impressed. His act would precede the star attraction, a popular male singer with a string of hit records. Grant's act was merely a stage-wait until the singer would appear, and he knew it. But that was his first crack at the big-time. That night, he had looked through the curtain peephole and surveyed his audience. His years of study and practice, the endless hours of perfecting his craft, paying his dues in smoke-filled cabarets, all of it now seemed to culminate in his New York debut before this audience, who had paid their cover charge to see someone else.

Grant had been booked for a one-week engagement, but if he failed to impress them, it was all over for him. He had learned long ago that audiences, at least the ones he had known, were not polite to showmen who failed to entertain them. They cast their ballot by looking away, by talking during the performance, or by the ultimate death verdict, getting up and leaving. Not that this audience would resort to such tactics. The Golden Muse was an upscale nightclub that catered to upscale patrons. This audience would merely reserve their applause to a soft, polite tapping of hands, which was just as deadly as booing. Everything was riding on that one performance. He heard the din of the crowd subside as the announcer came on stage. Grant took another deep breath, held it and let it out.

"Ladies and gentlemen, tonight we have with us a new kind of performer, a rising young star with a gift for reading minds. So you're now forewarned—think nothing but pure thoughts. The Golden Muse is pleased to present the latest sensation in mentalism, Grant Montgomery." With the drum roll as his cue, he walked on stage. The audience applauded politely, anxious to get the act over with so they could see the star. Grant smiled, observing them, their expressions seeming to say, "OK, young man, let's see what you can do, and don't belabor it."

Grant thanked and welcomed his audience, then gave a one-minute monologue, disavowing any psychic power and attributing the skill he was about to display as sleight of mind as opposed to sleight of hand. The faces in the audience were still looking at him with what he feared was boredom. A bald-headed man, sitting with a group of people at a table next to the stage, looked at him with glassy, alcohol-dimmed eyes. "Let's see if you can read my mind, hot shot," he said. The woman next to him grabbed his arm and said something to him in a low tone, red-faced and frowning. Grant knew this small outburst was unusual for patrons of the club. He had to be careful how he handled the situation.

Grant smiled at the woman. "No, don't be concerned, my dear," he said, "your husband is absolutely right. If I'm a mentalist, I should be able to do something that would impress him." Still smiling, he turned his attention to the bald-headed man. "Sir, may I borrow some personal item—a pen, a wallet, a watch, anything—although my telepathic ability tells me you don't have a comb." A few laughs in the audience. "I'll be sure to return the item to you." The man gave him a sarcastic glance, reached in his breast pocket and retrieved a pen. Grant reached for it and thanked him. He began to rub the pen with one hand, all the while looking at the man with penetrating eyes. If Grant kept his gaze fixed on the man too long, the audience would get restless. If he broke it too soon, he would lose the moment that he now commanded.

Grant extended the pen to its owner. At the precise instant that the bald-headed man took the pen with Grant still holding one end of it, Grant said, “Bill, I believe your daughter is going to be accepted to one of the Ivy League colleges. Harvard, to be exact. So you needn’t have any fear that she might settle for a school other than your own alma mater.” The man released the pen as if it were red hot.

With the pen still in his hand, Grant continued to look at the man with his soul-searching gaze. “You have a son who’ll reach college age in two or three years, and you’d love him to think about Harvard, too. I don’t think I’m revealing anything too personal by saying that you’re somewhat worried that college isn’t one of your son’s priorities right now. Have no fear about that. He’ll come around during his senior year in high school, and he’ll continue your family’s tradition at Harvard.” Grant stopped for a moment, aware that there was no sound at all from the audience, only eyes transfixed on him. He smiled at the man and returned his pen. “Am I correct, or have I missed anything?”

The bald-headed man was staring at Grant with an open mouth. He nodded, unable to speak. His wife, wide-eyed, placed her hand over her mouth. Grant heard several gasps in the audience. He smiled with the knowledge of what careful planning could do. Customer reservations made at the club, usually one to two weeks in advance of the show, gave Grant the names and addresses of people attending the early and late shows, and he arranged for certain customers to be seated at certain tables. Armed with that knowledge, his divinations of events in their lives were the result of painstaking research undertaken well in advance of the show. Once Grant knew several customers’ addresses, he could ascertain the names of neighbors in that area. Then an advance team of paid researchers, posing as salesmen, property insurance assessors, or even census takers, would canvass the neighborhood discreetly. Friendly residents were always willing to share information about their neighbors that seemed harmless, but was priceless to Grant. The rest was showmanship.

The remainder of his half-hour performance was equally as mesmerizing. The audience had come to see a singer; now they didn't want Grant to leave the stage. He closed his act that evening to thunderous applause. He had upstaged the star of the show, who later demanded a new opening act, but that was fine with Grant. He had taken his first major step toward stardom.

Since then, he had appeared before so many audiences, so many faces that blurred with the passage of years. Now, at the Benedum, those faces finally melted away, erasing time and memory, as if a lifetime of performances had been merely an intermission, and he was again waiting to be introduced to that same audience at the Golden Muse so many years ago.

The Benedum was now completely filled with patrons ready to see the great mentalist. Backstage, Grant arched his shoulders back, primed for the sea of faces waiting for him. But he would have felt better knowing Colette's face was among them.

Colette held the door open as Frank Hutchinson entered her apartment, flicking on his flashlight. "No need to keep the door open," he said, "I can see the fuse box." She closed the door and moved toward him to share his beam of light.

He opened the fuse box and aimed the light inside. He tried to depress one of the switches, but it wouldn't budge. A few seconds later he said, "Well, I'll be darned. Look at this."

"What is it?" she said and moved next to him, until she was inches from his face. He stepped back allowing her to take a closer look into the fuse box.

Suddenly the beam of light went out. In the instant snap of darkness, she was startled by the clasp of a cold, clammy hand over her mouth and an arm squeezing her waist.

"Don't make a sound," he said. His voice came in a rush of sour breath, and she braced herself like an iron bar.

God, what was happening? What was Frank doing to her? She started to struggle, but she couldn't budge from his grip. He suddenly twisted her around, and for a second she was free to break away and scream for help, but before she could, his rock-hard fist smashed into her face and she fell to the floor.

Colette was dazed, unable to move, vaguely aware of something being wrapped over her mouth, sticking to her skin. She felt rough hands turning her on her stomach, her arms held tightly in back of her as the same adhesive material secured her wrists. Within seconds she came back to full consciousness, and the full realization that she could neither speak nor move her arms, that something was restraining her. Then Frank Hutchinson turned her on her back, and she saw him put the roll of duct tape into his toolbox, never taking his eyes from her.

Her legs were free and she thought of kicking him in the groin, but realized her ankle-length dress would restrict her movement. Maybe she could lash out with both legs, hit the bastard where he lives with her high heels. But he might deflect the blow. She would have to catch him by surprise and strike with dead-on accuracy in the dim hallway, because she wouldn't have a second chance. Even if she could, she would have to quickly get to her feet, get past him to the door, open the doorknob with her hands bound behind her, and run into the hallway. And if she could manage to do all that, she had no assurance that anyone would be in the hallway to see her, and she wouldn't be able to scream for help. Chances were he would recover from a lucky blow in sufficient time to stop her from ever making the door. And he would hit her again, maybe this time beat her unmercifully. She had made this assessment of her predicament within seconds.

So she just lay there in the dark, afraid to move, bewildered.

Colette fought the panic rising within her. She had to remain rational. She was alive, aware that he did not intend to kill her, at least not yet. If he did, she would have been dead by now.

Then his flashlight snapped on, and the light beam fluttered with the movement of his hand, casting a giant, ominous shadow dancing eerily on the wall and breaking to a new angle on the ceiling of the foyer. She saw him remove a dark object holstered on the side of his belt.

Was it a gun? She held her breath.

He held a portable phone in front of him, and she started to breathe again. Hutchinson placed the flashlight under his arm, and punched in a number. Only four digits. She knew he couldn't be making an outside call.

"Bill, this is Frank. I found the problem. It's a short in one of the circuits. I can take care of it. Everything's copacetic." Short pause. "OK, see you later."

She figured he was calling building maintenance. *What does he intend to do with me?* she wondered. *Has he gone completely mad?*

He holstered the phone. In the beam of the flashlight, she could see that he was looking at her, smiling. Hutchinson took two steps toward her, standing at her side. Then he flashed the light in her face, and she squinted, suddenly blinded. "You and I are going to take a little ride," he said. "But first I'm gonna see to it that you don't give me any trouble." He placed the flashlight on the ground.

Colette tried to refocus her eyes. The light had impaired her vision with a yellow afterglow, but she still could see that he had taken something out of his toolbox, although she couldn't tell what it was. Suddenly the air was filled with a pungent sting. Her vision returned with sufficient clarity to see the bottle in his left hand and the saturated wad of cotton in his right. The cotton was coming closer to her until it covered her nostrils. She tried to shake her head, but his grip held it like a vise. Colette twisted her body, kicking out with her legs, but they caught only air. She held her breath until she thought her lungs would burst. Finally she had to inhale deeply, and her chest heaved with each breath she was forced to take.

Within seconds, she was breathing normally, then slowly, no longer able to struggle, her strength and will ebbing away. And in the final moment before unconsciousness, she thought she heard a far-away voice reverberating from deep within a tunnel, saying, “Sweet dreams, Colette, the best is yet to come.”

CHAPTER SIX

The stage was bare. The theater lights were dimmed, and a spotlight was thrown stage left, where he would make his entrance. Then an unseen announcer's voice filled the theater. "Ladies and gentlemen, on behalf of Children's Hospital, the Benedum Center is pleased to present the world's leading mentalist, a man who has come out of retirement for this one-time-only benefit performance. Please welcome Pittsburgh's own...Grant Montgomery."

A ruffle of curtains at his entrance point. The audience waited, ready for the star's appearance. A few more seconds' delay and another ruffle of curtains. A slight murmur skimmed through an anxious audience. Then, just at the point where the audience's anticipation was raised to a new level, Grant Montgomery appeared. He walked on stage with the confident smile and demeanor of an experienced showman as they greeted him with enthusiastic applause.

Grant welcomed everyone, praised the work of Children's Hospital and, as the audience settled in, he was back in the limelight he had abandoned two years ago. He gave the usual preamble to his act, denying that he had any psychic ability, then began to wink at that opening statement by mesmerizing his audience.

"I'm seeing the letter J vividly. There's someone in this audience—maybe a James or a Jean—who is celebrating a birthday. Is that correct?"

A middle-aged man in the fifteenth row raised his hand and stood.

"Sir, does your first name begin with the letter J?"

The man remained standing. "Yes, my name is Jerry."

"I thought so. And when do you celebrate your birthday?" Grant asked.

"Tomorrow," he responded.

"Thank you," Grant said. "You can't possibly be more than twenty-five."

Applause mixed with laughter.

Although the trick was old, it was good for a warm-up. Grant had relied on the law of averages. In an audience of almost twenty-nine hundred people, someone was more than likely to have a birthday that had just passed or is just coming up. And the letter J as a first name could apply to at least thirty male or female names, thereby increasing the odds for a hit. Using words carefully was also part of Grant's arsenal. He had *asked* the man when he celebrated his birthday and the man told him the day. After the show, when people would recount this feat, they would say Grant revealed the actual birth date because most people wouldn't remember exactly the way it happened. Audience members didn't come to such performances to be observant, but rather to be entertained.

Grant moved to one end of the stage, and raised his hand to his forehead as if in deep concentration. "Someone here tonight is distraught over losing a piece of jewelry. I can't be wrong about this, because I feel it too strongly." Grant purposely didn't mention any specific time; a piece of jewelry could have been lost yesterday or a year ago.

This time, two women raised their hands. Grant noticed that one of them seemed hesitant and only raised her hand half way. The other woman had her hand raised high and was waving it.

"I see two women have raised their hands, but something compels me to focus on you." He pointed to the woman who seemed hesitant. She was shy and therefore less likely to contradict him if he got some fact wrong. "You've lost an expensive piece of jewelry. I see a necklace ..." Grant watched her face closely for any subtle reaction and saw a faint frown. "No...wait," he said. "Not a necklace...I think it's a bracelet." The slight frown disappeared and the woman's eyes widened. A hit. "Yes," Grant said, "it's a beautiful bracelet but, at one point, you wanted to have a matching necklace made." He was reasonably sure she wouldn't challenge the last point, but he kept on talking without giving her any chance to do so. "Now, let me allay your fear. You haven't lost the bracelet permanently, it's only been misplaced. And I'm happy to tell you that you're going to find it in your home within the next two weeks." No one tonight could challenge such a prediction.

The audience broke into a spontaneous burst of applause.

Grant acknowledged the applause, but raised his hand. "Thank you, ladies and gentlemen, but like the song says, we've only just begun, so please hold your applause until the end of the performance. Otherwise we're all liable not to be just late for the reception, but to miss it altogether." The audience laughed on cue, and there were still a few pockets of applause.

Grant smiled, knowing they didn't realize that his smile was in appreciation for his years of training in how to obtain information through observation and other means and then time the revelation, so that it was accepted as a minor miracle.

"Before the show," Grant said, "some of you were asked to think of certain names, numbers, dates, anything at all that was meaningful to you, as long as it wasn't too personal. And this is an excellent group because I'm already picking up many vibes." Grant slowly walked to one end of the stage. "Someone in the audience is thinking of the number four-twenty-six. May I ask whoever is thinking of that number to please raise your hand."

A woman in the sixth row at the other end of the stage raised her hand. She was blond, in her mid-thirties, wearing a high-neck dress with a diamond choker.

"There you are," Grant said. The man beside her had his arms folded, looking at Grant. He had seen that look many times before.

Grant smiled, then focused his attention on the woman. "May I ask you to tell the audience what the significance of that number is?"

Her voice was low, well modulated. "That's the number of the new house we just bought."

Grant repeated her statement so that everyone was aware of what she had said. "Congratulations on your new home. I hope you'll be very happy there. You've made a wise choice, and I think you'll find Ellsworth Avenue in Shadyside a wonderful place to live. Am I right?"

The woman looked astonished. "Yes," she said. The man next to her looked at Grant with a befuddled expression. The audience applauded.

Quite unexpectedly, Grant rattled off a nine-digit number. "I believe that's a Social Security number. Whose number is it? Please raise your hand."

A man near the back of the theater stood with his hand in the air. "It's my number," he shouted.

Everyone turned to look at him.

Grant placed his hand on his forehead, trying to block out the glare of the spotlight so he could see the man. "Sir, would you please confirm that we have never met and that we had nothing prearranged between us?"

"That's true," the man said in complete honesty.

"Thank you, sir," Grant said, "and please forgive my formality, but I'm not going to call you by your first name, otherwise people will think we're both lying." More audience laughter and applause.

Grant had opened by saying that, before the show, some audience members were asked to *think* of certain numbers, names and other facts. That was true, but as customers entered the Benedum lobby, two ushers asked several of them to *write* this information on slips of paper mounted on clipboards. Although innocent-looking, the special clipboards made a secret carbon impression of what was written. The ushers asked these same audience members to keep the slips of paper so they wouldn't forget what they wrote and so that no one else would have access to the written notes. The carbon impressions were then slipped to Grant backstage, who memorized most of the information before the show. What he couldn't memorize due to time constraint, he wrote on a two-by-three-inch card, which he kept in his pocket where he could easily retrieve it, keeping it palmed.

Grant sensed that they were warming to him quickly. But these were only the preliminaries. Later, he would get into the heavy material, revealing facts that were *never* written down and were *not* obtained through assistants, whom he hadn't used since his early days in show business. His use of two carefully selected ushers tonight was a rare exception.

Tonight he would reveal births and deaths, victories and tragedies that had touched their lives, facts he couldn't possible know unless he actually was psychic; that's when he had to be careful. That's when they might start going over the edge, crossing the threshold from simply being entertained to suddenly believing, as he had witnessed so often in the past. That's what he wanted to avoid, but they didn't come to see a few tricks tonight. They came to see what made him the world's greatest mentalist, and he knew it.

Tonight, for the last time, he would have to walk a fine line, and he couldn't waffle, couldn't take a false step, or twenty-nine hundred faces in the audience would become one face, one pair of eyes. And it would be the eyes and face of the grieving mother of the ten-year-old boy who had been kidnapped more than two years ago. The boy Grant could not save in spite of all his skill.

He glanced at the empty seat in the first row by the orchestra pit. Hopefully, Colette would arrive soon.

His thick glasses had become fogged in the heat of his struggle with Colette, and he rubbed a handkerchief over both sides of each lens. With his thumb and index finger, Frank Hutchinson massaged the bridge of his nose where the weight of the glasses pressed the nose guards into his flesh, leaving two red indentations. Then he put his glasses on and checked the woman lying at his feet. He aimed the beam of his flashlight at her face. Unconscious from the chloroform, she was still beautiful, even with her eyes closed and her mouth wrapped in duct tape that extended around her head. He ran the light over her body. She was so lovely. He had to get her out of the building, and he knew just how he would do it.

"Sleep tight," he whispered, knowing she couldn't hear him. "I'll be back in a few minutes."

Hutchinson left apartment 522 and locked the door with his key. He walked to the elevator and pressed the "down" button, hoping he wouldn't run into anyone he knew who might want to chat or ask him where he was going, however innocent such an encounter might be.

He stood there for a minute, waiting for the elevator. It seemed like an eternity. He closed his fist, pressing his fingernails into the palm of his hand. *Come on, come on, come on.*

The elevator finally arrived, and the door opened. He was in luck. No one was on it. He stepped in and pressed the basement button. The elevator door closed in what seemed like slow motion. A few seconds later, the door opened to the basement.

He stepped out of the elevator, and looked around. No one there. The other two maintenance men were busy on other floors. He went to the master fuse box and restored the lights to apartment 522. Hutchinson walked to the other end of the basement by the service elevator, where he'd left one of the refuse bins, a rectangular metal container on wheels. He placed a thin wool blanket that had been discarded by one of the residents into the bin. Then he pushed it into the service elevator and closed the door. Within a few minutes, he was back on the fifth floor, wheeling the refuse bin down the hall toward Colette's apartment, hoping that he would remain unseen.

The door to apartment 520 opened, and Mrs. Marelli stepped out into the hallway in front of Hutchinson. She was carrying a plastic garbage bag.

The woman smiled at him. "Oh, I was just going to throw out my garbage before we go out tonight, and here you are like a guardian angel."

Hutchinson stopped pushing the bin and returned the smile. "That's me, your guardian angel." Damn bitch would have to come out just now. He motioned to the bin. "You wanna put your garbage in here?"

"If you don't mind. This'll save me a trip down the hall." She looked into the bin and placed her garbage in it. "It's empty except for the blanket," she said, surprised. "Are you here to pick up some garbage?"

That's all he needed now, some nosy bitch asking questions. But he was prepared for such an eventuality. "Yeah, garbage has been piling up in some of the refuse rooms, and a few tenants complained about it, so we're trying to take care of it."

"Oh dear, well I certainly wasn't one of them. I guess there's no satisfying some people. Do you know who complained?"

"Afraid not." He glanced at his watch. "I better be on my way, it's getting late."

"What time is it?"

"Twenty after eight," he said, calling the time ten minutes later than it was.

"Oh, I better get moving, too, or Paul and I will be late for our dinner reservations. You take care now, and don't let some of these tenants get your goat."

He smiled at her and pushed the bin down the hall toward the refuse room. When he was sure that Mrs. Marelli was back in her apartment, he turned and headed back, stopping in front of Colette's apartment. He put his key in the lock, opened it, and, with his back to the door, pulled the bin into apartment 522, then quickly closed the door.

She was lying on the floor, just as he had left her.

No more time to lose. He took Mrs. Marelli's garbage bag out of the bin and put it in Colette's garbage can under her kitchen sink. He didn't need any garbage stinking up that bin, getting the stench of refuse all over her. He wanted Colette to be fresh.

He picked up Colette, surprised that, for being slender, she was somewhat heavier than he imagined. Dead weight. Would she be this heavy when she really was dead? He lowered her into the bin, careful not to bump any part of her body on the metal rim that might cause her to bruise or bleed. Any bruising or bleeding was going to be inflicted with purpose, not by accident. He covered her with the blanket. The bin was four feet deep, so if he ran into anyone, no one would see her in there. Now he had to get her out. But what if he ran into that nosy Marelli again as he was coming out of Colette's apartment? She'd want to know what he was doing in there and where Colette was.

He opened the door a crack, then peered out into the hallway, looking in both directions. All clear.

He opened the door wide, pulled the bin out with one hand as he kept the door open with the other, then closed the door and locked it.

Hutchinson forced himself to wheel the bin at a normal pace to the end of the hall where he had the service elevator waiting for him. He pushed the bin into the elevator, unlocked it from its stationary position, and pressed the basement button.

So far so good.

When he reached the basement, he checked again to make sure no one was there. Then he pushed the bin out of the elevator as quickly as he could, and placed it by the loading dock only a few feet away. He unlocked the door to the loading area, and lifted it by its handle as the door rolled up on tracks attached to the ceiling. He maneuvered the bin down the loading ramp, holding on to it tightly. When the bin was on a flat surface next to the street, Hutchinson closed the door from the outside. He reasoned that when one of the maintenance men found it unlocked tomorrow morning, he would think that one of the other two just forgot to lock it and wouldn't report the violation to management. Loyalty among fellow workers.

Hutchinson was now on a public street, even though it was a small alleyway, and he knew that this was the most dangerous part of his plan—the possibility, however remote, of being seen. He surveyed the area. He was alone. His car was parked across the street, directly in front of the loading dock so he wouldn't have to take any unnecessary steps. But he had to act quickly.

Hutchinson reached in the bin, still careful to keep Colette covered by the blanket, and lifted her. He had to reach inside the bin from an awkward angle and raise her weight with his arms and back. He felt the strain in his lower back as he lifted her, but he managed to get her out.

Suddenly he saw the head beams of an approaching car dimly lighting the area, and his heart started to hammer. But the car was traveling in a perpendicular direction to where he stood and, at that angle, its driver would have no opportunity to see him. The car drove by.

Hutchinson ran toward his car with Colette draped over his right shoulder, wrapped in the blanket. He unlocked the trunk and quickly placed her inside. The heel of her right shoe was showing and he pulled down the blanket to cover it. He locked the trunk, then entered his car and pulled away.

Careful to drive within the speed limit, he felt protected by the deepening shadows of evening that stretched before him. The city streets seemed almost deserted with only a few headlights interspersed in the opposite direction and a clear road ahead of him.

With his heart still pounding, Frank Hutchinson smiled. He had completed the first phase of his plan. He was no longer the stalker. He was now the abductor.

And Colette Hershfield was finally under his control.

CHAPTER SEVEN

At the Benedum, initial laughter and curiosity had been slowly converted to bewilderment, then finally to tense silence among an audience held spellbound. Grant Montgomery was nearing the end of his performance. He had just revealed the name of a sixteen-foot cabin cruiser, The Winged Marlin, purchased by the man in the fourth row, who couldn't fathom how the mentalist could possibly know such a fact.

"One further note, if you'll permit me," Grant said. "Your wife's fear of water is well founded, based on the tragic drowning of her own father." He heard a few gasps in the audience, and the man's wife was looking up at him with tears in her eyes. Grant smiled at her, then turned his gaze on her husband. "Please don't become anxious about her wishes to avoid your new sea craft. In time, your wife will overcome her fear of water, and you will both enjoy many years of happiness with your cabin cruiser." Grant had learned long ago that his own research on a few select audience members was worth more than gold to his career. "It's time I was sailing off into the sunset, too," he said. He still had another five or six minutes of performing time left, but he decided to cut it short. Some members of the audience would leave the theater convinced that he had the gift to read the past and divine the future, and he knew it. No need to reinforce it. He had wanted to hold back, to temper his act, but he didn't know how to give less than his best, and he wondered if tonight he had stepped over that line he didn't want to cross.

He glanced again at the empty seat in the first row. What crisis could have caused her to miss the entire performance?

"Ladies and gentlemen, you have witnessed some revelations here tonight that on the surface appear to be unexplainable. I can assure you that they are all perfectly explainable, and none of them are attributable to any special powers, except the power to entertain you, hopefully. It's been my pleasure to be with you tonight. I hope you've enjoyed it and that I'll have an opportunity to meet many of you this evening at the reception."

Grant bowed, and the audience broke into applause. He took two curtain calls to a standing ovation.

Backstage, the stage manager shook Grant's hand. "That was a great performance, Grant. You had them eating out of your hand. Makes me wonder why you ever retired."

"It a long story, Joe," Grant said, patting him on the arm. "I'm going to freshen up for a minute. I'll see you at the reception."

"Me and half of Pittsburgh," Joe said.

Grant rushed to his dressing room, anxious to call Colette, accepting congratulations from a few stagehands on the way. When he entered the room, he immediately dialed her number.

He heard her voice. "This is Colette Hershfield. I'm not available at the moment, but please leave your name and number, and I'll return your call as soon as possible."

Grant was tempted to leave a teasing message, something like, "You didn't have to get cold feet and leave town at the last minute, you know," but he decided against it. Hell, she knew he would be disappointed, just as she knew he would be understanding about whatever business crisis kept her away. Most likely, he would connect with her at the reception, then he could tease her all he wanted about being ignored and abandoned.

He went to the sink and splashed water on his face, then patted it dry with a hand towel, still wondering if the doorman at The Halifax was the mysterious caller who reported that Colette would be late. Grant glanced at his watch. 9:35 P.M. No way to check on that now. The doorman wouldn't be on duty this late.

Hundreds of people were arriving at the Grand Ballroom of the Hilton. The cocktail/dinner reception was a sellout with sixteen hundred reservations. Grant arrived fifteen minutes after the reception was under way, and the ballroom was filled. He mingled among as many people as he could. At $250 a head, they deserved some attention. He spotted Tom and Marie Santucci chatting with the mayor, and he started to maneuver his way through the crowd toward them. By the time he reached them, the mayor and his wife had splintered off to another group, and the Santuccis were now with Emilio Vasquez and a dark-haired woman with flashing eyes whom Grant didn't know, but assumed to be Emilio's wife.

Santucci extended his hand to Grant. "Marie and I really enjoyed your performance tonight. Many thanks for the tickets."

Vasquez introduced his wife, Consuela. "We thank you for the tickets, too, my friend," he said. "We couldn't afford to be here if it wasn't for you." He stuck his finger under his collar and stretched his neck from side to side, uncomfortable in his rented tuxedo.

"My pleasure," Grant said. "It wouldn't have been the same for me without you and your lovely ladies here tonight."

"Speaking of lovely ladies," Tom said, "where's Colette?"

"I wish I knew. She sent a message that she'd be late, but she missed the entire performance. I thought I'd catch up with her here, but I haven't seen her yet."

Marie Santucci looked disappointed. "I was looking forward to seeing her this evening. I hope she shows up soon."

Grant suddenly tilted his head as he heard the name Sam Kassler, which sounded like someone was calling the name of a friend he hadn't seen in a while. He turned and spotted a member of city council pumping the hand of an overweight man, average height, in his early fifties with hair almost totally gray. The two men were standing about ten feet from Grant in a cluster of five or six others, and he overhead a snippet of their conversation about the stock market.

He looked at Kassler. *So that's the bum who's been bothering Colette.* Under other circumstances, Grant would have confronted him. He looked at Santucci and nodded in the direction of Kassler. "The man we had a conversation about the other day is standing behind me. The gray-haired overweight guy."

Santucci stood on his toes and looked over Grant's shoulder. "You mean the one who might have a strange telephone habit?"

"One and the same," Grant said.

Vasquez changed his position so that he was facing Grant and could observe the crowd behind him. "Yeah, I see him, the only gray-haired guy in the group. From the look of him, you wouldn't think he was a creep."

Consuela Vasquez, her dark eyes expressive with curiosity, looked at Tom Santucci's wife. "Marie, do you have any idea what these three are talking about?"

"None at all," Marie said, smiling, "but I know the drill. They're getting focused on police business." Marie was in her early forties and had black hair. In spite of her expanding waistline, which she fought constantly, she was still able to turn some male heads when she paid attention to her appearance.

"You're right," Grant said, smiling. "I want all of you to enjoy yourselves tonight, and forget about police business. We just had a momentary slip, ladies." Grant called one of the waitresses, ordered drinks for them, and started to mingle again. But throughout the evening, he kept glancing at Kassler, observing him, yet careful not to be obvious. Occasionally he would see the same woman with Kassler—a full-figured brunette with a dye job—but only for brief periods. Although he had never seen Sam Kassler before, the woman was vaguely familiar to Grant. Perhaps he had seen her or her photograph somewhere. He noticed that Kassler and the woman showed a forced politeness when they were together as though they were trying to hide an undercurrent of distaste at being in each other's company. When she wasn't with Kassler, she seemed to be working the crowd, anxious to be in most of the photographs being taken by commercial and newspaper photographers.

At the buffet dinner, the Santuccis and the Vasquezes sat at the same table with Mr. Manion and his wife, both of whom were in their late sixties. Edward Manion was a prominent banker who sat on the boards of several Pittsburgh companies. His wife, Lucille, who had been born into wealth, was seated next to Emilio Vasquez, although, for the life of her, she couldn't figure out how such a mismatch had happened. So much for open seating. She looked demurely at Emilio and said, "Tell me, Mr. Vasquez, what line of work are you in?"

Emilio, who was a fine police sergeant, suffered most of his life from an embarrassing habit. Whenever he became excited or felt he was in an uncomfortable situation, he would often silently—but uncontrollably—pass wind. That evening, sitting next to this lady of position and wealth, who obviously did not want to be sitting next to him, Emilio was feeling uncomfortable.

"I work for the city detective bureau in the investigations department," he said. "I'm a sergeant."

"Oh," she said, without looking at him, "and what does a sergeant in the city detective bureau do?"

Emilio knew she asked the question with no interest in his answer. "Well, we do a lot of things ..."

"Such as?" Her expression said she was expecting a *long* evening.

Emilio looked at Tom Santucci for help, but Tom was engrossed in conversation with Mr. Manion, while Consuela and Marie Santucci were chatting, unaware of his predicament. "We investigate crimes," he said, "and we try to solve them." He immediately felt stupid by his answer.

Lucille Manion looked at him with a raised eyebrow. "I gathered as much." She returned her attention to the small plate of food before her. "And have you solved any crimes lately?" she asked, her manner aloof.

He tried to smile. "Well…we're working on several cases now."

"My, my. You sound very secretive. But I'm sure we'll all sleep better tonight knowing that you're on the job."

Emilio didn't like to be toyed with, and he didn't like sarcastic snobs. "I'm working on a robbery and a murder case."

Lucille Manion wrinkled her brow and began to sniff. She started to say, "What's that horrible …" Then she brought her napkin up to her face. "Oh, oh, my Lord." She suddenly sprang up and headed toward the door.

Everyone at the table stopped talking and looked at Mrs. Manion as she was leaving, then at Vasquez.

Emilio smiled sheepishly. "I think my talk of robbery and murder might have upset her."

After the dinner, one of the newspaper photographers asked Grant if he could take a photograph of him and some of the officials of Children's Hospital. Grant obliged. The photographer was setting up the shot when Grant noticed the same woman he had observed with Kassler, walking toward them, smiling.

"Hello, Laurie, dear," Blanche Kassler said to one of the hospital directors.

She stepped in front of the photographer, to his chagrin, and faked a kiss on the woman's cheek. Blanche turned to the photographer. "Oh dear, I hope I haven't upset your photograph." She waved her small gold purse to the photographer. "Now, when you're done, I want you to take a photograph of me and Laurie. She and I served on a fund-raising committee." Blanche looked at Grant. "And I'd love to take a photograph with Mr. Montgomery. He's the star attraction, and I haven't been introduced to him yet." Laurie introduced them. The photographer, who was rolling his eyes, said to Blanche, "Look, why don't you just stay exactly where you are, so we can get this photograph taken."

"I don't want to horn in," Blanche said, still smiling, "but if you insist."

The photographer finally took the photograph, and Blanche immediately focused her attention on Grant. "Mr. Montgomery, you were so thrilling tonight. If you have a second, I'd like you to meet my husband."

Grant nodded. "Of course, I'd be happy to." He glanced at his watch. 11:40 P.M. What could have detained Colette this long?

Blanche took Grant by the hand and led him to one of the bars at the far end of the ballroom, where Sam Kassler was ordering a drink. She introduced her husband to Grant, who smiled as they shook hands. Kassler's palm was sweaty, and his forehead glistened with perspiration.

Blanche looked at her husband. "Wasn't Mr. Montgomery wonderful tonight?"

Sam Kassler picked up his drink and looked at Grant with a glimmer of disdain. "Yeah, I bet you'll even do private readings *if* the price is right."

"Wrong," Grant said, "but in your case, I'll make an exception, and I won't charge you a dime." Grant was no longer smiling. "You're a hard-working man. In fact, in the last several months, you've even taken on a new responsibility at your stock brokerage firm—public relations. And I can see that you're very impressed with your public relations consultant, Colette Hershfield, aren't you?"

The shatter of the glass hitting the floor when it slipped from Kassler's hand caused several people standing nearby to turn their heads quickly. They looked at him, wondering if he had too much to drink.

Shortly after midnight, the reception was over, and people were leaving the Grand Ballroom. The officials of Children's Hospital initially estimated that the evening had raised nearly $450,000, and they expressed their appreciation to Grant for all he had done.

With the evening's entertainment concluded, Grant went to the hotel manager's office, and placed another call to Colette.

He heard the same recording. Where could she be at this time of night? This wasn't like Colette.

Driving back to his home in Mount Washington, he tried to rationalize his uneasiness. Unexpected events happen in business all the time. After all, she's a big girl who knows how to take care of herself.

He unconsciously rubbed the scar on his chin with his left hand while steering with his right. She probably didn't call because she didn't expect to be so late. She obviously couldn't call him while he was performing, and she might have thought that it would be too difficult to reach him later in the evening when he was among hundreds of people.

But that uneasy feeling wasn't going to be swept away, no matter what kind of logic he applied.

When he arrived home, he dialed her number again, only to hear her recorded voice for a third time.

He decided to leave a message. "Colette, where have you been? I've been worried about you. The evening was successful for the hospital, but not nearly as good for me without you. Call me when you get in, no matter what time it is." He cradled the receiver and went to the picture window in his living room. He stood before it, and looked out at the starless night. The city below was outlined in a panorama of distant lights that, after a while, seemed to wink at him, as if to acknowledge the cause of his concern, to signal that somewhere out there, the darkness held a secret.

Grant tried to shake the thought, but his uneasy feeling was growing into a premonition that something had gone wrong.

The man who called himself Frank Hutchinson had been driving for several hours, stopping occasionally on deserted roads to check on Colette, who was still unconscious, and to let fresh air into the trunk. He was behind the wheel again and saw the turn coming up in the road ahead of him as he eased off the gas pedal. He looked again in his rearview mirror. No one in sight. At this hour, there wasn't likely to be any traffic on such a lonely, abandoned road. He was in north-central Pennsylvania on the outskirts of Wellsboro in Tioga County. Thousands of acres of Appalachian mountain wilderness seemed to surround him, but were many miles away.

He made a right turn, went a hundred yards or so, found the spot, made another right and drove several more miles on a dirt road that he guessed had been untraveled for months, maybe longer. No one would come to such a spot except to hunt, but hunting wasn't in season now. He took the last puff of a cigarette and snuffed it out in the ashtray under the dashboard.

He was soon in a virgin forest of white pines and hemlocks, some of the trees more than five hundred years old, towering into the black sky. Alive during the day with the music of wild birds and the rush of waterfalls, the forest at night was overwhelming in its silence as if it were a land frozen in time. A mountainous, wooded wilderness that could conceal him from the world forever.

Hutchinson was five or six miles north of Pine Creek Gorge on Route 6. He kept bearing to his right, and a few minutes later he saw his destination thirty yards or so in front of him—an old cabin faintly illuminated in the path of his headlights. Hutchinson killed his lights and slowed the car to a crawl until he was in back of the cabin where his car would remain unseen, even in the unlikely event that some lost soul should traipse through these dense woods.

He was confident that the woman in the trunk was still out, based on the amount of chloroform he had given her. He got out of the car and looked around.

A perfect spot.

Then he went to the trunk and opened it. Hutchinson looked down at the figure covered by a dark wool blanket. No movement. He flipped the blanket aside and looked at her. Colette's eyes were closed.

She appeared to be dead.

His heart skipped a beat and he felt a charge of adrenaline surge within him. What if he had given her too much chloroform? If she were dead everything was ruined. But he watched her for some sign of life and noticed that she was breathing softly. Hutchinson let out a sigh of relief. He could almost feel sorry for her, lying there so helpless with her mouth and wrists wrapped in duct tape. But the time for feeling sorry for anyone, particularly anyone dear to Grant Montgomery, had long since passed.

He reached in and lifted her, then draped her over his right shoulder as he closed the trunk. She didn't seem as heavy this time as he carried her to the cabin. He unlocked the door and entered. The cabin was more of a shack, musty with the stench of stale air and dirt trapped by log-cabin walls that were air-tight. Even the fresh fragrance of the woods couldn't penetrate the odor of years of neglect, which hung in the room like a shroud.

The only source of light was an old-fashioned kerosene lamp that rested on a three-inch-thick rectangular oak table. Two oak chairs were on one side of the table, facing the door. A cot with a dirty mattress was in one corner of the room, and at the opposite end was a door to a five-by-eight-foot bathroom with a toilet and sink that were corroded in spots. A coal-fired stove with a wrought-iron pipe that served as a chimney connection was next to the table near one of only two boarded windows in the cabin. At the base of the stove was a small mound of coal, wood chips and a hand-held shovel. On the far wall opposite the stove was a small cupboard used to house canned goods. The bare hardwood floor was cold. In fact, the room itself was so cold that Hutchinson could see the distillation of his breath as he exhaled.

He lowered Colette onto the mattress. Her five-ten frame filled every inch of the bed. Hutchinson rubbed his hands together as he put them to his lips, blowing. He went to the stove, opened the iron-grated loading door, and shoveled several scoops of coal into the firepot, then fired the stove. No one was going to see any smoke coming from the chimney in this forsaken wilderness, not at this time of night. And even if anyone did, who would care?

Soon the fire in the stove cast a ghostly crimson light that danced on the walls and ceiling as if the cabin had suddenly been awakened from its desolate slumber. Then he heard a stirring sound from the other side of the room.

He walked over to Colette and watched her as she turned her head from side to side, murmuring, trying to find her way back to consciousness. Her eyes began to open, but he could see that she couldn't focus, that she wasn't fully awake yet. Hutchinson went out to his car and returned a minute later with his toolbox. He removed a roll of duct tape and wrapped her ankles with it. Then he used the tape to wrap her legs and her waist to the cot.

He slapped the sides of her face a few times, only hard enough to help snap her out of her fog. "Listen to me, Colette. I have something to do, but I'll be back soon. You can't go anywhere. You can't even move very well. And if you struggle, the duct tape will only cut into your skin. No one knows you're here. No one in the world except me. You're quite alone, so you'd best be a good girl until I get back."

Hutchinson put his hand on her right leg and slowly ran it up over her body, feeling her stiffen to his touch. "When I get back," he said, "I'll have a surprise waiting for you and your lover."

The insistent buzzing ran through his brain like the whirring of a motorized saw cutting wood, forcing Grant to open his eyes, reach out to the nightstand next to his bed and turn off the alarm. He had set it for 6 A.M., but hadn't gone to bed until 1 A.M., then lay awake for at least another hour before fatigue took its toll and sleep finally came. He flipped the blanket off him and sat on the edge of the bed, rubbing his forehead. His sleep hadn't been restful, and he felt drained.

Suddenly his mind cleared. Colette. If she were home now, it was too early to call her. She'd be in bed exhausted from whatever appointment kept her from attending the affair last night. Even though he'd left the message for her to call him no matter what time it was, she'd probably gotten in so late that she didn't want to disturb his sleep. He decided to take his usual half-hour run, shower, and have breakfast. Let her have some sleep, then he would call her.

By mid-morning, he couldn't contain his anxiety any longer. He dialed her number and again heard her recorded message. Was she in her apartment still asleep? Or hadn't she returned yet? Either way she would have checked her answering machine and returned his call.

He didn't like it. The premonition he had fought the night before was with him again. But this time, he didn't try to rationalize why she would be so late in calling him.

Something was wrong.

He picked up the phone again and punched in the two-digit memory code to speed dial the number.

"Tom, listen, I'm concerned about Colette. Ever since last night, I've been calling her apartment, but I only get her answering machine."

Santucci's voice was calm. "Just because she isn't in her apartment, doesn't mean that anything's happened to her."

"I understand, but I know Colette. This isn't like her."

"When was the last time you talked to her?"

Grant thought for a second. "Last night, shortly after six. She called me to wish me luck. Never said anything about the possibility of being late."

"Well, don't get excited just yet," Santucci said. "She could've been called away on a business emergency, or maybe an out-of-town relative took seriously ill...maybe she's with a friend who's in some kind of trouble. It could be anything."

"I thought of all those things, Tom, and a few more. But the fact remains that she would've called me, no matter what the circumstance."

Santucci paused. "What do you think? She might've been in an accident?"

"I don't know," Grant said. "It's a possibility if she's been seriously hurt and can't call anyone. She has an aunt, but she lives in Virginia, and the hospital wouldn't know to call me."

Grant detected the slight hesitation in Santucci's voice. "Grant, I don't want to pry, but you and Colette didn't have an argument recently, did you?"

"Aw, for God's sake, would I be calling you if we did?"

"Okay, don't get angry, it's just that I've seen things like this happen before. Tell you what. I'll have someone make a check of all the hospitals just to make sure, and, if we discover anything, I'll call you. In the meantime, she'll probably show up."

"Thanks, Tom. I appreciate your help."

As soon as he hung up, Grant grabbed his car keys, went into his garage, and started the Lamborghini. He wasn't going to sit by a phone and do nothing while Santucci checked the hospitals.

He drove into the city and parked his car in an underground garage a block from The Halifax. When he reached the apartment building, he greeted the elderly doorman, who was dressed in his blue uniform with gold epaulets.

"Bill, do you know if Miss Hershfield is in?"

"No, I don't," the doorman said. "I was thinking that it's strange I haven't seen her this morning. She always takes a morning walk."

Grant looked at Bill, hoping for the right answer. "Did she ask you to phone the Benedum last night and leave a message for me that she'd be late?"

The doorman shook his head. "No, she didn't. Why?"

"Just wondering. I'll buzz her apartment and see if she's in."

Grant entered the outer lobby, and pressed the buzzer for apartment 522. No response. He pressed it again with the same result. If she couldn't hear a phone ringing, she couldn't hear that buzzer, either. He used the key he had to her apartment to take a quick look. Colette wasn't there.

He came out of the building. The doorman looked at him with a worried expression. "Is everything all right?"

"Everything's okay, Bill."

He decided to drive to city detective headquarters in East Liberty. Maybe by the time he arrived, Santucci would be able to tell him that she wasn't involved in an accident. Hopefully, he could put his mind at ease about that, anyway.

Santucci was on the phone, sitting behind his mahogany desk, which almost filled the width of his office. When he saw Grant, he motioned for him to come in and take a seat. Grant went to the makeshift kitchen in back of Santucci's desk and poured himself a cup of coffee. It was the strongest, most bitter coffee known to man, Grant often said, but that morning he needed it. He sat in one of the two metal folding chairs facing Tom and waited for him to finish his conversation.

Finally, Santucci hung up. "We still have a couple more hospitals to call, but so far we've come up empty." He lowered his glance, then looked up at Grant. "I know how you feel, but don't jump to any conclusions just yet. People get a little funny sometimes and do strange things, like getting lost for a while because something suddenly upset them."

Grant sighed. "You call that normal behavior? Colette's a normal woman."

"In my job, I don't usually deal with normal behavior." Santucci paused, turning down the corners of his mouth. "Okay, sure, you and I both know that Colette's normal. But she's human, too. And sometimes we humans do dumb things, like failing to keep someone informed about where the hell we have to go at the last minute. I've seen stranger things happen, believe me."

Grant took a sip of coffee. "I know what you're trying to do, Tom, and I appreciate it. But regardless of what you say, I'm still worried about her. I know her too well, and she just doesn't act this way. She was looking forward to last night."

Santucci leaned forward with his elbows on his desk. "Well, at least we know she didn't run away with that Kassler character," he said with a faint smile. "Incidentally, I saw you with him last night when he dropped his drink. What the hell did you say to him?"

"I was very discreet. I called him a shithead and said I'd shoot his balls off if he ever bothered Colette again."

Sergeant Vasquez rapped on Santucci's open door as he entered. "We've just completed our check of all the hospitals," Vasquez said, "and Miss Hershfield hasn't been admitted to any of them."

Santucci nodded. "Well, in a way, that's good news."

"That depends on how you look at it," Grant said.

Santucci took a deep breath. "Tell you what. Someone has to be missing for twenty-four hours before we can classify them that way. But rather than wait that long, we'll start checking around."

Grant took another gulp of coffee and placed his cup on Santucci's desk. "Where do you intend to start?"

"I'll have Emilio start contacting the airlines," Santucci said, "just in the off chance that she might've taken a flight last night. If he comes up empty, he'll follow up with the bus lines and train station. While he's doing that, I'll visit The Halifax to see if the management knows anything, and I'll check on who might've seen her last."

Grant rose from his chair. "If you don't mind, I'd like to come with you. It's better than waiting around for you to call me."

Santucci looked up at Grant. "I see you don't want to waste any time." He stood and buttoned his suit jacket. "Let's be on our way then."

Frank Hutchinson had a creased brow as he sat across the desk from the manager of The Halifax. "I just got the call last night, Mr. Mather. It doesn't look good at all. My sister lives alone in Pleasant Hills, and she's gonna need my help. She won't go to a hospital, wants to die at home, and we can't afford to have a nurse there twenty-four hours a day."

Phil Mather was in his late thirties, had dark, wavy hair, and was impeccably dressed in his gray Brooks Brothers suit, white shirt, and Italian-made paisley tie. He had been manager of The Halifax for the past seven months and was charged with improving profits, while maintaining good relations with tenants and employees. Mather shook his head. " I'm very sorry to hear about your sister. Cancer took my mother, so I know what you must be going through. Of course you can take the time off, and I'll see to it that you remain on full salary."

Still dressed in his work clothes, Hutchinson nodded gratefully. "Thanks very much. That'll sure help, and I don't think I'll be gone from the job too long. The doctors are saying that she has only a short time left, maybe a couple weeks at most."

"Don't worry about anything here, Frank. You just tend to your sister as long as you need to."

Hutchinson pushed his glasses up on his nose. "That's very generous of you, Mr. Mather. I'll let you know when I can come back to work."

Hutchinson stood and shook Mr. Mather's hand. He smiled after he left Mather's office. He'd had only a couple hours of sleep in his car the night before after leaving the cabin, but he was as fresh as if he had just returned from a month's vacation. Now he was free to initiate the second phase of his plan, to do what years of nurturing his hatred had compelled him to do.

As he was about to leave from the front entrance of the building, Hutchinson suddenly stopped. His smile was quickly replaced with a frown. About seventy feet in front of him, he saw Grant Montgomery and a man he didn't recognize walking in the plaza, heading toward The Halifax.

His initial reaction was to leave by the back exit, but he dismissed it. Why not walk right by Montgomery to confirm what he believed, that his former employer would never recognize him because his appearance had changed so dramatically after all these years?

Hutchinson observed both men as they approached. Their expressions were somber.

He opened the outer door of the lobby, mumbled a greeting to Bill, the doorman, and kept on walking toward Montgomery and his companion. The two men merely glanced at him as he passed them.

He wasn't recognized.

Hutchinson smiled again as he walked in the opposite direction, opening the distance between himself and his unwitting adversary, knowing that their paths were about to change as surely as the course of their lives would.

CHAPTER EIGHT

Colette lay awake in the dark with her mind racing. Throughout the night, she had tried several times to free herself from her bonds, but it was useless. The more she fought the tape, the more it chaffed and cut into her wrists. She was lying with her arms behind her, and the weight of her body had made her arms numb. She shivered with cold and fear.

Why was he doing this to her? What possible reason could he have? What did he want? Was he insane? Frank, the shy repairman. It seemed so unreal, a bad dream. *Please, dear God, let it only be a bad dream.* If she kept telling herself that, maybe she could believe it. That was the thing to do, the only defense mechanism she had.

Her eyes darted around the room. Where on earth was she? She could barely see the two boarded windows in the dark, and she didn't know if it was still night or how long she had been there. Hours, maybe a day. Time in the dark couldn't be measured with every minute punctuated by fear.

The thought that Frank Hutchinson might harm her, perhaps kill her, made her tremble in the cold, sunless room. Even in her drug-induced fog, she had been aware that he ran his hand over her body and leered as he did so. She also remembered that he had said something strange, that he had a surprise waiting for her and her lover. He knew about her relationship with Grant. He had seen them together often enough.

Where was her abductor now and why did he leave her? When would he return? The questions came spilling out, each one unanswerable, until she thought she would go mad.

Don't panic, she thought. *This is just a dream. You'll wake up soon, and you'll never go to sleep again. Never alone. Never, never again.*

Suddenly she heard a metallic sound, a key being placed in a door lock. She turned her head, looked at the door, her heart pounding.

The door squeaked as it opened, allowing a shaft of morning light to penetrate the musty room. Her eyes were wide with fear. *Wake up,* she told herself. *God, please let me wake up now.*

Hutchinson entered the room and looked at her, his eyes magnified to a grotesque proportion behind the thick lenses. He locked the door, went to the table, and lighted the kerosene lamp. Then he went to the cot and stared down at her for a few seconds.

His eyes seemed to dwarf the rest of his body. They loomed over her, inexpressive, but waiting. She couldn't protect herself from those eyes, but couldn't tear away from them, either, fearing she might trigger him into taking some violent action by merely breaking eye contact.

He cut the tape around her waist and legs that bound her to the cot. Then he turned her on her side for a few seconds, her back facing him. "You've been fighting the tape, haven't you?" His voice was stone-cold. "I told you you'd only hurt yourself if you did. But it doesn't matter." He turned her on her back again, her arms still taped behind her. Hutchinson dragged a chair from the table, placed it next to the cot and sat in it. In the dim light, he leaned toward her until his face was almost touching hers.

The rush of his foul breath washed over her like a frigid wave, jolting her into the reality of what she couldn't fully admit until that moment. Now she knew that she would not escape by waking, because the dream she imagined was fake. Her nightmare was real.

"I'm finally back," he said. "Now it's time for the surprise I promised you."

Grant and Santucci sat in the office of Mr. Mather, manager of The Halifax, who was shaking his head, frowning. "I'm afraid I haven't seen Miss Hershfield for several days. Why do you ask?"

Santucci crossed his legs. "It's nothing to be alarmed about. We're just making a routine check. We think that Miss Hershfield was called away on either a business or personal matter, and just neglected to tell anyone where she was going, that's all."

Philip Mather raised his eyebrows. "If that's all, then why is the police involved? Is there something you're not telling me?"

"Not at this point, Mr. Mather," Santucci said, "so don't let your imagination run away with you. But considering her status in the community, we'd rather err on the side of caution."

Mather nodded. "Well, I certainly hope she's fine. If I should see her, do you want me to contact you?"

"Have her call me or Grant," Santucci said. "In the meantime, we'd like to take a quick look through her apartment and talk to her neighbors."

"Well, I don't want our tenants to be needlessly alarmed, but I guess you gentlemen have to do your job," Mather said. He started to check a roster of tenants. "Let's see, she lives on—"

"The fifth floor," Grant said, "apartment 522."

Mather elevated his eyebrows again as he looked at Grant.

"I'm a friend of hers," Grant said, knowing that Mather was aware of that fact, but was attempting to be discreet.

Mather nodded. "I can accompany you gentlemen, if you wish, but I'd rather not. I wouldn't want any of our tenants to think that I singled them out to be questioned by the police."

Santucci rose from his chair. "I understand. Mr. Montgomery and I can handle it from here."

Returning from the grocery market, Mrs. Marelli saw the two men in the hall talking to Effie Givens, her widowed neighbor in apartment 519. She recognized Grant immediately, having seen him several times with Colette, but could not identify the man who was with him. She quickened her pace as she walked to her apartment so she could overhear their conversation.

"Oh dear, I hope nothing has happened to her," she heard Effie say.

"No cause for concern," the other man said, "we're just making a routine check."

Mrs. Marelli thought he looked like a policeman. She wondered who they were talking about.

"When was the last time you saw Miss Hershfield?" said the man who looked like a policeman. So they were asking about Colette Hershfield. She wondered what the problem was.

Effie's face was flushed, and she flattened the sides of her face with both hands. "Oh dear Lord, I don't think I can remember when I saw her last. Has anything happened to her?"

"Please don't be alarmed, Mrs. Givens," Grant said. "Everything's under control. Miss Hershfield and I just got our schedules crossed, and I'm checking with some of her neighbors to see if she might've mentioned where she was going."

Effie's hand was shaking. "But this man is a policeman," she said pointing to Santucci, "so something must be wrong."

Santucci shook his head. "No, we're not aware that anything is wrong. We just need some information."

Mrs. Marelli stood at her door, and the sound of her fumbling with the key in the lock caused both men to turn and glance at her for a second. She was sure, however, that her friend Effie was so flustered that she didn't even notice her. Mrs. Marelli finally unlocked the door and entered her apartment. So the other man *was* a policeman. Her curiosity was now piqued. She strained her ear at the door, but she couldn't make out what they were saying.

Both men saw her go into her apartment, so she surmised that they would want to question her, too. After they did, she could check with Effie to see if they asked the same questions. Then she could compare notes with any other tenants they questioned. A little detective work on her part. Just like the TV programs. She shivered with a tinge of excitement. Montgomery said he and Colette got their schedules crossed. A likely story. Maybe she's off having an affair with someone, and he's just jealous. This was going to make some of those ladies in the bridge club sit up and take notice.

She had to compose her thoughts now before Montgomery and the policeman questioned her. Let's see, when was the last time she saw Colette? Suddenly she realized that this may not be mere idle gossip for the next meeting of her bridge club. This might be serious. Maybe Colette was missing. What if something had happened to her?

The last time she saw Colette was just last night, when the lights in her apartment went out. She saw Frank, the maintenance man, enter Colette's apartment to fix her lights. But a short while later she peeked through an open crack of her apartment door and saw something she didn't understand. Frank had wheeled the refuse bin directly into Colette's apartment. It seemed a strange thing to do. How much garbage could Colette have accumulated? And why would she keep a lot of garbage in her apartment, instead of putting it in the refuse room? In any event, Frank must have seen Colette even after she did. The police would certainly want to know that.

But wait.

What if they told Frank that she was the one who gave them his name? The police promise not to reveal their sources, but she'd seen enough of those TV police shows and read enough novels to know that isn't always true. People usually suffer for their good intentions. They'd surely question Frank and only frighten the poor man. He wouldn't like that at all. In fact, he would probably get upset with her if he discovered that she had given his name to the police. Then the next time anything needed fixed in her apartment, he wouldn't be in a hurry to help her. He'd probably tell the rest of his friends in maintenance what she did, and they wouldn't like it either. They might boycott her. Word could spread to the office people and to Mr. Mather, who's relatively new on the job and doesn't want any problems. They might think of her as a trouble maker. She didn't need that kind of reputation.

If this is a matter for the police, maybe it's best not to involve anyone. Why allow the police to interrogate and frighten an innocent man? No, this was one time she was going to keep her mouth shut and mind her own business. Stay out of trouble. If they asked her, she'd simply say that she hasn't seen Colette in about a week or so. Let the police earn their salaries; that's why people pay taxes.

Mrs. Marelli heard the knock on her door. Mum's the word, she thought.

Sam Kassler opened the two suitcases he had placed on the four-poster bed, then started to pack them with enough clothes for at least two weeks.

His wife, Blanche, entered their bedroom where they slept together, but had not had sex for the past year. "Where are you going?"

He kept packing. "I have to go out of town for a few days."

She placed her hands on her hips. "Where out of town?"

"San Francisco. I have to check out a brokerage firm there we might want to acquire." He went into the walk-in closet, a moment later came out with three suits draped over his arm, and placed them on the bed. Then he went into the closet again and came out carrying three more suits."

Her tone was biting, accusatory. "Looks to me like you're packing for more than just a few days."

He didn't answer and continued packing the suits.

She took a step toward him. "Look at me when I speak to you."

Kassler narrowed his eyes as he looked at his wife. "Don't start with me, or so help me Christ ..."

"So help you Christ what?" she snapped. "Why didn't you tell me you had this trip planned, so I could've gone, too?"

"Because this is strictly a business trip, and I have to be with the principals of this firm day and night. I have no free time."

She sneered at him, her hands still on her hips. "Who cares whether you have any free time or not? I could've shopped and had fun while you were doing whatever the hell you had to do."

Kassler took a deep breath and let it out slowly. "Look, Blanche, I don't have time for an argument. My flight leaves in a couple hours. I'm staying at the Fairmont in Nob Hill."

"You don't have time for an argument? That's pretty good. Just walk away like you always do from any situation that's unpleasant. Well, not this time."

He closed the suitcases and locked them.

She walked around the bed and glared at him. "You're not fooling me for a second. You've packed enough clothes for a couple weeks. I don't believe you're going on a business trip. You're going to meet some woman, aren't you?"

"If you don't believe me, that's your problem." He turned from her and lifted one of the suitcases from the bed. "Now get the hell out of my space."

"Put that down," she said. "You're not going anywhere until you answer some questions."

He put the suitcase down and clenched his fist. "I said get out of my way."

Blanche stood in front of him and spread her stance. "Like hell I will. You're not going to make a fool of me. Who are you meeting in San Francisco? It's Colette Hershfield, isn't it? You acted like a scared rabbit when Grant Montgomery mentioned her name at the reception. I'll just bet it's your *public* relations that she's working on."

He raised his fist, ready to strike.

She started to laugh, that forced shrill laugh that pierced his ears and ripped through his brain, mocking him, stripping him of his manhood each time he heard it.

"Go ahead, hit me," she said. "Come on, let's see you do it. You know what would happen if you did. I'd have my lawyers on you so fast, you'd never make the front door, let alone the airport. I'd take everything you own, then spit on you when you were in the poorhouse. That's where you belong—in the gutter, not in the society I know. "

Kassler lowered his arm, aware that he was shaking.

She looked at him with disgust. "Look at you. What a pitiful excuse for a man. What did you promise Hershfield? That you'd divorce me and marry her? That's a joke. She's having some fun with you, playing you for a sucker. She'd never see anything in you. No woman would."

He took a step backward, and sat on the edge of the bed with his head bowed.

Blanche laughed again. "That's right. I guess a wimp can't help it if he's a wimp."

Now she knew that Colette was in his life, but he couldn't let that deter him. He had to stick to his plan and not let her play those mind games with him. He looked up at her. "For the last time, I'm going to San Francisco on business, and I'll return in a few days."

She seemed to tower over him as he sat there, looking up at her. "You're a liar," she said, "and not a very convincing one. But then wimps and failures never are."

He rose from the bed and faced her. "Do me a favor. Increase your dosage of sleeping pills, and wash them down every night with a lot of gin. Maybe when I get back, I'll be lucky enough to find you dead."

"You rotten bastard," she said and raised her arm back to slap him, but as she swung her arm forward, he grabbed her wrist and twisted it. Blanche winced and cried out. This was the first time in their married life that he had inflicted any physical pain on her.

Their nine-year-old daughter came running into the bedroom, out of breath. "Mommy, Daddy, what's wrong? Stop it. Please." She came around the bed, looked at both of them, tears welling up in her eyes.

Blanche massaged her wrist. "Daddy's just being the big fool that he always is, sweetie. He likes to hurt Mommy because it makes him feel better."

Emily began to cry and couldn't stop the flood of tears. Then she suddenly turned and ran out of the bedroom.

"Emily," Kassler said, but knew that calling her back was pointless. He turned to his wife. "Now look what you've done, you bitch."

Blanche slapped him so quickly that he was unable to dodge the blow. He stared at her, rubbing the side of his face. He wanted to kill her, to feel her throat in his hands as he squeezed it ever tighter. He had to put it out of his mind. He glanced at his watch. His flight was scheduled to depart in an hour and fifty minutes. Time to leave. Stick with the plan. Now he had the information he needed. And he was going to act on it.

Frank Hutchinson selected a can of peaches from the other cans he had stocked in the cupboard. He opened the can and began to eat the peaches with his penknife. He sat at the table and looked at Colette as he stuffed a half peach into his mouth, the syrup running down his chin. He knew she must be hungry, but considering what he intended to do to her, he also knew that hunger would be the least of her worries. He looked at her, lying there so helpless. That's the way he wanted her.

He finished eating the peaches, drank the remaining syrup from the can, and tossed it in the corner. It made no difference if the can had his fingerprints on it. When he was through, the police could have a field day in this place for all he cared. That is, if they ever found this place.

He dragged the wooden chair across the room again and placed it next to Colette. Then he went back to the table and picked up his toolbox. He returned to her side and sat, smiling at her. He could see the terror in her eyes, smell it in her scent as she watched him.

Hutchinson removed a pair of scissors from the toolbox and cut the duct tape from the back of her head, taking some of her hair with it. He ripped it from her mouth in one motion as quickly as if he had slapped her. The action seemed to startle her. Her chest heaved up and down as she gulped in air.

She began to hyperventilate, and he had to wait a few minutes for her breathing to become normal.

Colette looked up at him. "Please...can I have a drink of water?"

He titled his head. How strange, he thought. Of all the things he expected to hear from her, pleading, questioning, crying, she asks for a drink of water.

Hutchinson took a folding tin cup from his toolbox, went into the bathroom, and came back with the water. Then he threw it in her face. She half-screamed as the cold water splashed over her.

"That was to get your attention," he said. He went back to the bathroom, filled the cup with water and returned. "Now you can have a drink." He held the cup to her lips with one hand and lifted her head with the other. She gulped it down.

"Want more?" he asked.

She shook her head.

He placed the cup back in the toolbox, then sat in the chair next to her. "Now I want to explain why you're here. I want you to know why this is happening to you. That's the surprise I promised you."

"Please," she said, "I haven't done anything to you."

"No, of course you haven't," he said, still smiling. "You don't think I'd kidnap someone without explaining why, do you? Only a crazy person would do that. You've a right to know, and I'm—"

Colette lifted her head. "Please, Frank...I promise—"

Suddenly he slapped her face so hard that her head was thrown back onto the cot. That gave him satisfaction; it was almost like slapping Montgomery. Her lower lip, which was puffed from the punch she took in her apartment, started to bleed. "Didn't your mother ever tell you that it's bad manners to interrupt? I removed the tape so you could speak, but not until I give you permission. If you interrupt me again, I'll use my fist instead of my hand. Is that understood?"

She nodded as she lay there, looking at him with wide eyes.

He leaned back in the chair and folded his arms. "Now I'm going to tell you something that I'm sure you don't know. Your lover and I go back many years. You see, I was Grant Montgomery's agent when he was first breaking into show business. I was a good agent, too. I handled all of his bookings. He paid me the standard commission, fifteen percent of his gross. The more money he made, the more money I made. But I had a secret. I started to take narcotics— heroin to be exact—and I became addicted." He paused for a moment, watching her. She seemed to be paying attention. "I needed more money to support my habit. At first, I borrowed some money from Montgomery, but I couldn't pay him back and I couldn't keep asking him for more or he would've started to suspect something. So I began to steal money from him. It was easy, because as his agent, I handled the money. I learned to forge his signature on checks. But then he found out and fired me. My reputation was ruined. I was only human and made a mistake, but I couldn't get a job in the business anymore. That wasn't fair, was it?"

He waited for an answer. "I asked you a question."

Colette seemed to be confused. She opened her mouth as if to speak, but he heard no sound. "Oh yes," he said. "You have my permission to speak."

"No…it wasn't fair."

"I know you don't mean that. You're just trying to pacify me, because you're too frightened to say what you mean."

She lowered her eyes.

"I was a professional man, but I finally had to accept menial jobs to earn a living. I couldn't keep my wife and son in the same lifestyle they were used to. Finally, my wife couldn't take it anymore and she left me. She took my six-year-old son, Bobby, with her. I begged her not to go, but she wouldn't listen to me. Said she was ashamed of what I had done. She ended up divorcing me. All because I made a mistake and Grant Montgomery fired me. If he hadn't done that, I'd be a different man today. Look at me. I've lost my hair, my eyesight has gone bad, I've lost a lot of weight, and I have to make a living as a maintenance and repair man. That doesn't seem fair, does it?"

She shook her head.

He leaned forward in his chair, his arms still folded. "I'll tell you something else that no one knows. I got even with my wife for leaving me. I waited for her one evening when she came out of a movie with this guy she was dating. I followed them, thinking they were going to her apartment, but they weren't. They were going to his apartment. I knew what they were going to do. I use to follow them for a long time just like I followed you. I learned their pattern. One evening, I got into his apartment building and waited for them to get in bed. Then I broke in and killed both of them. With a knife."

He reached in the toolbox next to his feet and withdrew a dark leather sheath from which a gold handle protruded. He gripped the handle and slid out a double-edged dagger. He held it before him with both hands, blade up, as a priest would hold a chalice. The faint glow of the kerosene lamp glittered on the silver blade. Hutchinson looked at it with reverence. "This is the knife. The police never solved the case. They said it was the work of a homicidal maniac." He looked at her. "Can you imagine? Me, of all people, a homicidal maniac? What do they know? I've proved I'm smarter than they are."

He put the knife in his lap, still clutching the handle. "Do you want to ask me any questions?"

"What...what happened to your son?"

"Bobby went to live with his grandmother on his mother's side. He's a young man now, but I haven't seen him since he was six years old. He thinks I'm dead, you know. Isn't that a sad story?"

Colette nodded. "Yes, it is."

"Well, the story is going to get happier, because I like happy endings. Now I'm going to settle the score with Montgomery just as I settled it with my ex-wife. So you see, I have nothing against you. It's Montgomery I want. You're just a means to an end." He paused. "Would you like to know how I'm going to settle it with your lover?"

Her lips were trembling, her lower lip still bleeding. "How?"

Hutchinson leaned in closer until his lips were almost touching her right ear, then he whispered to her. "I'm going to make him pay by what I do to you."

CHAPTER NINE

Santucci extended the mug of coffee across his desk to Grant. Earlier, after a quick look through Colette's apartment, they'd finished their canvassing of most of the tenants on the fifth floor of The Halifax. Although a few recalled seeing Colette that week, none of them could shed any light on her whereabouts.

Grant accepted the coffee. "Where do we go from here, Tom?"

"We still haven't questioned everyone at The Halifax. I'll have a couple of our men go there this afternoon and talk to some of the folks who weren't in when we were there. Colette might show up in the meantime and surprise all of us."

Grant peered over the coffee mug, which he held to his lips. "What if she doesn't?"

"Does she have any relatives other than her aunt in Virginia?"

"Some distant cousins," Grant said, "but no one she's close to. Nobody I know."

"Then we'll call her aunt," Santucci said, "and if she doesn't know anything, we'll start calling her clients. We'll have to go into her apartment again to find a list of them." Santucci took a sip of his coffee, then placed the mug on his desk. He looked at Grant. "I'm hoping it doesn't come to this, but if we come up empty and Colette doesn't show up by the end of the day, I'm afraid we'll have to consider her as missing."

Grant lowered his gaze to his coffee mug. "I have a bad feeling about this. It's been with me since last night. Normally

I wouldn't worry about her just because I hadn't seen her in a while. We're not glued together twenty-four hours a day. But missing the affair last night and having someone else phone in that she'd be late just doesn't sit right with me."

Santucci cocked his head. "What are you talking about? Who phoned that she'd be late?"

"I thought I told you at the reception that someone left word for me that she was going to be detained."

"Well, hell's fire, maybe you did, but I wasn't on duty at the reception, so I wouldn't have made a mental note of it."

"Then I'm glad I mentioned it now," Grant said. "The stage manager said a ticket salesman took the call, but the caller didn't leave a name. It was a man's voice, though. That's all I know."

"I'll want to talk to that salesman and see if I can find out anything more, some detail he might've forgotten." Santucci drummed his fingers on his desk. "We know she didn't ask the manager of The Halifax to call, but maybe she left word with someone else in the office to call the theater."

Grant shook his head. "There are only two women who alternate hours in that office, and neither one of them has a man's voice."

Santucci's frown worked its way up past his widow's peak. He scratched the side of his chin. "They do have a doorman there. If she had to leave in a hurry, she might've asked him to call the Benedum."

"I've already checked with the doorman," Grant said. "He didn't place the call."

Santucci looked up at the ceiling, then at Grant. "Sweet Christ, you're a step ahead of me playing detective. Now is there anything else I should know?"

"Yeah, there is," Grant said, staring off into space, "but whether you want to admit it or not, I think you already know it."

"Know what?"

Grant returned his gaze to Santucci. "You don't have to wait until this evening to classify Colette as missing."

The sun dipped in a distant horizon, extending slow shadows over the forest.

Hutchinson returned from his car carrying a CD radio cassette recorder. He placed it on the floor next to Colette, and raised her in a sitting position on the cot. Her wrists and ankles were still taped, her arms behind her back.

He placed a tape cassette into the cassette player. The black rectangular player had an antenna, two built-in speakers, and could accommodate either a cassette or a compact disc. He turned up the volume control. With his forefinger, he pushed up his dark-framed glasses on the bridge of his nose and looked at Colette. The light from the kerosene lamp cast a dull orange glow throughout the shack. He sat in front of her, intrigued by the play of light on her face and body, but amused by her fear.

Frank Hutchinson was going to enjoy this. It's what he had lived for since that day two years ago when he made the biggest decision of his life. He remembered the moment well. It was early November in the cold gray haze of a Minnesota morning. He had been confined to a drug rehabilitation center in Minneapolis, where he had worked periodically at menial jobs, anything he could get to sustain himself. His health had deteriorated over the years, and he was struggling with his addiction to heroin. They had given him methadone, once a day, then every other day in smaller doses until the doctors believed his physical addiction could be kept under control if he had the will power to stay clean. And he did develop the will power, spawned by his determination to get even with the person he considered responsible for his condition.

While in the rehab center, he was alone frequently with time to think and to plan. He wasn't responsible for his unfortunate condition, he had told himself over and over until he believed it. No, all he was responsible for was making a mistake. Grant Montgomery was responsible. It all started with him. Montgomery didn't have to fire him because he stole money from him by forging his signature on checks. Montgomery had a lot of money. What did thirty-five thousand dollars mean to him? Nothing. *Montgomery could have looked the other way*, he thought, *let me pay off my debts. But no, he had to fire me when he discovered what I had done.*

On November 3, when his treatment at the center was finished, the doctors had told him that they could do no more for him, that the rest was up to him. His two months of confinement in the rehab center had allowed him to fantasize how he was going to get even. Yet up to that point, he wasn't sure if he could ever realize his fantasy. He had thought of a dozen ways to kill Montgomery. But with that simple admonition from the doctor, "The rest is up to you," he knew, at that moment, that his fantasy would become reality. It *was* up to him. After all, if he could settle the score with the woman who abandoned him and took away his son, why not the man who was the root cause of all his misfortune? He would have to change his identity and track down Montgomery. That's how he would take charge of his life again. The rest was, indeed, up to him.

Now at last his day had come.

Hutchinson looked at Colette. "You're probably wondering why I have this tape recorder here, aren't you?"

Her eyes never left his face. She only nodded.

"Well, you see, Colette, by now, your lover must be getting worried about you, wondering where you are. So I'm gonna call him and tell him that you're with me." He studied her for a moment and smiled. "Oh, no, I can see by that little gleam in your eye that you think I'm holding you for ransom. No, not all. I'm not interested in money. I'm only interested in making him suffer. I'll tell him that he'll hear a recording of your voice. Would you like to make a recording for your lover?"

He could see the fear still in her face, but now a new emotion, confusion, crept into her eyes, and he knew she was trying to respond to what she didn't understand.

Her voice quivered. "Please...I don't—"

He broke in. "No, I don't think you'll like making this kind of a recording, Colette, but you'll have no choice. You see, you won't actually speak to your lover. I'm only gonna let him hear you screaming. That way your pain will become his pain. You're merely an instrument to help me achieve my purpose—

you might say an innocent victim of circumstances, just like I was. You know, I once read that the longer revenge is delayed, the crueler it grows. Believe me, that's true. So now you understand, don't you?"

Grant was exhausted from only three hours sleep the night before, but mostly from worrying about Colette. He managed to get two additional hours of sleep that afternoon when he returned to his home after meeting with Santucci. He had decided that the best thing he could do was let the police continue their investigation of Colette's whereabouts. The afternoon sleep had refreshed him, but he was restless, still worried, unsure of what he could do, if anything, to help the police.

He went to the full-length picture window in his living room. Dusk began to shade the city as the waning light melted into a cinnamon sky. He had admired the scene countless times. The streets and bridges below were packed with the daily migration of cars heading into the suburbs. Tomorrow dawn would awaken the city, and the same cars would return to the downtown area as surely as they would leave again at the break of sunset. The world followed a predictable pattern of behavior, and only when a life was suddenly disrupted, that pattern was broken and the world spun off course.

Maybe her life wasn't disrupted, he thought. Maybe Santucci was right. Colette would just show up this evening and wonder what all the concern was about. He would like to believe that, but he couldn't.

The phone rang. Santucci might have uncovered some information.

He heard an unfamiliar voice.

"Listen carefully, Montgomery. I'm only going to repeat this once. I have Colette Hershfield with me."

Grant tightened his grip on the receiver. "Who is this?"

"I'm the person who left the message at the Benedum that Colette would be a little late," the voice said. "Well, she certainly is a little late, isn't she?"

Grant's heart began to pound. "Is this some kind of a sick joke?"

"Joke?" said the strange voice. "You'll soon see how much of a joke this is. Now keep your mouth shut and listen. I want you to know what it's like to lose someone close to you. I lost someone close to me once and you're the one who's to blame. Now I'm gonna make you pay—"

Grant interrupted. "What are you talking about? Where's Colette?"

"I told you to keep your mouth shut. Your girlfriend is with me, and I'm afraid she's rather helpless. Very soon you'll receive an audio tape, and I want to make sure you have a tape recorder handy."

Jesus, who's on the other end of the line? he wondered. "Is Colette all right?"

"She's just fine, and I'm sure she misses you. Sleep well tonight, and look for my tape. It'll be a message from Colette."

Grant clutched the receiver tighter. "Listen to me—" But he heard the click as the line went dead.

My God, he thought, *Colette's been kidnapped. I knew something was wrong. Damn it, I knew it. Is she hurt? Dear God, please don't let her be hurt.*

With the receiver still in his hand, he called Santucci, who was in his office. "Tom, I just got a call from someone, a man, who claims that he has Colette and that she's helpless."

"Jesus Christ," Santucci said so loudly that Grant had to move the receiver from his ear. "What did he say?"

Grant found himself running out of breath. "It was like a phone call from hell. He's the person who called the Benedum and—"

"How do you know?"

"He told me so. He said I'd receive an audio tape very soon, that it would be a message from Colette."

"Son of a bitch, she's been kidnapped. She's being held for ransom. Did he ask for money?"

"No, but he said something very strange...something about someone he lost who was close to him. Said I'm responsible, that he was going to make me pay."

"Do you have any idea what he meant?"

"I don't have a clue," Grant said.

A few seconds passed before Santucci spoke. "Did he say anything else?"

"I don't think so...I was caught off guard. He wouldn't let me say much."

Grant heard the urgency in Santucci's voice. "Grant, try to reconstruct the conversation as best you can word-for-word. Write it down now while it's still fresh in your memory. We're dealing with a federal offense here, so I'll have to bring in the FBI. You just stay put. We'll try to get to your place as soon as we can." Santucci paused. "This is a long shot, but did the voice sound at all familiar to you, even vaguely familiar?"

"No, I've never heard it before."

"Could you detect any accent?"

"Nothing. His voice sounded strange, like he was disguising it. At first, I didn't know whether or not to believe him. But I'm now convinced of one thing."

"What?"

Grant was breathing heavily. "Colette's in the hands of a man who knows me—or thinks he does."

Within an hour, Tom Santucci, Sergeant Vasquez and three FBI agents were in Grant's Mount Washington house. Grant had written a transcript, recalling as best he could each word of his conversation with the caller, and the FBI agents reviewed it while questioning him. Jim Dowling, the special agent in charge, was in his late forties, had blond hair combed straight back, and spoke in a soft voice. His partners, Tony Lapanski and Dan Merrick, were a few years younger. Tony, with dark, wavy hair and a trimmed mustache, seemed to have a perennial smile. He brought equipment with him, which included analog and digital scanners, a computer, and a tape recorder. Dan, at six-foot-three, was taller than the other two, and had shoulders like a football lineman. His chestnut-colored hair was showing signs of receding.

Grant knew that Dowling was now in charge, and that Santucci and Vasquez would give the FBI every cooperation possible, both having worked well with the Bureau on other cases.

Dowling, who was sitting on the living-room sofa, placed the transcript that Grant had prepared on the coffee table. Lapanski was sitting next to him and Merrick was perched on the armrest of the couch. Santucci and Vasquez were settled in easy chairs next to Grant.

"Good work, Mr. Montgomery," Dowling said. "Most people getting a call like that would be so excited that they wouldn't be able to get their facts straight. I'm glad you kept your wits about you."

Grant instinctively traced the scar on his chin with his thumb. "I just hope it helps. And please call me Grant. What's our next move?"

Dowling gestured toward Santucci. "The first thing is that Tom's people will work with our boys in checking out Colette's apartment. In fact, they're already on the job. They'll dust the place for prints and check for hair or fiber samples, possibly blood, anything that might indicate if a stranger was in her apartment and if a struggle took place."

"You'll probably find my fingerprints all over the place," Grant said.

Dowling nodded. "We're aware that you and Miss Hershfield had a relationship."

Grant shifted his weight in the chair. "I wish you wouldn't put that in the past tense."

Dowling half smiled. "Sorry, it was just a matter of expression. While Miss Hershfield's apartment is being checked, we're going to set up a wiretap of your phone here. Agents Lapanski and Merrick are experts in that area. We initiated a court order to do the tap as soon as I got the call from Tom." Dowling dropped his gaze for a second, then looked at Grant. "But I want you to understand something. As we're doing our job, you'll have the hardest job of all—and that's waiting. We know the kidnapper is definitely going to make contact with you again. Although we'll be with you every step of the way, you'll still have to tough it out."

Grant nodded. "I realize that, but my concern is not for what I have to go through. It's for Colette and what she's going through."

Dowling said, "And that's exactly what's going to make it toughest on you. I've been down this road before, and I've seen people in your situation fold and blow the whole thing in spite of the instructions we give them. We don't want that to happen here."

Santucci interrupted. "Jim, I don't think you're going to have that problem with Grant. I've known him a long time, and he'll do whatever it takes."

"Good," Dowling said. He returned his attention to Grant. "Now, here's what we need you to do."

Grant leaned forward, ready to absorb every word.

"The chances are this tape recording from Miss Hershfield is to let you know that he's not bluffing, that he does have her," Dowling said. "I say 'he' but there could be more than one kidnapper involved, so we don't assume anything. He'll probably give her a written message to read that pleads for her life and asks you to follow instructions. That's designed to soften you up. We don't know if you'll get any immediate demand for money, so we'll have to wait and see. How he has this tape delivered is another matter. Maybe by mail or maybe he has you pick it up somewhere."

Grant took a deep breath. "All right, assuming there's no immediate demand for money on the tape, what do you want me to do?"

Dowling tightened his lips in thought. "I don't think he'll continue to communicate with you by tape. The delivery or pickup of a tape takes too long. I don't have a crystal ball, but if my intuition is right, you'll get follow-up phone calls from this guy." He stabbed the air, pointing at Grant. "It's important that you keep him on the line as long as possible. If he demands money, ask him to repeat the amount. He might tell you to deliver the money to a remote location. Even if you know where it is, pretend you don't. Ask him how to get there.

If he doesn't go for that, tell him that you don't want anything to happen to Miss Hershfield, that she means everything to you and that you'll do anything to get her back as long as they promise not to hurt her. Saying all that eats up time, and the more time we can get to trace the call, the better."

Grant frowned, looking at Dowling. "He's bound to know you guys are on the case, unless he's an idiot. If he was smart enough to kidnap Colette, don't you think he'd be smart enough to detect a stall like that?"

"Maybe," Dowling said, "but we can't assume that. We still have to try. And don't lose sight of the fact that you have something going for you that most other victims don't. As an entertainer, you know how to convince people that you're being sincere. So I'd say that if he calls you, you've got the biggest acting job of your life facing you." Dowling rose and walked to the mantel. He turned and faced Grant. "I don't mean to put that kind of pressure on you, Grant, but we need to get a fix on this guy."

"Don't worry about pressure on me," Grant said, "and I don't think I'm the victim here. But what if this creep calls from a pay phone somewhere? Even if you could trace it, that's not going to tip you off on where he's hiding Colette."

"No," Dowling said, "but we might be able to tell if he's in a certain area of the city. If he calls you a second time, hopefully we can trace it and find out if he's in the same area of town or a different area. That tells us whether he's on the move or not. And chances are he'll call you a second time, maybe more. Sometimes the first call demands a certain amount of money. The second call gives instructions on the drop point. He might threaten to kill her if you don't cooperate. But not all kidnappers work alike. So we have to stay flexible and expect anything. How he operates will tell us what kind of a person we're up against." Dowling went behind the couch and placed his hands on the backrest. "I just wanted to alert you to what you might expect."

Grant stood, rubbing the back of his neck. "I understand completely, Jim, but I can't guarantee that I can keep him on the phone for as long as you need."

"Do your best. That's all we can ask of you." Dowling gave a nod to Lipanski, who rose and started to unpack and set up the equipment with Merrick helping him. Dowling sat on the couch again, shot a glance at Santucci and Vasquez, then focused on Grant. "My people are going to be here for as long as it takes. We'll sleep in shifts."

Santucci rose from his chair and looked at Dowling. "Emilio and I will help relieve the three of you."

Grant jumped in before Dowling could agree. "Like hell you will, Tom. You've got a wife and two daughters. You're going home to your family tonight. Same goes for you, Emilio. I can see you two guys tomorrow." Grant motioned to Dowling and his two agents. "The four of us can handle it."

Santucci started to object, but Grant raised his hand to silence him and turned to Dowling. "I'm not trying to interfere with what you have to do, but I don't want to take these men away from their families, unless you absolutely need them here all night."

Grant sensed that Dowling didn't like his quick reaction on who was going to sleep where, but noticed the concession in Dowling's expression.

"We all have families we'd rather be with tonight," Dowling said, "but we also have a job to do. I don't think Tom and Sergeant Vasquez have to keep a vigil with us tonight, but I do want them here early tomorrow, no later than seven. If I need them earlier, I'll call."

Santucci looked at Dowling. "We wouldn't stay away from this one if you ordered us to. We'll be here at six."

Grant shook hands with Santucci and Vasquez, and walked them to the door.

"Grant, I appreciate your concern for us," Santucci said, "but this is no time to worry about me and Emilio. We're in this all the way with you."

Grant managed a smile. "That's why I need both of you to get a good night's sleep."

That evening, Tom Santucci waited for his two teenage daughters, Carol and Kathy, to go up to their rooms to do their homework after dinner, which was their nightly ritual strictly imposed by him and his wife, Marie. She kept her hair pulled back in a bun when she wasn't out having dinner with Tom or attending a PTA or some social function. She looked a little older than Tom, although she was three years younger. Still, he found her as attractive as the day he married her, and often told her so. Tom stood at the sink, helping her dry the dishes.

"What's the matter, Tom?" Marie asked. "You seemed preoccupied throughout dinner." Very little about Tom escaped Marie's attention.

"I waited for the kids to leave because I didn't want to discuss this in front of them."

Marie was about to hand him a plate to dry. "Discuss what?"

"Someone's kidnapped Colette Hershfield."

The plate slipped from Marie's hand and shattered on the floor. "My God, you're not serious."

"Afraid so. I just found out about it this evening."

Tom picked up the cracked pieces from the floor; Marie was wide-eyed. "I can't believe it," she said.

"Grant got the call from the kidnapper this evening, and he called me right after that." He put the pieces in the garbage can under the sink. "I knew you'd be shocked. I was, too. The kidnapper said Grant would receive a tape with a message on it from Colette. This is the same guy who called the Benedum and said Colette was going to be late." He filled her in on what little details he knew.

Marie sat at the kitchen table. Her eyes teared. "Oh, Tom, I'm sick about this. I just can't believe it."

He stood next to her and put his hand on her shoulder. "I know, honey. Kidnapping is a federal offense and I had to bring in the FBI, so at least we've got an experienced team working on this. Normally, they handle this kind of case on their own, but Dowling and I've worked together before, and he wants me involved on this one. Maybe because I'm close to Grant."

"What are they going to do?" she asked through her tears.

"Tap Grant's phone to trace any more calls. If the kidnapper demands a ransom, I'm sure they'll set a trap for him."

"How's Grant taking it?"

"He's putting up a good front," Tom said, "but I know what he must be going through."

"That poor guy." She looked up at Tom. "This is going be all over the media. The girls are bound to hear about it," Marie said, wiping her eyes. Her daughters were as fond of Grant as Tom and his wife.

"I know, but I'd rather it not be tonight."

Emilio Vasquez had explained the kidnapping to his wife, Consuela. The dark-haired woman with flashing eyes had never met Grant's girl, but she sympathized with her as if she had known Colette for years.

"It's so terrible," she said. "She must be going through hell." She looked at Emilio. "What are her chances of coming out of this alive?"

They were sitting on the sofa in their living room. He took her hand in his. "I don't know. I've never been involved in a kidnapping case. The FBI has those statistics."

Consuela shook her head. "Grant seems like such a nice man," she said, only having met him for the first time at the reception. "He must be going through a similar hell."

"Yeah, he's a good man, though," Emilio said. "You know, when you help to save a man's life, you feel close to him. That's why this case bothers me so much."

"If they're holding her for ransom, he has the money to pay, doesn't he?"

"He does now, but he didn't always. Grant grew up in a poor neighborhood, and he knows what it's like to struggle for a buck. Tom told me that Grant worked his way through college doing a mentalist act and some magic. He hasn't forgotten his roots."

"I know, but it's more than that," she said. "He has a certain strength of character. You can see it in him."

Emilio nodded, then looked into space. "There's something else you can't see in him, though."

She looked at him. "What?"

"He has the capacity to kill, if he has to. He's been in Vietnam. And he's had to kill since then to save his life. Working with us hasn't been easy for him. Remember the Hernandez and Florentine cases?"

"I remember," she said, "but the war was the war. And his life was in jeopardy with those two cases he worked on. You can't blame him for defending himself, can you?"

"No," Emilio said. "A man does what he has to do—only this time, there isn't much he can do."

Grant made three bedrooms available for the FBI agents. Tony Lapanski took the first two-hour shift, sitting in the living room by the wiretapping equipment and tape recorder. Dowling would take the second shift, Merrick the third. If the phone rang, the plan called for Grant to get into the living room in seconds. All four phones in the house were tapped, but Dowling wanted Grant to answer the phone in the living room, where the agents would be stationed, so that Dowling could give him hand signals if necessary. They had the signals worked out. If Dowling moved his closed thumbs and forefingers in opposite directions as if he were stretching a rubber band, it meant they needed more time to complete the phone trace. Gesturing as if he were coaxing someone to come forward meant that Grant should try to get more information. Showing his opened hand in a stop gesture signaled Grant to stall or remain silent.

Grant lay on his bed fully clothed. He looked at the phone on the nightstand next to his bed. Sleep wouldn't come. His senses were sharpened to every sound in the night, a distant car somewhere, the rustling of leaves against a drain pipe, the almost imperceptible footsteps of one of the agents in the carpeted hallway. He was like a compressed spring ready to release.

The thought of Colette in the hands of a kidnapper burned into his brain. Why would someone have done such a thing? Someone he apparently knew who wanted to make him pay for the loss of a loved one. *Who in the name of God could it be,* he wondered, *and why would he think I was responsible?*

He ransacked his mind, trying to remember everyone he ever knew who had lost a loved one, anyone who might have ever lamented his loss, anything from the past that might serve as a clue. The FBI had questioned him about it at length. But he still couldn't remember anything that might help them. Nothing he ever did would have triggered such an act in another person. No one he knew was capable of such a crime.

He stared at the ceiling. His mind kept turning back to Colette. How terrified she must be. Dowling said there might be a threat of harm to Colette if he didn't cooperate. He would pay any price to get her back. He would give all he had and, if necessary, beg and borrow the rest for her safe return. If her kidnapper gets what he demands, there was hope that he would free her. As long as she couldn't identify him. *And whoever the bastard is,* Grant thought, *he has to be smart enough to mask his identity or keep Colette blindfolded.*

He kept telling himself that the abductor would have no reason to harm Colette if he got what he wanted. Grant had to hold on to that hope. The alternative was unthinkable.

CHAPTER TEN

Colette lay shivering on the cot. Her captor was sitting at the table, watching her. In the faint light of the lamp behind him, she could only make out his outline. But she could still see those eyes, those terrible, luminous eyes behind the thick lenses observing her. He hardly moved, except for an occasional shifting of his weight. It seemed as though he had been looking at her like that for hours. But he hadn't spoken to her in all that time.

She remembered the last thing he told her, that he had the tape recorder because he wanted Grant to hear her screaming, that her pain would become Grant's pain. What did he intend to do? She was at the mercy of this crazy savage. It had taken her countless hours to admit the fact that he *was* crazy. If he had kidnapped her for ransom, that would have been terrifying enough. But this—to harm her in some way so he could make a recording of her screams to torment Grant—this was sadistic insanity.

Colette was numb with fear and exhaustion. She didn't know how long it had been since she had slept. When would Hutchinson make good on his threat? She heard the creek in the chair again as he changed his position. It was a sound that seemed to rip through her body, making her tremble. Each time she heard it, she thought he was getting up to approach her, to begin torturing her. Her heart would start to throb until she realized that he had only moved in his chair, that he was still watching her. Waiting for what, she didn't know.

She was almost that frightened only once before, when she was six. She and three other girls had made fun of a classmate's mother, who had a prominent, hooked nose. They teased the woman's daughter that her mother looked like a witch. The mother, who was on the Hartwood Elementary school playground one afternoon, decided to teach them a lesson. She told Colette and the other three girls that, as a witch, she would put a curse on them for the grave sin they had committed in taunting her daughter. She told them that when they went to bed that evening, she would conjure up an evil spirit to come into their bedrooms and take them far away to a dark place where they would never see their parents and friends again. Colette was petrified at hearing such a curse, and the fact that it had come from this woman, who looked like a witch, proved that she must be a witch.

After school that day when she went home, she refused to go into her room to do her homework. She was afraid to tell her parents that her sin brought a terrible curse on her. She had no appetite for dinner, only picking at her food, and tried to delay going into her room until her parents forced her to go to bed. In bed, she was too afraid to even move. The pale night light next to her bed offered little comfort. She prayed that the evil spirit would not come, that the guardian angel her mother told her about so often would protect her. But she had never seen this guardian angel, who now might have abandoned her. Then she heard noises outside of her room.

There it was again, like footsteps getting closer.

This was the evil spirit that the witch told her would come to take her. She threw the blanket over her head and started to cry. "Mommy, Mommy," she whimpered, her body shaking. Then she felt the blanket being wrested from her grip, the evil monster about to grab her, and she screamed until she thought her lungs would burst. But she was rescued from her living nightmare by the familiar warmth of her mother's hand stroking her hair and her soothing voice telling Colette that she only had a bad dream and it was all over. And she soon realized that there was no evil spirit and that the guardian angel she prayed to was her mother. That night she slept in her parents' bed, secure in the protective presence of her father and in the warmth of her mother whom she held tightly.

But that was long ago. She could never be that little girl again with a father to safeguard her and a mother to comfort her. Now she was alone. Bound and helpless. With a madman staring at her.

If only Grant knew where she was being held captive, he would come for her with the aid of the police, with the entire U. S. Army and Navy if necessary. But he didn't know. How could he when she didn't know where she was herself?

Colette's exhaustion began to overtake her fear. She didn't think it was possible to sleep, no matter how long she had been awake, but she felt herself fading, her body paralyzed with weakness. The outline of the man watching her seemed to blur. She fought to stay awake, but the foggy cobwebs in her brain were being pulled down like a blind shutting out the last residue of light. And she finally let go, retreating into the protective darkness of sleep.

The heel of his boot crushed out the cigarette on the wooden floor as the kidnapper watched Colette sleeping. Let her rest for a few hours. She wouldn't be any good to him if she were too exhausted. He needed her to be alert, to understand the full impact of what was happening to her, so that when Montgomery heard her on tape, he wouldn't hear a whimper or the groggy sob of a woman who was exhausted. Instead, he would hear the terrifying screams of a woman fully awake, fully aware, feeling the full intensity of her pain.

So as Colette slept, bound to the cot, unable to move, Hutchinson decided to get a few hours sleep, as well. He could sleep right there in the chair. In the middle of the night, he would awaken her when she was refreshed, and phase two of his plan would begin. Then it would be time to turn on the tape recorder.

Dowling was sitting in front of the picture window in Grant's living room. He had been an FBI agent for eighteen years. Eighteen long, hard years. His job frequently took him away from his family for weeks at a time. He knew those absences were not fair to his wife, Susan, or to their two children, Billy, eleven, and Linda, nine. He missed them terribly when he had to be away from them for long periods. Now he was on a kidnapping case, and God knows how long he would have to be gone this time. Susan, bless her, was understanding, and never put any pressure on him to find another line of work. She knew he loved being an agent.

On those occasions that they both dreaded, when he had to tell her that he was given another assignment that might keep him away for weeks, she would merely smile and make him promise that he would be extra careful and come back to them as soon as possible. Those occasions were becoming more frequent, and he was beginning to love his job less. Billy and Linda were growing up, and he had to miss too many of the small events in their lives that were really big events—the final little league game, the school play, the annual church family picnic. He was lucky, he told himself. So very lucky to have Susan, Billy, and Linda. What would he ever do without them? He couldn't bear the thought of losing them. And that made him think about Grant Montgomery.

What must Montgomery be feeling now? Only a small percentage of those ever kidnapped for reasons other than ransom came out of such an ordeal alive. And if the kidnapper was deranged, no telling what might happen. God, if anything like that ever happened to Susan or to one of his children, he didn't know what he would do. He wouldn't be able to stand it. At that moment, he no longer wanted to be a special agent in charge of anything. He suddenly wanted to be back with his family, to hold Susan and Billy and Linda in his arms so tightly that he could crush them. He wanted desperately for this case to be over.

Grant went into the living room, where Jim Dowling was on the second watch. Dowling seemed like a lonely figure, sitting in front of the window. He was either admiring the night view of the city, Grant surmised, or wondering what would be on the kidnapper's tape. Or maybe he missed his family tonight.

Dowling turned when Grant entered the room. "Couldn't sleep?"

"Afraid not," Grant said.

Dowling got up and went to the couch. "Hope you don't mind my rearranging some of your furniture." He had moved one of the chairs in front of the window. "That's a hell of a view you have here."

Grant approached him with his hands in his pockets. "Were you admiring it or thinking about the same thing I am?"

Dowling feigned a smile and eased his weight onto the couch. Grant remained standing.

"Jim, give it to me straight. What are Colette's chances?"

Dowling smoothed the crease on his trousers, avoiding eye contact with Grant. "That's a tough one to call. It depends on what type of person kidnapped her. If he's strictly after money and doesn't want a murder rap hanging over his head, then her chance of being released is good—if he gets what he wants."

"What if she can identify this person?"

Dowling looked up at Grant. "Usually kidnappers keep themselves masked or the victim blindfolded. Look, I know we've been over this a dozen times, but if you could just continue to search your memory for anyone who could possibly blame you for the death of a spouse, a friend, or anyone for that matter. That's the key to finding the identity of the kidnapper."

"I've racked my brain trying, believe me, but I keep coming up empty." Grant hunched his shoulders. "There's no one I know who ever blamed me or could blame me for the loss of a loved one—not a friend, not a relative, not a business associate, not even a fan."

"All right," Dowling said, his voice heavy with weariness, "give it a rest for tonight. Maybe tomorrow you'll remember something that might help us."

Grant went to the picture window. A thousand lights in the city and suburbs formed an iridescent tapestry against the darkness. "What if this guy isn't after money?"

Dowling released a deep breath. "Then we're faced with something else."

Her body was limp, belying the fact that her wrists and ankles still were tightly bound with duct tape. Frank Hutchinson continued to observe Colette. He had been awake now for fifteen minutes after having slept for four hours in his chair.

She was much too lovely for that ingrate he had once worked for so many years ago. He watched her breasts move with each breath she took, slowly ran his eyes over her body, found himself breathing heavier.

He felt his heart jump start again just as it did every day when he saw her for the first time in the morning as she took her walk. Lying there on her side in her long velvet dress that conformed to the shape of her body, she was the most desirable woman he had ever seen. But he had decided that he would not ravage her sexually. Not that he didn't desire her, God only knows, but he didn't want Montgomery to think for a second that his kidnapping of Colette was partially motivated by his physical lust for her. That could only be construed as a sign of weakness by the man he hated. On the contrary, he wanted Montgomery to know the bottomless depth of his hatred, which was focused completely and singularly on the mentalist. Satisfying his lust for Montgomery's woman would only allow his immense hatred to be misunderstood and, therefore, diminished.

Hutchinson glanced at his watch. 4:35 A.M. She'd had more than four hours of sleep, enough to refresh her so that she could have strength enough to resist and to scream her head off.

He positioned the tape recorder on the floor next to her cot, then grabbed her arm and shook her. "Wake up, you've had enough sleep." He waited for a couple of seconds, but she didn't respond. He shook her again. "I said wake up." He was surprised to find her exhaustion so deep that she couldn't easily be awakened.

Hutchinson raised the back of his hand and swept it down hard across her face. Colette grunted as her eyes opened wide. He knew she was disoriented for a few seconds. "You're awake now, aren't you? That's right, you're with me. Everything's copacetic."

She looked up at him, and he saw the terror return to her face as she became fully aware again of her predicament.

"You had a refreshing little sleep, Colette. Now it's time to make a little tape recording for your friend and lover, Mr. Montgomery. I'll bet you wish he was here now."

He kneeled on one knee to activate the tape recorder.

"I have to go to the bathroom," she said.

It hadn't ever occurred to him that she might have to relieve herself. But in order for her to do that, he would have to free her hands and feet. He didn't like the idea, but the alternative was to risk an accident in the cot.

"All right, goddamn it, but be quick about it." He retrieved a pair of scissors from his toolbox on the table, then cut the tape from her ankles. He allowed her to sit up while her wrists were still bound behind her. Hutchinson sat next to her. He tapped the scissors on her shoulder. "There's no window in that bathroom and only one way in and out through the door. So if you try anything tricky, I'll know it and you'll pay dearly. Understand?"

"I understand."

"If you're not out of that bathroom in exactly three minutes, I'm coming in. And you'll wish I hadn't." He turned Colette toward the wall and cut the tape from her wrists. He heard her moan as she brought her arms forward. She rubbed her arms and wrists.

"Stop wasting time," he said.

Colette rose from the cot and seemed unsteady on her feet. She massaged the knotted muscles in her thighs for a few seconds.

Hutchinson remained seated on the cot, watching her. "Remember, you've got just three minutes."

She limped into the bathroom and closed the door.

"How many kidnapping cases have you handled, Jim?" Grant sat opposite Jim Dowling in the living room, neither one of them capable of sleep.

"I've been in charge of three, and I've worked on two others in my eighteen years with the Bureau. Merrick and Lapanski have worked on several cases, as well." Dowling gave Grant a sideways glance. "You don't have an inexperienced team here, if that's what's on your mind."

"No, I realize that. The only thing that's on my mind is Colette's safety. Fill me in, will you. How do these cases normally go?"

Dowling took a shallow breath. "They vary, Grant. If Miss Hershfield has been kidnapped for ransom, the kidnappers—if there's more than one—will more than likely keep her at one location. Then, at some point, they'll give you a specific time and place that you're to make the drop, that is, deliver the money. That's where a kidnapper is most likely to get nailed, because he has to expose himself to pick up the ransom. But the ones who are easily caught are usually inexperienced hoodlums, half of the time drug addicts, who are desperate for money."

"I have the feeling our man isn't inexperienced," Grant said.

"You may very well be right. Experienced kidnappers won't release the victim until the money has been safely picked up. And the pick-up man doesn't return to wherever they're holding the victim for fear of being followed. But, through good surveillance, they're usually apprehended, no matter where they go."

"If they get the money, is the victim usually returned unharmed?" Grant asked.

"Sometimes. I don't have the statistics on it."

Grant noticed that, for the second time that evening, Dowling avoided eye contact.

Dowling said, "If any harm is inflicted on the victim, that becomes aggravated kidnapping, which is even a more severe felony."

Grant knew that Dowling purposely didn't give a direct answer. "What if the kidnapper isn't after money, but something else—like revenge?"

Dowling rested his chin in his hand, but his voice betrayed his casual manner. "You asked that question before, and, like I said, then we'd be faced with a different animal. We don't know what we're faced with yet. We just have to wait and see."

Grant leaned forward in his seat. "That doesn't answer the question, Jim, and you know it. You and I can't afford to be less than honest with each other. What you're thinking, but haven't said, is that we could be up against a crazy who's unpredictable, someone who might harm Colette to pay me back for whatever he thinks I've done to him. And if she can identify him, her life isn't worth much. Isn't that right?"

Dowling hesitated, then finally nodded. "I'm beginning to wonder if you really *can* read minds."

Colette had been in the bathroom for a full minute, frantically looking for anything that might serve as a weapon. Before she entered, she had said a silent prayer that the bathroom would have a medicine cabinet containing a man's shaving razor, or a drinking glass she could break, anything she could use as a weapon. But the bathroom was bare except for the stained commode, a pedestal sink that was cracked at the base, and two rolls of toilet paper. Colette was on the edge of hysteria as her eyes searched every inch of the bathroom. Nothing.

At least she was out of his sight, free from his tyrannical presence, even for a few minutes. But the door had no lock, and she was afraid he would open it any second and see her frantically scrounging around the room like a starved rat searching for food.

She knew he was timing her. She looked at the gold watch that Grant had given her. Another full minute had passed. One minute left. One minute before the madman would open the door, drag her to the cot and do God knows what.

Her prayer to find some sort of weapon went unanswered. She had to face it. She was totally defenseless against this brute, this man she had trusted, someone she had actually let into her apartment several times. This person she had thought was so shy.

Less than a minute remaining.

Colette looked up. An exposed light bulb was hanging from the ceiling. If she could get the bulb, maybe she could smash it against his face and run like hell. She stood on her toes. The bulb was more than a foot beyond her reach. Maybe if she stood on the toilet she could brace herself with one hand on the wall and unscrew the bulb with the other. But the light bulb was in the far end of the ceiling and the toilet was at the other end of the room, so she would have to stretch to reach it. She would have to position herself at what seemed like an impossible angle.

She glanced at her watch. Thirty or so seconds left. She had to work fast.

Colette took off her high-heeled shoes, stood on the toilet seat, braced herself with her left hand on the wall and leaned forward, reaching for the bulb. It was still three, maybe four inches beyond her reach.

If she could stretch just a little more.

She extended her body as far as she could without losing her balance, and the bottom of the light bulb was finally in her hand. She twisted it counter clockwise. The bulb burned her fingers, and she grimaced against the pain, but she didn't care how much it burned. She had to keep unscrewing it, and she could feel it loosen, thread by thread. The muscles is her arms and legs were aching. Only a few more twists and it would come out.

One last twist. Suddenly the bathroom was flooded in darkness, but the bulb was free of the socket and in her hand. She felt an exhilaration surge throughout her body. Colette leaned back to adjust her balance and looked down.

She froze.

He was standing there, framed in the doorway by the dim light of the kerosene lamp on the table, looking up at her with piercing eyes that seemed to be elevated from their sockets. His whisper cracked the silence like a scream in a graveyard. "Put it back."

She dropped the light bulb and it exploded on the floor. Colette kept looking down at him, unable to move.

Hutchinson took several steps toward her, grabbed her thighs and pulled her forward. She was suddenly smashed against him as he held her with both arms around her thighs. A second later, he relaxed his hold just enough to allow her to slide down his body until her feet were barely touching the floor.

Pressed against him, Colette winced from his hot breath in her face.

"What did you intend to do with that light bulb?"

She didn't answer.

"It doesn't matter," he said, still holding her with both arms around her waist.

Suddenly he released her, grabbed her hair and twisted her right arm behind her back. "It's time to entertain your lover with our little performance," he said and forced her into the other room toward the cot.

She began to struggle, but he twisted her arm harder and she screamed, "Stop!"

Hutchinson threw her on the cot face down. He placed both hands behind her back, and she couldn't hold back her sobs as she felt her wrists being wrapped tightly again with duct tape. He turned her on her back.

She watched him as he went to his toolbox, withdrew the gold-handled dagger and approached her.

Dear God, he was going to kill her. Her heart tried to hammer its way through her chest.

He stood before her, smiling, his horrid eyes showing a flash of excitement for the first time. She held her breath as he put the knife to her throat.

But he placed the knife at the neckline of her dress and sliced it down to her waist. He ripped the rest of her dress apart with both hands. A second later, her body stiffened at the touch of cold steel on her calf as he positioned the knife in the side slit of her full-length dress, held the end of the dress taught and ripped it open like an envelope.

Hutchinson knelt by her side, and pressed the record button of the tape recorder. Then he stood over her and she could feel his eyes burning through her body as he placed the knife under her bra and cut it open in a quick upward sweep.

Within seconds, Colette felt his clammy hands on her body. Her eyes were frozen on him, her mouth open but silent, the scream chocked off in her throat.

"Go ahead and scream all you want," he said, and ran the razor-edged cold steel along the supple flesh of her stomach.

CHAPTER ELEVEN

Sam Kassler still had a half hour before his morning meeting with Reinhardt and Hopkins, one of San Francisco's oldest law firms. He sat in a rose-colored Queen Anne chair in the plush lobby of the Fairmont Hotel, where the beige carpeting was an inch thick. Kassler watched people browsing through various shops in the hotel, which was a shopping village in itself. He often said that with enough money, one could live in the Fairmont and never have to leave the premises. And although the thought of doing just that appealed to him, he knew such a lifestyle was totally impractical.

A Japanese tour group entered the lobby, several of the members with cameras hung around their necks. One of them went to the registration desk while the others surveyed the luxurious surroundings. The one who registered them returned to his group, said something in Japanese, and escorted them to the back of the building, where the glass elevator was riding guests up to the twenty-second floor of the Fairmont Tower.

Kassler smiled with bitterness in his heart. The Japanese could afford such opulence; money was immune to race or nationality or religion. It could buy anything—companies, power, men. Now the Japanese owned the brokerage firm of Marshall, Sterns and Nobel, where he had worked for seven years. A Japanese conglomerate had acquired the firm eight months ago. The conglomerate ran the business by its own rules, calling the shots and demanding obedience and respect from the Americans who worked for them, whether the chairman or the janitor. Kassler felt as if the Japanese owned him. He hated them.

He remembered that day six months ago when he was summoned to his boss's office. Edward Marshall, president and chief executive officer, was sitting on one of the upholstered chairs in his palatial office like a visitor. Sitting behind the president's desk, however, was Toshimitsu Sangura, one of the principals of Sangura Industries, the Japanese conglomerate that had acquired Marshall, Sterns and Nobel. Ray Sterns had retired from the business two years ago, Floyd Nobel had died more than a decade ago, and Edward Marshall still kept the names of his former partners as part of the business, but only because that's the way Sangura wanted it.

Marshall rose when Kassler entered the office. "Come in, Sam. You know Mr. Sangura." During the takeover, Toshimitsu Sangura and several of his top lieutenants had visited the brokerage house often. After completion of the acquisition, their visits had become less frequent. The employees all knew what was expected of them.

Kassler was surprised to see Sangura in Ed Marshall's office. He was even more surprised to see him sitting at Marshall's desk.

Sangura smiled and nodded to Kassler, but he did not rise from Marshall's chair. Kassler guessed that if Sangura had stood, he would be shorter than Marshall, but sitting there in Ed Marshall's chair, he loomed like a giant.

As the head of one of Pittsburgh's top brokerage firms, Ed Marshall looked like anyone but an investment executive. He was five-foot seven, portly, and partially bald. He dressed well but, no matter how expensive the suit, it did not complement his stocky frame. He had, however, one of the best minds in the business and, therefore, was respected by clients and colleagues alike. Now he seemed nervous. "Have a seat, Sam," Marshall said, motioning to a chair in front of his desk. "The reason I called you is—"

Still smiling, Sangura raised his forearm with his palm open, his elbow resting on the desk. Marshall stopped in mid sentence. "If you don't mind, I'll take it from here."

Kassler sat in one of the chairs facing Sangura. The oriental was half Marshall's age, dressed in a dark blue suit, white shirt and print tie. His black hair was slicked back as if he had applied a pound of grease to it. His eyes were slits that seemed menacing, the perennial smile masking steel.

"I know you're a busy man, Mr. Kassler, so I'll make this brief." Sangura spoke perfect English, without the trace of an accent.

Kassler remembered from reading Sangura's biography that he was educated at Harvard. What the hell was up, he wondered.

"Since you're the man in charge of new business," Sangura said, "I thought it best that we speak face-to-face. To cut to the quick of it, you need to attract more investors. Income for last year was only four percent above the previous year." The smile disappeared. "So far this year, this firm is not meeting its financial goals. Your figures for the last quarter are below expectation. That's not acceptable, Mr. Kassler. I've already explained to the management of this organization—so you've heard this before—that Sangura Industries expects a minimum bottom-line increase this year of twenty percent. We wouldn't have acquired this company if we didn't think that was possible. This company has the potential. It's well established, has excellent portfolio management and solid accounts, all of which comprises a sound foundation for growth. Not status quo performance, but growth. This firm has to become much more aggressive in pursuit of new business if it's to meet our expectations. Do you agree?"

Kassler changed his position in the chair. "Yes, I do, however—"

Sangura raised his arm again. "I'm glad we agree on that point. Now, what are your plans to achieve our mutual objective?"

"Well, I've initiated a marketing and public relations program to strengthen our image and increase the portfolios we manage and—"

"And the result doesn't indicate much success, does it?"

Kassler shot a glance at Ed Marshall, who looked away. Clearly, Marshall was no longer in charge. "But the program has just started," Kassler said, "and it needs time to achieve results. I've hired one of the best public relations—"

"I'll give you three months, Mr. Kassler. Then you and I will talk again. I must make clear to you that, at that point, I'll have to see respectable if not dramatic improvement."

He wanted to tell him that three months wasn't sufficient time for "respectable if not dramatic improvement," whatever the hell that meant in terms of numbers, but he knew the conversation had ended. With the mere drop of Sangura's gaze, he had been dismissed, given his marching orders. Meeting adjourned. And Ed Marshall, with whom he had always had at least a fair relationship, had lost control of his company and couldn't give him any support. The pressure would become worse by the day. He had enough of that kind of treatment at home. He couldn't accept the new ownership of his firm, and he knew he could never rise any further in the organization. With Blanche on one side of him and now Sangura on the other, Sam Kassler wanted out, and he intended to get out. But he had another problem to solve first.

Kassler checked his watch. More time had passed than he thought, and he would be late for his meeting if he didn't hurry. He left the lobby of the Fairmont and entered a cab in front of the hotel. Traffic was unusually heavy and what should have been a five-minute ride took fifteen.

He entered the law offices of Reinhardt and Hopkins ten minutes late for his meeting.

"Sorry to be late, Bill," Kassler said as he approached the slender gray-haired man who came from behind an oak desk to shake his hand. The wood-paneled office was furnished with wine-colored Chippendale wing chairs and a matching sofa. An oval conference table by the far window overlooked the high-rise glass office buildings in the Financial District.

"Not a problem," said Bill Reinhardt, displaying his professional smile usually reserved for clients and prospects. They had met years ago at a cocktail party hosted by someone they both had long since forgotten, and remained at least casual friends. But they never did business together.

Reinhardt was in his mid fifties, wore a neatly trimmed gray mustache, dark gray suit with a gold checkered tie, and matching handkerchief in his lapel pocket. Impeccably tailored, he could have passed as a model in *Gentlemen's Quarterly*. "How's Blanche? I haven't seen her in a while."

"Frankly, that's the reason I'm here."

Bill Reinhardt studied Kassler for a few seconds, then motioned to one of the two leather chairs in front of his desk.

Kassler eased himself into the chair as though he had just finished a hard day at physical labor. He rested his elbows on the armrests and steepled his fingers, looking at Reinhardt. "I won't waste your time or my own exchanging pleasantries, because what I have to say isn't very pleasant."

Reinhardt blinked. "I gathered something was wrong when you called me and figured this wasn't a social visit. We've known each other a long time, Sam, so please speak freely."

"Blanche and I have had our differences for quite some time, and I'm afraid I've reached a critical point. I want a divorce."

Reinhardt's head bobbed up on the word "divorce." "I'm sorry to hear that. Divorce is a serious move."

Kassler began tapping his fingers together. "She won't consent to a divorce. But I recently checked the law, and I understand that with sufficient grounds, like proving mental cruelty, I don't need her consent."

Reinhardt's expression was somber. "Technically, that's true, Sam, but if she doesn't want a divorce, she could contest it and make the situation very unpleasant for you." Reinhardt smoothed his mustache with his thumb and forefinger. "With all the attorneys in Pittsburgh, why did you come to me?"

"Because I want to keep this as quiet as possible until the divorce is final. Blanche and I know too many people in Pittsburgh."

"I see." Reinhardt cleared his throat. "Well, you know, our firm primarily practices corporate law, and divorce isn't something that we normally get involved with."

"Come on, Sam. Let's cut the bullshit." Kassler crossed his legs and continued tapping his fingers. "Some of the best attorneys in San Francisco are right in this firm. Even if you don't like to get your hands dirty with divorce cases, you've arranged a few quiet divorces for some of your big corporate clients and settled with their spouses, who wanted to cut their balls off. Not to mention that you've kept their names out of the headlines."

Bill Reinhardt's voice took on a slight edge. "That may be true, but those are special cases. Their companies are clients of this firm, and we work in the best interests of our clients. We have an obligation to protect them. But we don't accept divorce cases from people off the street—or even from friends, for that matter. And I consider you a friend, Sam."

Kassler stopped tapping his fingers. "And how do you consider Blanche?"

Reinhardt leaned back in his chair. "What do you mean?"

"It's a simple question."

"Well, since you're a friend of mine, naturally I consider her to be a friend, too. It distresses me to hear that the two of you aren't getting along."

Kassler smiled. "As simple as that, huh? Are you sure you're not concerned that my divorcing Blanche—with you as my attorney—might cause her to force your hand?"

Reinhardt knitted his brow. "What are you driving at?"

"You know, Bill, I've always suspected that Blanche was unfaithful to me. But I was never able to prove it. That is, not until a couple days ago."

"You're accusing your wife of infidelity?" he asked, his voice raising an octave.

"Oh, now don't play innocent with me." Kassler looked at him out of the corner of his eyes. "I just came across a certain letter you wrote to her a while ago."

Bill Reinhardt's eyes went wide and his mouth fell open.

"How I found it is unimportant," Kassler said. "What is important is that you wrote it, and some of the things you wrote were quite incriminating. I've had to do a lot of traveling lately, so both of you had plenty of opportunity to get together. Did she go to San Francisco or did you come to Pittsburgh?"

Reinhardt looked as though he had suddenly been stricken, unable to speak.

"Well, it doesn't make any difference," Kassler said. "The only thing that counts is that now I have the proof, something I've wanted for a long time." He smiled again. "You know, you surprise me, Bill. You're quite a passionate fellow, although no one would ever know it to look at you. I'm also surprised because I thought an attorney, of all people, would've had better sense than to put something incriminating in writing. Just goes to show you, if a stiff dick has no conscience, it has no brains, either."

Reinhardt slunk in his chair. His voice cracked. "Please listen to me...it's just something that happened, and I wish to God it never did. I give you my word I'll never see her again. This is the only time in my life that I've done anything like this. I don't know what came over me. I lost my head."

Kassler was still smiling. "You might lose your ass, too. People pay for their passions one way or another. And you owe me. You know what would happen to your own marriage and to your distinguished career and to the reputation of this venerable law firm if I released this letter to the media, don't you?"

Reinhardt didn't answer.

Kassler was no longer smiling. "Don't you?"

The color drained from Reinhardt's face. "Yes...yes, I know."

"Good. Now that that's settled, you're going to arrange one of those quiet, discreet divorces for me that your firm is so good at doing." Kassler leaned forward. "Listen carefully, counselor. I want custody of my daughter Emily. That's first and foremost. Next is money. Blanche and I never had a prenuptial agreement, but I'm not willing to give her fifty percent of my assets or anywhere near that. I'll only do what's reasonable, but if she demands more, then it'll have to come out of your pocket. *You've* had her, *you* pay her. Seems fair, doesn't it?"

Reinhardt took a deep breath, his face pasty white. "If you release that letter, you'll bring disgrace on yourself, as well. Surely you realize that?"

Kassler poked a finger at his chest. "Me? I'm the innocent, victimized husband. That's how people will see it." He winked. "But just between you and me, I really have someone else I'm interested in."

Reinhardt said, "There's nothing between me and Blanche anymore. It was all just a mistake. Please don't be unreasonable...don't resort to blackmail. You and I can work this out, if you'll just give me a chance."

Kassler shook his head. "No, I'm afraid you're going to have to handle this divorce on my terms, and you'd better be successful. But you're also going to have to handle Blanche at the same time, and she's not going to be very happy with you. You'll soon discover what a barracuda she can be." Kassler leaned back in his chair. "You know, you two deserve each other. What the hell you ever saw in her, I'll never know. She's not even a good lay, but this'll bring new meaning to your relationship."

Reinhardt put his elbows on the desk and placed his face in his hands.

Sam Kassler smiled. "They say love and hate are just different sides of the same coin. Well, you've had the love side, now I'm going to turn over the coin for both of you." He laughed. "I'd love to see the look on her face when you tell her. You of all people. Can you imagine, an attorney who has an affair with another man's wife is forced to handle the aggrieved husband's divorce on his terms? That's one for the law books, isn't it, counselor?"

Grant glanced at the clock on the wall. 6:15 A.M. How long had it been? Each hour seemed like an eternity. Still no word from the kidnapper. He hadn't slept the night before. From the kitchen he entered the living room, where Dowling, Lapanski, and Merrick were talking in low tones. Did they know something he didn't?

"I put some coffee on, guys. It'll be ready in a minute." Grant didn't think they had slept much, either.

Dowling looked at him. "Thanks. You look like you could use some yourself. I guess we all could."

Several minutes later, Tom Santucci and Emilio Vasquez arrived and went into the living room. Santucci had a questioning look on his face.

"Nothing yet, Tom," Grant said. "Take the load off and have a cup of coffee."

Santucci gave a half grin. "You look like you need the kind of coffee I make." He and Vasquez went into the kitchen.

A second later the phone rang. Everyone in the living room froze. Santucci and Vasquez quickly returned to the room. Dowling turned to Grant and raised his hand. "If this is our man, just remember to keep him on the line as long as you can." The phone rang again. Merrick and Lapanski, who were wearing earphones, had activated the phone tracing equipment, both for wire and cellular transmission.

Grant picked up the receiver.

He heard an exuberant voice on the other end. "Hello, Mr. Montgomery. I won't take much of your time, but Premier Publications is offering a one-year subscription to any of its three magazines. We have a special reduced price for a limited time only. Are you familiar with our publications, sir?"

Grant's first impulse was to tell the caller to get the hell off the line. But this might be the kidnapper, testing them somehow. Yet the voice sounded different.

"I'm not familiar with your publications," Grant said. "What are you offering?" He glanced at Dowling who was signaling him to keep the caller on the line.

The caller described the three publications and the special discount on each one, including a savings of fifty percent if he were to subscribe to all three. Grant and Dowling maintained eye contact and finally shook their heads, convinced that the caller was a salesman. Grant politely refused the offer to the dismay of the salesman, and hung up.

Grant took a deep breath. "At first, I thought this might be our man disguising his voice."

Dowling nodded. "You did the right thing. We can't cut off anybody who calls. If possible, we want to trace every call that comes in, no matter who it is."

Sergeant Vasquez rubbed his chin. "I thought this guy was supposed to send a tape here, rather than call."

"That's right," Dowling said, "but we have to be prepared for anything." He glanced at his watch and looked at Grant. "If the phone rings within the next hour or so, stay loose. I'm expecting our people to report if they found any clues in Miss Hershfield's apartment. It's almost too much to hope for, but you never know."

Twenty minutes later, the phone rang again. Merrick and Lapanski went on the alert, and Dowling motioned for Grant to answer it. Santucci and Vasquez were at Grant's side.

This time the voice was familiar, but still disguised. "You've been waiting for the tape, haven't you?"

Grant's heart began to race. He glanced at the three FBI agents. "Yes, I've been expecting it. Is Colette all right?"

"I decided to let you hear the tape on the phone," the voice said, "rather than send it to you. I hope that didn't upset any plans you had with the FBI and the police. I know they're with you."

"Tell me how Colette is doing. I'll pay whatever ransom you demand, but I have to know that she's unharmed."

"Judge for yourself," the voice said. "So listen to her now." Grant heard a faint click on the line, wondered for a second if it came from the wiretap, then realized it was a tape player being turned on. He listened to a recording of a man's voice say, "Go ahead and scream all you want."

Grant's knuckles turned white holding the receiver as he heard the terror in Colette's voice. "Stop...please don't do this. Don't cut me. Stop...Oh, God, don't." Her scream slashed through him like a buzz saw ripping his flesh. She cried out twice more. Then her screams stopped and a strange noise came on he couldn't decipher. A moment later, he realized that it was the sound of Colette sobbing.

Grant was suddenly aware that Dowling was signaling him to keep the caller on the line. He swallowed and tried to speak.

His voice cracked. "What have you done to her? You son of a bitch, why are you doing this? I told you I'd pay you whatever you wanted."

"I am being paid," the voice said. "That was your girlfriend getting a taste of my knife. There's more to come."

The phone went dead.

For an instant, no one moved.

"Damn it," Dowling said, swinging his fist in the air, "we couldn't complete the trace."

Grant stood there, clutching the receiver, staring into space.

CHAPTER TWELVE

The room was cold and damp, washed in a faint amber glow by the kerosene lamp on the oak table. A musty odor lingered in the cabin from lack of fresh air. The early morning sounds of the dense woods were blocked out by the two boarded windows and the airtight log-cabin walls.

When Hutchinson had turned on the tape recorder and run the knife blade across Colette's bare stomach, he'd felt a sense of power. He was in control of his life again. His plan was working. He left a red trace of the blade across her abdomen, barely cutting the outer layer of skin. He didn't want her to bleed heavily. Not just yet. But Colette had screamed in panic at what she thought was about to happen. And that's all that mattered. He got the recording he wanted. Montgomery had to be convinced that his woman was being tortured.

When he turned the tape recorder off, he'd told Colette that her screams were so convincing, he had no need to cut her just yet. He could keep her fresh for the time being. But he assured her that her time would come.

Now Hutchinson looked down at Colette lying naked on the cot. He called on every ounce of his will power to keep from violating her. His plan would not permit it. From the trunk of his car, he had retrieved the blanket he used to hide her in the trash bin. He placed the blanket on top of her, carefully tucking one end under her chin and molding the rest of the blanket around her as if trying to make her as comfortable as possible. Her hands were still taped behind her back and he had retaped her ankles together.

He smiled. "I wouldn't want you to catch cold."

She turned her face to the wall.

"Now, is that a nice way to treat your host? Turning away from me like that. But that's all right. I won't punish you for being insulting because you did your job when you screamed on the tape. That's what I wanted." He pulled a chair over and sat next to her. "I could just picture Montgomery's face as he heard you screaming. I could see him as clearly as a vision. How he must've suffered, hearing you like that. If only I could've made a videotape of his reaction. Then I could savor that moment as often as I wanted, and it wouldn't be necessary for me to continue to hurt you."

Colette still faced the wall.

He rubbed his hands together. "Tell me what you think was going through his mind when he heard you screaming."

She didn't respond.

"I asked you a question."

Colette slowly turned her head toward him.

He could see the tears welling up in her eyes.

"I'm sure he was tormented," she said. "You got what you wanted. Now please let me go."

"Let you go?" He threw his head back, laughed and slapped his thighs. "Colette, I'm surprised that you still can maintain a sense of humor after all you've been through. Let you go? That's a good one. Why, my dear, like the song says, we've only just begun."

She started to weep, and flinched as she bit her lower lip, which was already swollen.

He shook his head. "Now, now, try to calm yourself. You should try to get some rest, because God knows you're going to need it. You see, very soon we're going to make another tape for your boyfriend."

Colette sucked in her breath and looked at him, her tears causing her mascara to paint her face in spidery streaks.

"This time you managed to avoid getting cut. Next time it's going to be different."

Grant stood in his living room facing Jim Dowling and his two assistants. Tom Santucci was on the phone talking to headquarters, while Emilio Vasquez was next to him, making a notation in his notepad.

"I've killed as a soldier," Grant said to Dowling, "and I've killed as a civilian to protect my life, each time with remorse, but if I ever get my hands on that son of a bitch, I'm going to kill him for the sheer pleasure of seeing him die."

"I understand how you feel," Dowling said.

"What went wrong with the phone trace?" Grant asked, an edge to his voice.

"We're tracing for both wire and cellular transmission, but he used a digital cell phone," Dowling answered.

"So? What the hell does that mean?"

Dan Merrick and Tony Lapanski exchanged glances, but remained silent. Dowling said, "A digital transmission is a lot tougher to trace than an analog transmission from a cell phone. We had a problem trying to locate the cell site where the call originated. I don't think it's within a close radius."

Grant took a deep breath. "I'm sorry, Jim, but I've got to do something to help her. I just can't sit here and wait for this maniac to call again."

Dowling showed his open palms. "Believe me, by being here to take his calls, you're doing everything you can do. You're allowing her abductor to establish contact with you, which is exactly what we need."

"This lunatic knows not to stay on the line too long," Grant said and started to pace the room. "He knows you guys are on the case. You heard him."

"Yes," Dowling said, following Grant with his eyes, "but sooner or later he might make a mistake. People like that sometimes get a little too sure of themselves. They think they're too smart to get caught, and that's when they trip up."

Grant continued to pace. "Without some background on this creep, I can't understand his psychodynamics, but I can tell you one thing. He's clever. First he tells me that I'm going to receive a tape, but instead of sending one, he calls and plays one. He's trying to keep us off balance, so we can't figure out his next move."

"True enough," Dowling said, "but we're further ahead than we were yesterday. Now we know we're not up against an extortionist. We're up against a psychopath—that's a different ballgame."

Grant sat on the edge of the sofa and slammed his fist on the coffee table. "I've racked my brain trying to figure out who he could possibly be and why he holds me responsible for someone he lost. But I can't come up with an answer to save my life." *To save her life,* he thought.

"Keep trying, anyway," Dowling said. He motioned to Lapanski. "Tony, you continue to stay with the phone in case he calls back." He looked at Grant. "Dan and I are going to replay the tape to see if we can detect anything—the trace of an accent, background noise we might've missed, his manner of speech—anything that might give us a clue. Our people at headquarters will also see if they can determine his race and possibly get a fix on his age, nationality, and anything else. They'll even try to bracket his level of education by the choice of words he used. We're now running a computer check to determine if his modus operandi fits any other kidnapper in our files."

"I hope you can come up with something soon, but I need to listen to the tape again, too," Grant said. "Maybe the voice will ring a bell."

Santucci came from across the room. "Grant, given the nature of that tape, I don't think it's a good idea that you put yourself through that again."

Sergeant Vasquez rose from his chair. "He's right, Grant. You haven't recognized the voice up to this point. You won't be able to now, either. He's disguising his voice. Why torture yourself? That's just what the bastard wants."

"I appreciate your concern, guys," Grant said, "but I have to do it. There's still a slim chance that something might register."

Santucci ran his fingers through his receding hair. "Have it your own way." He looked at Dowling. "I was just on the phone with headquarters. Neither your people nor mine have found any kind of trace evidence in Colette's apartment. No sign of a struggle. No nothing. If he abducted her while she was in her apartment, then he worked out all the details very carefully. It isn't easy to kidnap somebody while they're in an apartment building where people are coming and going all the time."

Dan Merrick turned to Santucci. "Who said she had to be kidnapped from her apartment?"

Santucci's head jerked back, then he shrugged. "We can't say with certainty but, as far as we know, that's the last place she was before we discovered she was missing."

Merrick shook his head. "She also could've been taken off the street."

"How?" Santucci asked.

"For all we know, she could have gotten into a taxi and been abducted by some crazy cab driver. Or maybe she was offered a ride to the Benedum by someone she thought was a friend, who turned out to be a nut. I could go on. Stranger things have happen."

Tony Lapanski jumped in. "We're even checking into Miss Hershfield's background to see if she ever jilted anyone. Our man could be some ex-lover who snapped and thinks Grant's responsible for his breakup with her. Just on the theory that maybe that's what this nut means when he said he lost a loved one."

Vasquez sneered. "My sainted mother used to say that for every unexplained fact, there are fifty answers."

Dowling rubbed the back of his neck. Susan and Linda and Billy seemed so far away. "We'll investigate any angle that seems reasonable, but we're getting into conjecture here, guys, which doesn't prove anything. Let's not lose our focus."

Grant turned and started to walk out of the room.

"Where are you going?" Santucci asked.

"Into the kitchen. I think all of us could use that coffee now."

She lay on the cot, covered only by the blanket, in the cabin that had become a prison from which there was no escape. Hope for a rescue, for a change of heart by her abductor, for some miracle that would free her from this nightmare was fading fast. Although Colette had not been seriously hurt by the monster's knife, she now understood the violation of dignity, the debasement that other kidnap victims must have felt.

He was sitting there, observing her, but she couldn't look at him. She was petrified when he said he intended to use the knife on her. Was that an hour ago? Or only a minute ago? How could she tell? *God in heaven,* she thought, *please help me. Don't let him kill me.* But she feared her prayer remained trapped in her mind, unheard.

If only she could go to sleep and never wake up again. That would be better than what this madman had in store for her. She couldn't take any more of his wretched insanity.

Let me die, she thought. *Please, God, if you won't help me, then let me die.*

She thought of her mother and father and wanted to cry out for them, as if she could summon them for help from beyond the grave. But now her parents seemed like strangers faded in a crowd, their once comforting voices a distant memory echoing through the chamber of time.

She thought of Grant, of the tenderness he had always shown her, of their deep love for each other. But now when she needed him more than ever, he was as helpless as she was, unable to even find her and that God-forsaken shack, let alone rescue her. She knew that he must be nearly out of his mind with torment and worry, trying desperately to uncover her whereabouts. But all his frustration would only play into the hands of this psychotic, who was still looking at her, still gaping with those monstrous eyes.

What is he waiting for? she wondered. *He's trying to torture me with the thought of what he's going to do to me. If he's going to kill me, let him do it now. Only please, please make it quick.*

Colette became nauseated. For a second, she thought she was going to vomit, but the urge passed as quickly as it came.

From her peripheral vision, she was suddenly aware that he had risen from his chair.

She felt a lump in her throat.

He went to the cupboard on the far wall opposite the coal stove, opened it and withdrew several cans, then went back to the table. He opened his toolbox on top of the table, withdrew some gadget Colette couldn't recognize, and opened one of the cans. It wasn't a can opener, at least not like any one she had ever seen, but it was sharp.

If she could just get to that toolbox. The dagger and other sharp instruments could serve as weapons. Then she might have a chance. But how? She was bound and never out of his sight.

She flinched at the unexpected sound of his voice. "Would you like something to eat, Colette? Have to keep your strength up, you know."

Her first inclination was to say no. She couldn't possibly keep any food down. But she hesitated. If she said yes, he would have to free her hands so she could feed herself. And maybe, just maybe, she could get her hands on something, anything in that toolbox. It was a long shot, but she had to try.

"Yes, yes, I'd like to eat something."

His tone of voice mocked her. "Now that's being sensible. Little girls are always rewarded for being good."

Let the bastard demean her all he wanted. Just as long as he freed her from her bonds.

He picked up one of the cans. "Now, let's see. Would you like some peaches, which are good for you? Or would you prefer a can of beans, which can help reduce your cholesterol?"

She ran her tongue over her lips as if she were hungry. As incredible as it seemed to her, she actually was becoming hungry. It didn't seem possible, when only a moment ago she was nauseated, but maybe she could hold some food, after all. It might help to give her the strength she was going to need. "Anything will be good. The beans, if I can have it."

"If you can have it? Why, of course you can have it. Would I have offered it to you otherwise?" He picked up the instrument and opened the can.

She had to get closer to the toolbox. "Can I eat it at the table?"

He raised his eyebrows, which made his hideous eyes appear even larger and more menacing. "Getting a little tired of lying there, are you?" He paused for a few seconds. "Well, you've been a good girl so far, so I guess there's no harm in it. Looking at the same surroundings from a different angle can be refreshing, I suppose."

Thank God. Now he would have to free her. She would get some food in her and then she would strike. She would grab something—that dagger, a tool, a fork, even the jagged edge of an opened can of beans—and so help her God, she would strike out at the mad bastard with all her strength or she would die trying. It had come to that.

"I'm afraid you'll have to settle for eating the beans cold," he said, smiling. "I don't want to fire up the old coal stove just yet."

"That's all right. I'll eat it cold."

He set the can of beans down, left the open toolbox on the table, and approached her. "Come on, Colette, it's time to stretch those gorgeous legs and join me at the table for a little bite to eat."

Sweet Lord, this was the moment she had prayed for. Where only a moment ago she had given up, now it seemed her prayer was answered. And it happened in a flash. She was almost breathless and wondered if she could pull it off.

Colette sat on the edge of the cot, and the blanket fell on her lap, exposing her breasts. She clenched her jaw. *The hell with it. Just get me to the table.*

Hutchinson knelt in front of her and cut the tape around her ankles with his penknife. He wrapped the blanket around her so she was no longer exposed, held one of her arms, which still were taped behind her, and walked with her to the wooden table as though he were escorting a date. "You sit right here," he said and placed her in the chair directly in front of the toolbox. "And I'll sit here, opposite you, so we can have a nice chat while we eat. Or should I say dine? Well, I suppose a lady of your means has had a lot better than this humble table can offer you, but I'm sure you'll enjoy it nonetheless."

She waited for him to cut the tape from her wrists.

He looked at his can of peaches. "You know, you had a good idea there. Rather than peaches, I think I'll have some beans, too. It makes for a little more substantial meal." Hutchinson went to the cupboard.

While he began rummaging through the shelves, Colette looked at the open toolbox. She saw the dagger in its sheath. That would be perfect, but it would take a couple seconds to unsnap the leather loop around the handle and remove the knife from its sheath. And a couple seconds might be all he needed to disarm her. But other tools she saw could be retrieved quicker—a hammer, a file, a putty knife, screwdrivers in various sizes, all within easy reach. And God knows what else was in there that she couldn't see from where she was sitting. If she timed her move properly and acted quickly enough, she could snatch any one of those tools and strike in an instant. She didn't want to get caught staring at the toolbox and looked away.

Hutchinson returned to the table empty-handed. "Now wouldn't you know it. Just when I got a hankering for beans, that was the last can we had." He placed his hands on his hips, looking at Colette. "Well, I hate to act in an ungentlemanly-like fashion, but I'm afraid I'm going to have to take that can of beans from you. Hope you don't mind."

She shook her head. "No, I don't mind. I'll have anything."

He took the can of beans in front of her and placed it on his side of the table. "We certainly have enough cans of peaches here. I'm partial to peaches, you know. You can have that, if you like."

"Yes, that'll be fine. Thank you." *Anything, you son of bitch, just cut me free.*

Hutchinson pushed up his heavy framed glasses on the bridge of his nose. "All right, then, peaches it is. He took the open can of peaches and placed it in front of Colette. "Just let me know when you want to eat." He sat at the other side of the table, opposite her.

She hesitated for a few seconds. Let me know when you want to eat? What the hell was he talking about? "I'd like to eat now, please."

He shrugged. "Oh, all right. Mine can wait. It's not as if my beans are going to get cold." He chuckled at his own joke. Hutchinson positioned his chair in front of Colette, sat in it, and took a half peach out of the can with his penknife. "Open wide like a good girl."

She looked at him. "Please, I don't want to eat like that. Couldn't you just untie—"

He smiled at her. "Now, now, Colette, you didn't think I was gonna untie your hands so you could try to attack me with one my own tools you've been eyeing. I'd have to be very foolish to fall for a trick like that, don't you think? First of all, I doubt that you have the strength to do it, but why should I take a chance?"

Colette slumped in the chair. The bastard. The rotten bastard had been toying with her all along. That was even crueler than terrifying her as he recorded her screams. To let her think she had an opportunity to save herself, and then to take it away at the last moment.

She was defeated. She had never known such defeat in her life.

She knew now that she would never be able to free herself of this monster.

Colette lowered her head, fighting her tears. She heard Hutchinson laugh.

CHAPTER THIRTEEN

Grant agonized over the thought of Colette being tortured physically and mentally by a maniac. He had just listened again to the FBI tape of the kidnapper's call, but he couldn't recognize the disguised voice or anything even vaguely familiar about the kidnapper's manner of speech or choice of words. Except the obvious fact that the son of a bitch was enjoying himself. And Grant heard for the second time Colette's screams and sobs. He could hardly stand it. He had excused himself from the group of federal agents and city detectives, and gone downstairs into his den to be alone.

Now he sat on the edge of a recliner with his elbows on his thighs, his folded hands tapping his chin.

It seemed that all his skill as a mentalist, his highly developed insights into human nature, in reading people, were useless against this cunning psychotic, who remained a phantom. Grant knew the maniac was laughing at him, drawing this torment out as long as possible, and relishing each moment. Who could carry out such a terrible vengeance? Sure, a few people disliked him, and in his occasional consulting work with the police, he had no doubt made a few enemies. But they were criminals, who were now behind bars. He never made a bitter enemy otherwise—no one who would ever be crazy enough to abduct and abuse Colette or anyone else.

Colette. Innocent Colette, who was being made to suffer. Grant felt weighted in guilt as if an anchor had been placed around his neck. She was the last person in the world he wanted to see hurt. And the one responsible was a coward. If he were a man, he would face his adversary, not take it out on her. *Cowards never face their adversaries,* he thought. *They either strike at your back or get someone else to fight for them. Or, worst of all, harm someone close to you.* If only the maniac had taken the first two options, then Grant would have had to deal with him, and Colette would be free. But the coward chose the last option, because he knew that would be the worst one for Grant. That meant this maniac with his imagined vendetta must have some knowledge of Grant and his character make-up. It was doubtful that he was a complete stranger.

At the FBI's request, Grant had made a list of everyone in the last ten years he might consider to be an enemy or to even have a minor grudge against him. He had given the short list and the background on each one to Jim Dowling.

Grant didn't believe that any of those on the list had anything to do with Colette's kidnapping, but the FBI wanted to check out each of them. He knew Dowling and his people were doing all they could and that the city detective force would give this case top priority because of his friendship with Tom Santucci. But none of that seemed to be enough. They weren't any closer to finding the kidnapper, and they still had no clues. Colette remained at the mercy of this demon, who would continue to torment her to satisfy his lust for revenge.

Grant rose and went to a window that overlooked the city. He stared at the sweeping landscape that he loved to observe, but saw nothing. There was a score to be settled for what this madman has done to Colette. For what he might do.

And there was something else.

Until this moment, Grant hadn't permitted himself to think about it. But, God forbid, if the unthinkable should happen, if the maniac kills her, the only way that score could be settled was in the death of one of them.

The moment Jim Dowling heard his wife answer his cell phone, he had an almost overpowering urge to run home and hold her. He couldn't remember when he had felt this alone. Maybe the job was starting to get to him.

"Hi, baby," he said. "I just wanted to see how you and the kids are doing."

"We're doing fine, honey, but we miss you. How's it going?"

"About as well as can be expected. Montgomery's a real trooper, but I know he's going through hell."

Susan knew not to press him for information on a case he was handling. Wives could be privy to only so much; there was a line they couldn't cross, and sometimes it became a wall between spouses. "Do you think you'll be home anytime soon?"

"It's hard to tell, Suzy, but I have a feeling that I might be in for a long haul on this one."

He heard the disappointment in her voice, if not in her words. "I understand. Do you want me to wake up the kids so you can say hello?"

"No, let them sleep. Tell them tomorrow at breakfast that I called and that I want them to be good while I'm away."

"Linda came home today with an A-plus in her reading assignment, and Billy got a little jealous. I think he's going to apply himself a little harder at school."

"Good. Nothing like a little sibling rivalry." An awkward silence passed between them.

"Jim, I know this isn't the time, but do you think we could have a serious talk about a change in your career when this is all over? The kids are getting older and they need their father. I need their father, too."

Dowling swallowed hard. This was the first time she had ever broached the subject. He had thought about it several times, but then what else would he do? He didn't want a desk job. Yet he knew he needed to spend more time with his family if he wanted to keep them, and he wanted to keep them more than anything else in the world.

"I think we need to discuss it, honey."

"I'm glad you're at least open to discussing it. We've needed to for a long time."

"I know, baby, I know." Dowling checked his watch. "I can't talk any longer. I don't know when I'll be able to call you again."

"I know, but try," she said. "Please try. I'll be here." Susan paused. "Jim, you know our prayers are with you always, but tell Grant Montgomery that our family will pray for him and his girl."

"I'll do that. They're going to need all the prayers they can get." So would he. Dowling lowered his voice. "Suzy, I want you to know that I love you." He didn't think he had told her that in a long time.

Her voice tried to control a sob. "I love you, too, Jim. Come home safely to me."

Jim Dowling cradled the receiver, and the room seemed to darken.

Dolores, the maid who also substituted as a cook, approached Blanche Kassler with a tentative look. Her floral house dress, partially covered by a white apron trimmed in lace, seemed more appropriate for an older woman than the shapely twenty-four-year-old who wore it. "Pardon me, Mrs. Kassler, but will your husband be home for dinner tonight?"

Blanche Kassler sat in her living room in an oversized cranberry-colored easy chair with her legs propped up on an ottoman. The lavish room was decorated in antique vases displayed on special ceramic stands in every corner. A stone-façade fireplace that looked as though it could almost serve as another room was deeply recessed into the far wall, opposite Blanche.

She placed her martini on the end table next to her, and adjusted her left diamond earring. "No, Dolores, my husband will be out of town for the next couple of days. As a matter of fact, I'll be having dinner at the club tonight, so you can leave when you're finished with the rest of your work."

"Should I prepare anything for Miss Emily?"

Blanche lighted a cigarette and blew the smoke at the ceiling. "No, she and her friends are at the movies tonight, so I suspect they'll find a McDonald's somewhere." She picked up her martini glass and took a sip.

Dolores, who had been raised in a low-income neighborhood, was still awe-struck by her opulent surroundings in spite of her eighteen months of service to the Kasslers. She half curtsied before she left the room.

Blanche smiled. She liked subservience. Too little of it was left in society these days, where servants and other employees didn't know their place. Dolores could keep her job as long as she didn't forget that. She knew that Dolores had grown up in a poor neighborhood, and Blanche could empathize with that. She, too, had lived in a household where every dollar counted and too few of them were available on payday, because her father would stop at his favorite bar on his way home from the mill and squander money on liquor and women. Money that was needed for food and for the mortgage and for bills that remained unpaid from month to month. Her mother was right when she told Blanche at the age of fifteen that men were pigs, interested only in their own pleasure, and when Blanche married, she should marry into wealth because a rich pig was better than a poor one.

Blanche also learned at an early age that men could be manipulated through sex. She'd had her first sexual encounter at fifteen. They were in the woods near the home of her sophomore classmate, both of them hidden by the full maple trees and the deep grass; the sun had just set. Neither she nor Freddy Lyle, who was also a virgin, knew what they were doing, but each wanted the other to think that this was not the first time. Freddy had a life-long problem—he stuttered. And just before they were about to commit The Mating Act, as Blanche called it, she said, "Tell me you love me or I won't let you do it."

Freddy seemed befuddled. He opened his mouth, but made no sound. Then he began to stutter; the more he tried, the more he was unable to utter a coherent word. She was mesmerized by his desperate attempt to say the words that stood between him and his need for blessed relief. In the grip of frustrated passion, Freddy could only blurt jumbled sounds that she couldn't understand. His face flushed and, for a few seconds, she was afraid he was choking. Then his predicament suddenly struck her as funny, and she momentarily forgot about her own sexual curiosity, fascinated by the sight of Freddy Lyle lying beside her in the grass with his pants pulled down, his eyes wide, head bobbing with jackhammer rapidity, spittle and grunts spewing from his mouth as if the fate of Western civilization depended on his ability to say three little words.

She didn't experience The Mating Act with Freddy that evening. But she learned something. She couldn't verbalize it then, but she eventually came to realize that if all men could be made that desperate, they could be controlled. The promise of sex, the giving and withholding of it, were weapons she could store in her arsenal. Blanche began to test her sexuality on other high-school boys with success, while Freddy Lyle's parents couldn't understand why his stuttering was getting worse. Later, she graduated to affairs with grown men. But with each experience, Blanche learned how to get what she wanted from men, a latent talent that, with practice, blossomed into full power. And finally she met Sam.

Blanche glanced at her watch. 1:10 P.M. She figured that without dinner to prepare, Dolores would be gone by 5 P.M. at the latest, so there was no way the servant would run into Bill Reinhardt. He had called Blanche earlier in the day and told her that he needed to see her, that he would catch an early flight and be able to meet her at her home at 7:30 P.M. He was passionate for her, unable to stay away for any length of time. He didn't have to tell her that. She could read it in the urgency in his voice. She smiled again. In business and social affairs, William Worthington Reinhardt was the personification of conservatism. In bed he was a starved animal. Men were so easy when it came to sex. She had given him everything he wanted, everything his proper, pristine wife had denied him. She loved to listen to him moaning, totally controlled by her. And in only five encounters, he had become Blanche's slave. In return he could give her the attention, the passion that had been missing from her life for so long.

Blanche took another sip of her martini. Poor Sam. If he only knew.

She was aware that her husband was enamored of Colette Hershfield. That was obvious from his inability to deny it. She also knew that Sam had no chance at all with Colette. He was out of his league and, as usual, he would end up a frustrated fool. As for her own tryst, Blanche had no intention of getting emotionally involved with Reinhardt or of ever leaving her husband. Reinhardt was merely a stop-gap measure, a means of temporarily fulfilling her craving for a man's attention, of satisfying her own sexual needs and experiencing the excitement of new passion. But one day, like always, it would end, and they would part like two civilized, cultured people, who had obtained what they needed from each other and would remain distant friends. Then she would go on the prowl for the next one.

If that's the way it had to be in a loveless marriage, then that's the way it was, and she was going to make the most of it. But she would never divorce him. And in selecting her playmates, she would never step out of her class and lower herself with a brute, like one of the women in the ladies auxiliary did, who resigned in disgrace. Blanche had had enough of brutes as a young woman. Only the Bill Reinhardts of the world were now worthy of her attention.

She picked up her martini and went into her bedroom. She wanted to read again that passionate letter from Bill. Blanche had never expected such a letter. He had sent it to her home marked "personal" in care of one of the charities in which she served as a board member. Funny that he was careful enough to do that, but still blindly committed himself in writing.

Blanche laughed. Men were not only easy, they were fools. Tonight when they finished an after-dinner cocktail, she would take Bill Reinhardt by the hand and lead him like a child to her bedroom. And there she would reward him for coming all the way from San Francisco just so he could be with her again.

She opened her dresser drawer and withdrew a richly polished rectangular wooden box with a gold nameplate where she kept the letter locked with her diary. It was a two-page letter hand-written on his personal stationary. She wasn't going to read the entire letter, just that sentence that titillated her. She had committed it to memory, but still needed to see it in his handwriting again as if each time she read it she were reading it for the first time.

I've never known such total passion with another woman, and no one will ever be able to replace what I've found in you.

Her husband had never expressed such a sentiment, not even when he was courting her. She unlocked and opened the jewelry box.

She flipped through her diary.

The letter was gone.

She checked the diary again. Where the hell was it? Did she misplace it? No, that letter always remained locked in that jewelry box. What could have happened to it?

Then Blanche froze. *Sam found the letter. That's why he went to San Francisco. To confront Bill Reinhardt with what he knew.*

That letter gave Sam all the ammunition he needed to divorce her. He wanted a divorce all along, and now he had a piece of paper that could make it all possible for him. He left her. That's why he had taken so many of his clothes with him.

She started to pace the bedroom, then suddenly stopped. That's why Bill sounded so urgent, wanting to see her tonight. Not because he needed to be with her. Because he had to tell her that Sam knows and wants a divorce.

She had to be sure. She ran to the phone and called Bill Reinhardt. His secretary said he was gone for the day. Blanche slowly cradled the receiver. He's probably already en route, she thought. How was she going to get through the rest of the day until Bill Reinhardt arrived? She was unsteady and braced her back against the wall. In the lapse of a minute, her world was beginning to crumble.

Frank Hutchinson sat in his car parked in back of the cabin. Even in the thick woods, the morning was as serene and radiant as sun reflecting off a lake. He listened to the sounds of the woods, the birds caroling, a faint wind whispering through the burly pines and hemlocks, the sudden crunch of underbrush signaling the movement of an animal. He could appreciate such sounds. They were a pure part of nature, uncontaminated by man. And they triggered memories of his youth.

As a boy, he loved to play in the woods, to pretend he was a hunter stalking his prey, aiming at imaginary targets with the fallen branch of a tree that became a deadly high-powered rifle. And he brought down everything he aimed at because he was an expert shot without equal. Sometimes his adversaries were savage mountain lions, other times they were ferocious bears or tigers or charging rhinos. Even bad men got their due with a bullet perfectly equidistant between both eyes. He was king of his world then.

Jesus Merciful Christ, whatever happened to that world? he wondered. *How did it become so complicated?*

Now his world was a dark place. The woods he looked at and listened to were strangely beyond his reality, as if he were only permitted to observe the scene as it rushed by, but never to be a part of it again. Never to recapture the joy and innocence of that boy in the woods.

Suddenly, unexpectedly, he screamed. It was the tormented cry of a soul on fire. Startled by his own action, he covered his mouth with his hand. Then he imagined he heard his scream echoing throughout the woods until it faded away unheard. And he was profoundly alone, lost in his solitude, rejected by a world he no longer understood, a world that had betrayed him.

But he had a mission.

Hutchinson looked at the cabin, and the sight if it snapped him back to the task at hand. He took off his wristwatch and placed it on the dashboard. He would keep the call to under one minute, which would make it more difficult to trace, particularly in the mountains. When the second hand reached the fifty-second mark after he called, he would hang up. That gave him enough time.

He picked up the cellular phone, punched in the number, and kept his eyes on the second hand of his watch. The phone was answered after the first ring.

He recognized Montgomery's voice.

"I see you're keeping a vigil by the phone," Hutchinson said. "Hope I'm not interfering with your social life."

"Turn her loose, and I'll pay you anything you want."

"You don't seem to understand, do you? I'm not after money."

"Turn her loose," Grant said, "or I'll hunt you down and kill you if it's the last thing I ever do."

Hutchinson chuckled. "Temper, temper. Hot heads never think clearly. Colette's with me now, and she's naked. I love to look at her and touch her—in all the private places that you thought were exclusively yours."

"You sick son of a bitch. What did I ever do to you to make you act this way? Tell me. Tell me what I can do, but don't hurt her anymore."

He could hear Grant breathing hard. "I want you to know what's in store for Colette. You see, I'm going to inflict a great deal of pain on her. When I'm through with her, she won't look as good as she does now. Eventually, she's going to die. You'll get a tape of all this fun so that you'll have something to listen to besides classical music and jazz."

He heard Grant say, "Wait a minute—" as he hung up and clutched his watch. Fifty seconds. Not enough time for a trace. How did it feel not to be in control, mister mentalist? No more than he had felt over the years. But now, for the first time, he *was* in control, and he felt reborn.

Hutchinson got out of the car and walked to the front of the cabin. He liked to open the door slowly because it squeaked when he did so, and he knew the sound frightened Colette.

He stepped inside, allowing a shaft of daylight to enter, then closed the door and the room was in semidarkness again.

He walked over to her and sat on the edge of the cot. Hutchinson patted the side of her face. "Don't look so forlorn. I haven't forgotten you."

CHAPTER FOURTEEN

Grant smacked his fist into his palm. "You heard him," he said to Dowling, "that comment about something for me to listen to besides classical music and jazz. He has to be someone who knows me well enough to know my preference in music."

Dowling nodded. He hunched his shoulders and sucked in his breath. "We've got to get a fix on his identity. Whoever the bastard is, he's playing mind games with you. He wants to torture you. I know it's easy to say, but try not to let him get to you. There's a chance that he may only be bluffing, just threatening so that he drives you crazy with worry."

"He's already made good on one threat," Sergeant Vasquez said.

"Maybe just to convince us that he'll act on the second threat," Grant said, "but I'm not so sure that he will just yet. He's having too much fun with me to kill her. If he kills her now, the game's over. That's why I responded to him the way I did, to let him know that he's getting to me."

Dowling arched his eyebrows. "You sure as hell convinced me. You're beginning to get a step ahead of him, aren't you?"

"I'm trying, but I also meant what I told him. At some point, he's going to get tired of playing the game. That's when he'll want to keep his promise."

Tony Lapanski, who had lost his perennial smile hours ago, was rewinding the tape of the kidnapper's call. Dan Merrick was in the hallway, huddled in conversation with Santucci and Vasquez.

Dowling walked over to Grant and placed a hand on his shoulder. "Did any one of those on your list know what kind of music you liked?"

Grant hesitated for a second. "I doubt it."

"Of course, that information could've appeared in the media at any time, so it would've been public knowledge."

"It's possible," Grant said, "but my personal life wasn't the subject of much publicity. It's not as though I was a big Hollywood star. My publicity was mostly confined to my performances."

Dowling shot a glance at Grant. "Don't be too modest. I seem to recall reading some personal items, like the women you used to go out with."

Grant shifted his gaze to Santucci, who entered the room with Vasquez and Merrick.

Santucci pursed his lips and cleared his throat. "We were wondering if you had invited anyone besides me and Emilio to your performance and the reception."

"No, you two were the only ones, besides Colette, of course. Children's Hospital and the Benedum coordinated the invitations. Why?"

"Like you say, this guy has to be someone closer to you than you think, someone you don't suspect. We thought you might've invited someone in good faith, who may not be the friend you think he is." Santucci rubbed his chin. "If someone like that got tickets and didn't show up...well, Colette disappeared at the same time, so it might've been a lead for us."

Grant shook his head. "No, Tom, nothing like that happened."

"It was a long shot," Santucci said, "but we don't have much to go on."

Merrick looped his thumbs over his belt. "Why not make another list of everyone you can think of who knows that you like classical music and jazz. I know it looks like we have a one-track mind on lists, but we have to get a fix on this guy. That means narrowing down the possibilities one by one."

"I understand," Grant said, "and I'll do anything to help you, but most of the people who know what kind of music I like are friends of mine."

"At this point," Dowling said, "we don't care whether they're friends or not. Just jot down names and identify each one. Then we'll review it with you. We're trying to build a profile of this guy and see if it matches anyone in our computer files or anyone you know, friend or not."

Grant traced the scar on his chin with his left thumb. "I wasn't able to keep that creep on the line long enough. I don't think he's going to fall for the wiretap. This is the second time now. He says what he has to say and hangs up abruptly. I think he has his calls timed."

Dowling nodded. "I wouldn't doubt it, but we're still going to maintain the tap. In the meantime, we'll work with Tom and his people in following up on the names you gave us, but we need the other list, too. When can you have it ready?"

"I'm on it now," Grant said, trying to suppress his fear that Colette's predicament was becoming more desperate by the hour.

Sam Kassler left the law offices of Reinhardt and Hopkins with a smile he couldn't restrain. He walked along Montgomery Street in the cloudless San Francisco morning, savoring a sense of relief. He was ebullient after the action he took in his meeting with Bill Reinhardt. He would have the divorce he always wanted—and on his terms. At last he would be free of Blanche. She would never get custody of Emily, and she wouldn't get the kind of financial settlement that would keep her in the pampered lifestyle she had grown to love. And his wife's lover, the well-respected San Francisco attorney, would get what was coming to him; he'd soon find out what Blanche was really like.

He decided to take a long walk before returning to the Fairmont Hotel. It was such a wonderful day. He couldn't remember the city looking so vibrant in the morning sun. Previous business trips to the city were always confined to business offices and hotel suites, and never allowed him time to enjoy weather or scenery. Today was different. For the first time in his life, he acted against Blanche. He was a new man. Soon to be a free man.

He had to initiate one more element of his plan. But first, he would complete his cathartic walk, working his way around the Financial District to the massive Gothic inspired Grace Cathedral and past the well-manicured Huntington Park with its sand-covered children's playground. He would enjoy the tranquility of the easy morning and the refreshing sun. Then he would return to the hotel and make the final move before Reinhardt gave the news to Blanche. He would call his office and sever the relationship with his employer. He had enough stock in Marshall, Sterns and Nobel to quit now, and with prudent investing, he and his daughter could live quite comfortably.

But he did not intend to live without a mate. And there was only one he wanted or ever would want.

He would win Colette no matter what he had to do, no matter what sacrifice he had to make.

At a newsstand, Kassler picked up a copy of the *San Francisco Chronicle* and decided to browse through it leisurely over a cup of coffee before returning to the hotel and calling his office. Might as well enjoy his new-found freedom and the luxury of leisure. He walked a block further and entered a coffee shop. He sat in a booth, ordered his coffee, and began to read the paper.

Suddenly Sam Kassler's back stiffened.

He saw the four-paragraph wire service story headined "Pittsburgh Socialite Kidnapped." The story announced that Colette Hershfield had been kidnapped, that her captor had been in contact with Grant Montgomery, and that the FBI was on the case with the city detective bureau. The story noted that neither James Dowling, FBI special agent in charge, nor Thomas Santucci, head of investigations for the city detective bureau, had anything further to report.

He jumped up from his seat just as the waitress was serving his coffee, knocking the cup from her hand and spilling the coffee on her uniform.

The waitress screamed. "Hey, what's wrong with you?"

"I'm sorry," he said. "I'm very sorry ..." He threw five dollars on the table. "Here, get your uniform cleaned," he said and ran out.

Grant had made a list of everyone he could think of who knew his preference for classical music and jazz. He had dozens of names listed, which he reviewed name by name with Jim Dowling, but he felt at the start that it was a useless exercise.

He was sitting in his living room, staring out at the city from his picture window. Jim Dowling was on the phone conferring with FBI headquarters with his two assistants at his side. Santucci and Vasquez were sitting on the couch, looking at Grant.

Dowling hung up the phone and started to walk toward Grant, but Santucci caught his eye and waved him off. Dowling kept his distance, but broke the silence. "Grant, we've been able to check out those names you gave us fairly quickly, and we can rule out each one of them. The names on the other list are going to take a lot longer."

Grant rose. "You're going to come up empty there, too. Take my word for it." He turned to Dowling. "Sitting around and waiting for this bastard to call is getting to me. I need to get out of here for a while, take a break and clear my head."

"I understand how you feel," Dowling said, "but I don't think it's a good idea. Better you stay here and tough it out."

"I need to get out and I'm going," Grant said as he walked to the hall closet.

Santucci broke in. "I think Grant needs a break, and we should let him take it."

"What if the kidnapper calls when Grant isn't here?" Dowling said. "Did you think of that?"

Grant gestured to Dowling. "You're here. He knows the phone's tapped. Make up some excuse. Tell the bastard I've become physically ill with worry and can't talk. He'll love that. Tell him anything."

"Where do you intend to go?" Dowling asked in a tone of voice that indicated displeasure.

"No place in particular, maybe take a long drive."

Dowling waved his hands in the air and looked at Grant. "Okay, okay. Just don't make it too long. Take my car, the Buick. Leave your Lamborghini here."

"Why?"

"I'll explain later." Dowling tossed his car keys to Grant.

Grant didn't understand Dowling's request, but didn't want to take any more time to question it. He checked his watch. 9:35 A.M. "I'll be back before anybody misses me."

When he left his home, Grant drove toward the city in a downpour. Sheets of rain slapped at the windshield of the Buick, blurring Grant's view of the road. He reduced his speed and headed toward The Halifax in Gateway Center. He wanted to thoroughly search Colette's apartment for some clue that might point to how she had been abducted or who might have been with her that evening. Grant knew Dowling wouldn't permit him to take such matters in his own hands, arguing that Colette's apartment already had been thoroughly searched by professionals. So he used the excuse that he needed to take a break.

Maybe he wouldn't be any more successful than the FBI and the city detectives had been. Probably not. After all, they were experts. But taking some action was better than making lists of possible suspects who weren't suspects and waiting for the next call from Colette's abductor. The truth was he did need a break. Doing at least this much might prevent him from going crazy with worry.

He had his key to Colette's apartment, and he was confident that Bill, the doorman, would let him into the building. And if any member of The Halifax's management questioned his presence there, he would tell them he was working with the police on the kidnapping case.

Grant parked the car in the Gateway Center garage, across the street from The Halifax. As he ran in the rain toward the building, he spotted the doorman behind the glass door of the small outer lobby where visitors announced themselves on the intercom system. Bill opened the door as Grant ran into the outer lobby.

"You're drenched," Bill said. "You should've parked in our garage." The Halifax management frequently allowed Grant to park in the building if the garage wasn't full.

"No problem, Bill," Grant said as he brushed the rain from his suit jacket.

"Have you learned anything about Miss Hershfield?" Bill asked.

"No, but we're working hard on it. That's why I'm here, Bill. I want to make another check of her apartment. You've let me in before."

Grant noticed Bill's slight frown and momentary hesitation. "I know, but we're really not supposed to let anyone into the apartments without approval of the tenants," Bill said.

"Could you get permission from the main office?"

The doorman thought for a second. "Nah, hell, in your case, I don't think the rule applies. You're working with the police. So if anybody gives me any grief about it, I'll just say I didn't want to be accused of obstructing justice."

Grant smiled and patted Bill on the arm as the doorman slid his card in the lock to open the door to the main lobby. He took the elevator to the fifth floor, and entered apartment 522 unseen.

As soon as he closed the door and looked at the empty suite, he took a deep breath. The apartment suddenly became a mausoleum, leaving him with an aching void in the pit of his soul. The silence of the living room screamed at him.

He wanted to drop to his knees and promise God anything to return her unharmed.

He was jolted by a crack of thunder and went to the living-room window. The ominous sky cast a dark shadow over the city, and the storm erupted with the force of a dam-burst.

He remembered that Colette liked to watch storms. He remembered the first time they made love during a storm. But he couldn't think about that now. Grant turned his back to the window and surveyed the apartment. Where would he begin? Having had experience with police work on several cases, he knew this place had been checked for fingerprints, shoeprints, fibers, hairs, blood stains, outside soil that might have been tracked in, furniture out of place or any damage that would indicate a struggle, any kind of clue that could give the police a starting point. But they had found nothing. Nevertheless, he knew this apartment much better than the police did. And he knew Colette and her habits better than they did, too. Like her penchant for keeping everything neat and in its place.

If this *was* the scene of the crime, then he still had to be careful that he didn't disturb anything, no matter how thoroughly the apartment had been examined.

Grant walked around the living room, observing each piece of furniture, each item in the breakfront that he knew by heart, careful not to touch anything. Nothing was missing or out of order. He went into the dining area and studied it, calling on his memory and observation skills. Everything was neat and in place the way Colette kept it; nothing disturbed that might have indicated the presence of an intruder. For a moment, he felt foolish, as if he were trying to be Sherlock Holmes when he should really be back home, helping Dowling and Santucci do their job.

He entered the bathroom and used his handkerchief to open the medicine cabinet to the left of the sink. Ointments, band-aids, a lady's razor, a half-full bottle of aspirin. He opened the drawers of the vanity. A hair dryer, combs, several brushes, countless make-up items, curlers, but nothing out of the ordinary. Nothing that didn't belong.

Her office seemed intact, as well. Grant checked her desk calendar. It was opened to Wednesday, August 20. "Benedum, 8 P.M." was written on it in Colette's handwriting. No other marking was on the page. She had no other appointments that day, Grant thought. She *had* to be abducted in this apartment. If she had returned the following day, she would have turned the page of her calendar. Colette was meticulous about such things. But the FBI and city detectives would have already noticed such an obvious fact and must have come to the same conclusion. Yet Dan Merrick seemed to think that she could have been taken off the street. Grant locked his jaw. Was he a step ahead of them or a step behind?

Colette's briefcase was on the round glass conference table and, using his handkerchief, he carefully opened it. He spotted the appointment calendar she always carried with her, and opened it. It was filled with meeting dates. He came to Wednesday, August 20. The same notation in her handwriting: "Benedum, 8 P.M.," but nothing else noted for that day. He shook his head. The briefcase wasn't in police custody because it had been previously checked, and obviously hadn't given them any clues. He was merely covering old ground.

Grant stood in the doorway of the bedroom. He felt the lump in his throat as he thought of Colette. How often had they made love there? He looked at the photograph on her dresser, both of them standing arm-in-arm in front of the high school. It was taken at the school's honors function in which one of Tom Santucci's daughters, Kathy, had received an award for scholastic achievement. Later that evening, when they had returned to Colette's apartment, they held each other closely in bed. Her eyes were tearing.

"Grant, I love you with all my heart, but I don't want to be hurt again." Her failed marriage to a husband caught cheating with her best friend still left an unhealed wound. "Please don't hurt me. I couldn't take that again."

"I would never hurt you. You must know that."

She smiled through misty eyes. "Yes...yes, I do know that. I don't know why I said it. I guess I just had to hear you tell me again."

"It's all right," he said, his hands caressing her body. "I'll tell you as often as you want to hear it. I love you." After the lovemaking, she fell asleep in his arms, while he listened to her slow, rhythmic breathing. "As often as you want," he whispered.

Now Grant stood there looking at the empty bed. If he could trade places with her now, take her out of harm's way, he would. He turned and started to leave the room, then decided to search it anyway. He wished he had taken a pair of latex gloves with him. Using his handkerchief to search through dresser drawers was awkward. Several minutes later he left the room, convinced all was in order.

Grant rubbed his left arm. Might as well give it up. This wasn't a very good idea in the first place.

He checked his watch. An hour and forty minutes since he had left his home. Colette's abductor had not called since he left, or Dowling would have called him on the cell phone Grant had in his pocket.

The last room to be checked was the kitchen, and he merely went through the motion of looking inside each wall cabinet, expecting to find nothing that would help him. Kitchen knives were in the wooden holder on the counter top; none were missing.

He opened the cabinet beneath the sink and found only dishwashing detergent, a box of cleaning pads and the trash can. Grant was about to close the cabinet when he suddenly stopped. He looked again at the open plastic trash container, which had a banana peel on top of the rubbish.

Grant lowered himself on one knee. That's strange. Colette never ate bananas. She didn't like them. And it definitely wouldn't have been placed there by the pros who searched the apartment.

Grant started to go through the rubbish with his bare hands, unconcerned now about his fingerprints. He found an advertising flyer for a set of sterling silverware addressed to Mrs. Rose Marelli, apartment 520. Underneath that was a bank letter, offering an introductory low rate on its credit card, addressed to Mrs. Marelli. He examined the rest of the garbage and found a fashion magazine and two advertising brochures, each addressed to Mrs. Rose Marelli in apartment 520.

Grant frowned. What the hell was Mrs. Marelli's garbage doing in Colette's garbage container?

CHAPTER FIFTEEN

Bill Reinhardt's voice cracked. "Blanche, please, you've got to be reasonable about this."

"Be reasonable? You miserable son of a bitch, you're asking me to be reasonable?"

When he broke the news that he had to represent her husband in divorce proceedings, she had gone into a rage. She threw two martini glasses and an ashtray at him, screaming out of control. In her rampage, she smashed a three-thousand-dollar vase against the wall as if it were a cheap toy, missing him by inches.

"God, stop it," Reinhardt said. "Try to be rational. There's nothing either one of us can do, except make the best of a rotten situation. Please understand, I'm forced into this, but I'll do everything for you that I can."

She was frightening with her bloodshot eyes glaring at him, her pent-up anger about to explode again into violence. "You lying son of a bitch. I let you share my bed, and now you're going to represent my husband in filing a divorce against me. You're working for him, and you're not going to do *anything* for me, you lying bastard."

Reinhardt would have never believed that she was capable of such vehemence. He stood before her, but was careful to keep a safe distance away, fearing she might lunge at him. "But there's nothing I can do. He has the letter and he can ruin me with it. He can ruin both of us. Why didn't you destroy that letter or at least keep it in a safe place?" He suddenly dropped his weight in a chair and lowered his head in his hands. His voice sank into a tone of defeat. "Why in the name of God did I ever write it? How could I have been so stupid?"

He was aware that she had taken several steps toward him. "Because you loved what I used to do for you in bed. That's why you wrote it. You couldn't get enough of it because you can't get that kind of sex at home. You'd lie there and beg for it, you little wimp ass. That's why you wrote it."

He observed her as if seeing her for the first time. Who was she? This couldn't be the same woman with whom he had an affair. This was a total stranger. An animal that turned on him. "Please," he said, "please let's try to face this like two civilized human beings."

She placed her hands on her hips. "Civilized? I'll show you how civilized I can be. You're going to get for me at least half of everything he has, and he's never going to get custody of his precious daughter either."

Reinhardt gripped the armrests of the chair. "If you insist on that, he'll release the letter and ruin both of us. Don't you understand? At that point, you wouldn't get a dime. What good would that do you?"

Blanche approached him, and he cringed in the chair. Suddenly her mood changed as if she had reached inside her psyche and snapped on another personality. She smiled as she sat on one of the armrests and gently wrapped a lock of his gray hair around her finger. "Then you only have one other alternative," she said softly.

He looked up at her, unbelieving the sudden metamorphosis. He was hesitant, leery. She was up to something. "What alternative?"

Blanche smiled again. "Let Sam have his divorce and his daughter and his money, everything he wants. But if that's what it takes to buy his silence, then you're going to divorce your wife and marry me—or I'm going to tell her everything about us." She suddenly pulled the lock of his hair and he winced, then ran her fingers tenderly over the side of his face. "Your choice, lover boy."

"Please speak freely, Mrs. Marelli," Grant said.

Rose Marelli sat in an easy chair in her apartment facing Grant, who sat on the couch. She had difficulty maintaining eye contact with him and kept twisting her wedding ring.

"Well, I don't know why my garbage should end up in Colette's apartment, but I think I better tell you what I saw. I didn't give it a thought when you and that policeman questioned me the other day. I'm not even sure if it'll help you now." She paused. "I read about Colette's kidnapping, and I feel just horrible about it."

"I'm grateful for your concern. What can you tell me?"

"Well, last Wednesday night, the lights went out in Colette's apartment, and she asked if she could use my phone. Colette was dressed formally so I knew she was going out that night. She called maintenance and Frank came right up—"

"Who's Frank?"

"He's one of the maintenance men. Frank came up and apparently fixed her lights. I later saw him picking up the garbage on this floor, and I put my garbage in the big refuse bin he had. He said some of the tenants complained that the garbage wasn't being picked up on time." She creased her brow. "But a moment later I saw something I thought was strange."

Grant leaned forward. "What was that?"

She stopped twisting her ring. "Frank went down the hall, then turned back like he had forgotten something and went into Colette's apartment with that big refuse bin. I didn't understand that. We're supposed to put our garbage in the refuse room down the hall. The only thing I could figure out is that she must've asked him to take some large item out of her apartment, but I didn't watch long enough to find out what it was." She dropped her gaze. "I didn't want to get caught peeking." She looked at him again. "But I still don't know why he'd put my garbage in her garbage can. That doesn't make sense."

"Did you see Colette let this man into her apartment?"

"Yes, the first time when he fixed her lights. But not the second time when he went in with the refuse bin." Mrs. Marelli started to twist her ring again.

"Do you know if he used a key to enter her apartment?"

She shook her head. "Well, employees are not allowed to do that, unless it's some sort of an emergency. They have to get our permission to enter our apartments. So Colette must've let him in. I just didn't see her. When I peeked through my door, I only caught a glimpse of Frank when he returned with the garbage bin and took it into her apartment. I don't remember if he used a key."

"Did you see Colette after that?" Grant asked.

She frowned again as she searched her memory. "Come to think of it, I didn't."

"Do you think your garbage was in this refuse bin when he entered her apartment?"

"Oh yes, it had to be. I gave him my garbage and then he went down the hall a short distance, turned around and then came back and entered Colette's apartment, but he didn't see me peeking through my door. I hope you don't think I was being snoopy...wait a minute...maybe he did use a key. I think he did, but I can't be sure."

Grant nodded and crossed his legs. "About what time was this?"

"It was twenty after eight. I do remember that I asked Frank what time it was because Joe and I—he's my husband—we were going out to dinner and we were running a little late." She touched her lower lip with her forefinger. "Actually, it was ten after eight. When I went back to my apartment, I remember checking my kitchen clock, which is accurate to the minute. Frank's watch must've been about ten minutes fast." Mrs. Marelli hesitated. "You know, I'm telling you all this now because I don't want the police to question me again."

Grant smiled to reassure her that everything was all right. "The police might want to talk to you again, Mrs. Marelli, but they won't give you any trouble. I'm sure of that. Would you describe this maintenance man for me?"

She cocked her head slightly. "Well, let's see...he's about average height and slender. Bald. He must have poor eyesight because he wears very thick glasses. Maybe he's in his late forties or early fifties. I'm not good at guessing people's ages."

"Anything else?"

"No, not really. He's very nice, a rather shy person. I haven't seen him in a few days." Suddenly Rose Marelli sat upright. "Surely you don't think he's responsible for Colette being missing? I only gave you his name because he might've been one of the last people in the building to see Colette that night."

Grant raised his open hand and smiled. "No, I don't suspect anyone at this point, Mrs. Marelli, but I'm certainly grateful to you for sharing this information with me."

"Will the police question him?"

"Yes, but we won't reveal your name. We'll merely tell him that we're talking to everyone in the building who might've had contact with Colette on Wednesday evening."

Mrs. Marelli continued to twist her wedding ring. "But you have to tell the police who gave you his name, don't you?"

"They'll be grateful for your help. They need all the information they can get."

"Please tell them not to use my name with anyone, just to leave me out of it."

Grant leaned back and interlocked his fingers around his knee. He hoped his casual posture would relax her. "If you'll forgive me for saying so, you seem reluctant to talk to the police. May I ask why?"

"It's my neighbors. I wouldn't want them to talk."

He doubted that was the real reason. "We'll be discreet, believe me. What's the maintenance man's last name?"

She thought for a moment. "I think it's Hanison...no, it's Hutchinson. He's really a gentle soul. Very shy, you know. Did I mention that?"

"Yes, you did. Is there anything more you can tell me?"

"No, that's everything I know."

"You're sure you didn't see Colette after the maintenance man entered her apartment the second time?"

She shook her head. "I'm sure I didn't."

"And you think he used a key to get in," Grant said.

"I think so, but I'm not sure."

Grant was careful to modulate his voice, trying not to sound accusatory. "Mrs. Marelli, why didn't you give us this information when we questioned you earlier?"

She lowered her eyes again. "I...well, I guess I was too excited to remember it then."

He knew she was lying. He surmised that she simply didn't want to get involved, but felt forced to when he questioned her about her garbage in Colette's apartment.

She looked at him, still twisting her wedding ring. "You don't think I'll get in trouble with the law for not telling them about this sooner, do you?"

Grant feigned a smile. How often did this woman need reassurance? "No, you won't get in any trouble."

They stood and Grant extended his hand. "Thanks for all your help." They shook hands.

"We might be back in touch with you," Grant said, "but don't worry. We'll respect your request for confidentiality."

Mrs. Marelli escorted Grant to the door. The color seemed to have drained from her face, and her hand on the doorknob was shaking. "I'm so worried about Colette," she said. "You don't think whoever kidnapped her is going to hurt her or...or do something worse, do you?"

Grant held her gaze for several seconds, his expression sober. "I don't know," he said.

The oak-paneled study of his home in Pacific Heights, one of San Francisco's most elegant neighborhoods, was always a place of respite for Bill Reinhardt, a sanctuary where he could relax, browse through a book, or simply gather his thoughts at the end of the day, undisturbed. Now the room seemed like a black hole. His career was in jeopardy. If Sam Kassler ever released that letter, it was all over. And what if Blanche shot her mouth off? He wouldn't be able to face his colleagues, his clients, his friends. His wife. Phyllis. How the hell could he ever explain it to her? If only he had never met Blanche. If only he hadn't been so stupid. Even if Phyllis never found out, he couldn't deceive her any longer. He never meant to hurt her.

He had to make a clean breast of it, get it off his conscience, wipe it off his soul and beg her for forgiveness or he would find no peace within himself.

Reinhardt left the study, and found Phyllis sitting on the love seat in the living room, reading the latest best-selling biography. She loved biographies of contemporary figures, which provided an in-depth view of their lives and their motives, and revealed some of their closest-held secrets. He felt a slight tremor. How was she going to like this one?

She looked up at him when he entered the room. "Ready for a drink?"

"No, not just yet." He sat in a chair, facing her. He took a deep breath and let it out. "There's something I need to tell you."

Phyllis took off her half glasses, and put her book on her lap. "You look worried. What is it?"

"Well, it's just that...you know, I've been working awfully hard lately, and sometimes when you push yourself and you're under stress, you...well, you do dumb things."

She cocked her head slightly, watching him. "What do you mean? What kind of dumb things?"

"I guess what I'm trying to say is that...people make mistakes that they later regret." Jesus, he never faced anything so hard in his life, not even in a courtroom. He suddenly was aware that she was staring at him coldly.

"You *did* make a dumb mistake, didn't you?"

He blinked. She couldn't possibly know. But why did she say that? Why was she looking at him like that?

"I never meant to hurt you—" he started to say, but stopped when he saw her struggling to contain a smile. What the hell was so funny?

Phyllis put the book on the love seat, rose and went over to her husband. She leaned forward and kissed him on the forehead. "I know you've been working very hard lately, and I decided I wasn't going to say anything," she said, smiling.

"You did?" he said, looking up at her, bewildered.

"Yes, I wanted to see how long it would take for you to remember."

He hesitated. "Remember what?"

"Oh, don't be coy, about it, you faker," she said. "You suddenly remembered this evening that you forgot my birthday last week, didn't you?"

He looked at her dumbfounded. "Yes...yes, I did forget and—"

"And I forgive you," she said, still smiling, "but only if you make it up to me with an evening of dinner and dancing. Do you know how long it's been since we were out dancing?"

He shook his head, his anxiety draining, but he was still speechless.

"Well, don't sit there looking at me like you're Quasimodo watching Esmeralda," she said. "It's been *too* long, and a relaxing evening of dancing will put a little fun in your life. You know what they say about all work and no play."

He kept staring up at his wife. He *had* to tell her, to confess his deception so he could be free of it. He couldn't continue to live like this. God knows, he didn't want to hurt her, but what choice did he have? He had to tell her now. Bill Reinhardt looked at the sweet, forgiving face of this woman who had always placed her complete trust in him. It was now or never. He swallowed hard. "When would you like to go dancing?"

Jim Dowling looked at Grant incredulously and shook his head in disbelief. "God, I'm telling you, we went over every foot of her apartment with all the evidence-gathering equipment at our disposal, and what happens? We overlook her garbage can. That's sloppy work." Dowling glanced at Dan Merrick and Tony Lapanski, who were sitting on the couch in Grant's living room. They both nodded, indicating they understood his frustration.

"They had no reason to check it, Jim." Grant said. "It's an understandable oversight."

Tom Santucci approached Grant, and placed his hands in his pockets. His tie was loosened at the neck and he looked like he needed a shave. He had dismissed Vasquez to attend to other business at headquarters. "What do you make of it?"

"I'm not sure, Tom," Grant said, "but I don't like it. On the way back here, I kept asking myself why this maintenance man would wheel a big refuse bin into Colette's apartment and then put someone else's garbage in her garbage can. I don't like the answer I keep coming up with."

Dowling cleared his throat. "Let's have it."

"I'm trying not to let my imagination run away with me," Grant said, "but I see it like this. First of all, you don't wheel a dirty garbage bin into a tenant's clean apartment, particularly someone as fastidious as Colette. She wouldn't allow it. If she had some big item to throw out, she would've had the maintenance man carry it out to the refuse bin."

Dowling nodded. "I'll buy that. Go ahead."

Grant looked first at Santucci, then at Dowling. "No offense to either one of you, but I know what's in Colette's apartment better than you or your people do. There's nothing she'd want to discard that's big enough to require a bin to be dragged into her apartment. Any of the bigger items, like furniture, are all expensive pieces that she'd have no intention of throwing out."

Merrick and Lapanski were still sitting on the edge of the couch, listening to Grant. Dowling folded his arms. "We're certainly going to check out Frank Hutchinson but, remember, what you say is only conjecture. So he's not really a suspect yet, but he might be a material witness."

"But it's a starting point for us," Grant said. "And, who knows, we might be further ahead than we were just a few hours ago." He paused. "There's something else, too."

"What?" Dowling asked.

"Let's take what you call conjecture logically to the next step," Grant said. "A minute before Hutchinson enters Colette's apartment, Mrs. Marelli gives him a large plastic bag filled with her garbage. He accepts it, pretends to go on his way, then backtracks and enters Colette's apartment when he thinks he's not being observed by anyone. Mrs. Marelli's not sure if he used a key to get in, but I think he had to. The fact that her garbage ends up in Colette's garbage can tells me that he wants to get rid of it. Why? Because collecting garbage isn't the reason he's entered Colette's apartment. He wants to put something else in that refuse bin other than garbage. Something a large bin could accommodate."

Dowling hesitated before he spoke. "Like a body?"

Grant nodded. "He would've had to tie and gag her, maybe knock her out so she couldn't make any noise."

Santucci broke in. "I understand your logic, but it just seems like a hell of a stretch." He sighed. "Don't get me wrong, though. Your theory deserves to be checked out."

Grant sat on the armrest of a chair and ran his thumb over the scar on his chin.

"I've seen that look before," Santucci said. "Something else is on your mind. What?"

Grant looked out into space as if he were in a trance, talking only to himself. "Mrs. Marelli first said that the maintenance man entered Colette's apartment at eight twenty. She remembered this because she asked him the time. Then she said she went back into her apartment and checked the time, and it was really eight ten, not eight twenty."

"What does that prove?" asked Dowling.

"Maybe nothing," Grant said. "But Mrs. Marelli is known in the building for being a nosy person, who loves to gossip and will talk your leg off. If the maintenance man was up to no good and in a hurry, he might've told her that it was ten minutes later than it was, just to get rid of her."

Dowling turned down the corners of his mouth. "You sure know how to draw conclusions, but it might also mean nothing more than the fact that his watch was ten minutes fast."

"Maybe. I also don't like the fact that he moved down the hall before he returned to Colette's apartment. That tells me he didn't want to be seen going in."

Dowling took a deep breath. "I think it's time we had a talk with Mr. Hutchinson."

Grant kept a vigil in his home with Dan Merrick and Tony Lapanski, while Dowling and Santucci headed into the city to meet with the manager of The Halifax. They wanted to check on Frank Hutchinson's background before questioning him.

Several hours passed that seemed like an eternity. Dowling had established a code of one phone ring, then silence followed by two more rings to identify himself from any other caller. But no call was forthcoming from Dowling or Santucci.

Grant paced the living room, aware that Merrick and Lapanski were watching him, both of them trying to appear unobservant. Earlier, they had tried to make conversation with Grant, but he was too preoccupied to make small talk. The more he thought about his theory, the more convinced he was accurate. Perhaps he had cracked open the door to this case, just enough to let a small shaft of light slice through. If so, then at least there was some hope. If not, they were at a stalemate. Either way, Colette was running out of time.

He heard Merrick say, "Take it easy, Grant. If this guy's our man, we'll know."

"But will we know soon enough?" Grant asked.

Just then, Jim Dowling and Tom Santucci entered through the front door and came up the short flight of stairs leading to the living room. Dowling was carrying a large manila envelope.

"We met with Philip Mather, the manager of The Halifax," Santucci said, "and we have some information on Hutchinson." Dowling sat on the couch, opened the envelope, and started to spread out papers on the glass coffee table. Everyone gathered around him.

Dowling unbuttoned his jacket and loosened his tie. "Mather told us that Frank Hutchinson has been working at The Halifax as a maintenance man for the past seven months. We have his personnel file here." He handed a four-by-five-inch black-and-white photograph to Grant. "Do you recognize him?"

Grant studied the image of Frank Hutchinson. "No, I don't think I've ever seen this man before."

Dowling let out a sigh. "I was hoping you would have. Mather told us that Hutchinson met with him last Thursday and requested some time off to be with his unmarried sister, who's on her deathbed. She has cancer and lives alone. Mather granted him some time off and kept him on full salary. He said he's never had any complaints about him. He comes from Minneapolis. He worked different places there as a general handyman. Seems to be a bit of a drifter, but Mather said he's a good, reliable worker."

Grant continued to study the photograph. "Were you able to question him?"

"No, he hasn't returned to work yet."

"When is he due back?" Grant asked.

Dowling shrugged. "Mather left it open-ended with him, said he could take as much time as he needs. The doctors think his sister only has a short time left. He said maybe a couple weeks at most." He crossed his legs and placed his hand on his ankle. "Mather only remembers that the sister lives in Pleasant Hills, but he never got an address or phone number. Didn't think it was necessary since Hutchinson would keep him posted."

"Why isn't she in a hospital or a hospice?" Grant asked.

"Apparently, they can't do anything for her," Dowling said. "She's too far gone and can't afford a full-time nurse. Probably no health insurance. We'll get in touch with Hutchinson at his sister's place, if that's where he is. And we know from his personnel file that he has an apartment in Brookline. So we'll check there, too. But before we do anything, we wanted you to see this photograph. Grant, are you sure you don't recognize him?"

Grant checked the photo again. He didn't know this man. And yet, there was something about his eyes that was strangely familiar. Or was his imagination playing tricks on him? Was he trying too hard to recognize someone who was a complete stranger? He finally shook his head. "No, I don't know him."

Dowling slapped his knee. "Well, if you don't, you don't. We'll still check him out." He turned to Santucci. "Tom, can you have your people check his sister's home in Pleasant Hills and also his apartment in Brookline? If he can leave his sister for a couple of hours, bring him in for questioning. If he can't, contact me and I'll send a couple of agents to his sister's place."

"No problem," Santucci said. He went into the kitchen to use the phone. A few minutes later, he returned. "My people are on it now," he said. "Vasquez completed his assignment, so he'll follow through and use whatever help he needs." He looked at Grant. "We should have some word on Hutchinson soon." Santucci rubbed his hand over the twenty-four-hour growth on his face. "You don't recognize this guy, Grant. That suggests that Hutchinson's not our man. If he was, that begs the question, how does he know you? From reading about you in the newspapers or seeing you on TV? Hardly. That's too casual. The kidnapper blames you for the death of someone close to him. So he'd have to know you personally from somewhere. And that means you'd know him, as well. But if you've never met Hutchinson, then he can't be our man. He has no motive."

Dan Merrick leaned forward. "You're discounting the possibility that the kidnapper could be a nut who doesn't know Grant at all, but thinks he does."

"I'm not discounting anything," Santucci said. "In fact, I believe he *is* a nut, whoever the hell he is. But something in the pit of my gut also tells me that he knows Grant, and that he hasn't fantasized this whole thing. Not completely, anyway. I think he *has* lost someone he loved. If he's fantasizing anything, it's obviously his grievance against Grant."

"Since when did you earn your degree in psychiatry?" Merrick asked.

Grant put up his hand. "No, Dan, I think Tom is right. I've felt it all along. Somehow, this person is connected to my past, but I'll be good and damned if I can make the connection." Grant rose from the couch. He noticed that Dowling seemed to be preoccupied. "When was the last time you called your family, Jim?"

Dowling turned to Grant with a slanted eyebrow, surprised by the question. "I don't know. I lose track of time. Yesterday, I think."

"Why don't you give them a call now?" Grant said. "I'm sure they'd like to hear from you." He looked at the others in the room. "That goes for the rest of you. Don't lose contact with your families."

They nodded and mumbled agreement as Dowling went to the phone.

Grant picked up the photo of Frank Hutchinson and studied it again.

Several hours had passed. Santucci had just taken a phone call, and returned to the living room with a grim expression.

Grant caught the look that passed between Santucci and Dowling. He rose from his chair. "What's the matter?"

"I just talked to Vasquez," Santucci said. "Hutchinson isn't at his Brookline apartment. His landlady doesn't know where he is, and hasn't seen him in days."

"What about his sister in Pleasant Hills?" Grant asked.

Santucci shook his head. His words were measured. "There's no such person."

Hutchinson was back in the forest primeval, sheltered from the world. He was ninety or a hundred yards from the cabin, sitting near the edge of a seventy-foot gorge, his arms wrapped around his legs. He was entranced by the most magnificent wild country he had ever seen. The white pines and hemlocks, worth life itself to woodsmen a century ago, towered before him proud and unconquered. He drank in the sweet fragrance of mountain laurel until it filled his lungs, and held it there, intoxicated by its purity.

At the peak of sunset, the wilderness absorbed vibrant hues as if unwilling to relinquish the day. With dusk, pale shadows deepened throughout the woods as trees wailed to the punishing lash of the wind. He shivered as much from the grandeur of it all as from the biting cold. He turned up the collar of his windbreaker.

How long had he been sitting there? Minutes? Hours? A lifetime? Such natural beauty could only be a dream. And as night covered the massive foliage and hushed the wildlife, he was afraid his dream was ending, that his paradise would disappear, and he would be left with the harsh reality of a cold concrete world that demanded punishment for crime. Suddenly his fear came true. His dream was gone, ended by darkness, and the only vestige of his lost paradise was the mournful cry of a wild animal against the howling wind. He was once again back in the real world.

Hutchinson rose and stood in the dark. The real world was ninety or a hundred yards behind him, locked in a cabin, waiting helplessly for his return.

He walked briskly with his hands in his pockets, the condensation of his breath keeping cadence with his stride. At night, the wind in these mountains was penetrating and, in the winter, with snow and freezing temperatures, the weather could be deadly. His ankle-high boots crushed the underbrush as he worked his way through the woods. Several minutes later, he could see the old shack outlined in shadow.

Hutchinson was about to enter the cabin, and opened the rusty hinged door slowly so it would creak. He went in and looked at Colette.

She was a pathetic figure, lying there freezing with nothing but a thin blanket wrapped around her. She must be hungry. She hadn't had anything to eat in...how long had it been? He was losing track of time. Even so, he was still in control.

"Want something to eat, Colette?"

She only nodded. He knew she was afraid to make eye contact.

"I'll bet you do. But before you eat, you're going to sing for your supper." He looked inside his toolbox, still on the table. If he used the knife on her now, she would bleed to death, and his game with Montgomery would be over. He didn't want it to be over just yet.

He removed his windbreaker and withdrew a pair of pliers from the toolbox. Then he placed the tape recorder on the floor by her head. He activated the recorder and turned up the volume.

Holding the pliers, Hutchinson went to the foot of the cot and flipped up the blanket, exposing her bare feet. "Now, Colette, you tell me which toe you'd like me to crush, and I'll accommodate you."

"Oh, God. Please don't."

He ran the pliers across her toes as she recoiled from the sudden brush of cold metal.

"I see you can't make up your mind, so I'll just have to make the decision for you. Let's see ..." He placed the prongs on the big toe of her right foot.

Colette tried to muffle a scream.

He wiggled her toe in the vice-grip of the pliers. "This little piggy went to market ..." Then he removed the pliers from her big toe, placed the prongs on her little toe and began to wiggle that one. "And this little piggy stayed home. Well, since this little piggy is still at home, it looks like that's the one we'll go to work on."

CHAPTER SIXTEEN

Sam Kassler got out of the taxi, and walked past the manicured hedges and up the stone steps leading to the entrance of his Fox Chapel home with a mixed sense of trepidation and relief. He wasn't eager to confront his wife, who by now must know about his divorce proceedings, but he wouldn't have to put up with her much longer. His real fear was for Colette, and he still could hardly believe that the woman who dominated his thoughts had been kidnapped.

He took a deep breath, put his key in the front door, and entered.

Having seen the taxi pull up, Blanche was waiting for him in the foyer.

He had barely closed the door when he heard that well-known voice that was always an octave higher when she had too much to drink. "So the son of a bitch decided to come home, did he."

Kassler closed the door, turned and looked at her. "Yes, the son of a bitch is home, but not for long," he said. "I'm here to get the rest of my things." He tried to walk past her, but she stepped in front of him and placed her hands on her hips. She reeked of gin.

"I burned the rest of your things," she said. "Nothing in this house belongs to you."

He wondered if she were bluffing, but he knew she was vicious enough to destroy his clothes. "You can burn thousands of dollars in clothes," he said. "I wouldn't put it past you. But there is something very precious in this house that *does* belong to me...my daughter. And I intend to take custody of her, no matter what you try to do."

"Like hell you will," she said, unsteady on her feet. "Over my dead body you will."

"It might come to that, Blanche, so don't tempt me." He moved past her and started to walk up the stairs. He was aware that she was following him.

She belched as she worked her way up the steps, trying to steady herself with both hands on the railing. "Where the hell do you think you're going?"

Kassler ignored her and went into their bedroom. He opened the door to his closet. It was bare. He turned and faced her as she stood in the doorway. "You rotten bitch. You really did destroy my clothes."

Blanche smiled. "You didn't think I would, did you? Well, you're in for a lot more surprises, buddy boy. Think you're so goddamn smart, trying to force Bill into filing divorce papers against me." She braced herself with one hand on the doorframe. "Well you can try every trick in the fuckin' book, but you're gonna end up holding the shit end of the stick, fella. You're not half the man Bill is. He wants me, and he and I are gonna take you for every nickel you're worth. And you'll never see your daughter again. I'll see to that. How do you like that, big shot?"

He didn't believe her. It was the liquor talking. Reinhardt knows what would happen if he tried to cross him. Or does he? Was Bill Reinhardt so enamored of Blanche or so frightened by her that he would try to double-cross him?

"Where's Emily?" he asked.

"Somewhere where you'll never find her." She was slurring her words.

Blanche came into the bedroom and held on to one arm of the four-poster bed. "I know why you came back. You heard on the news that your lover, Colette Hershfield, has been kidnapped. That's why you're here, isn't it? Why don't you admit it, you bastard? Somebody kidnapped the tramp...well, it serves her right. I hope she gets what she deserves, just like you're gonna get what you deserve."

Kassler found himself walking toward her, but he felt strange, ethereal, like someone else had taken control of his body and he was merely a puppet being manipulated.

She took two steps back and stumbled to the floor. She looked up at him, her eyes wide. "Sam...stay away from me."

Before he understood what was happening, he was on top of her, his hands around her throat.

Blanche screamed. But no one was in the house to hear her. "Stop...Sam, please ..." She grabbed his wrists and tried to free herself, but she couldn't break his grip.

He could feel his hands tightening around her neck, but it was the hands of someone else, and he was only a bystander, watching his wife being choked. Her screams seemed to fade in and out, first muted, then ear-splitting. Blanche's eyes bulged and her face turned red. Kassler bared his teeth as he continued to squeeze the soft, pliable flesh in his hands as if it were putty.

Suddenly her body went limp.

His mind blanked and, for a second, he could only see blackness. Kassler released his grip. He looked down at her blurred body. Then his vision slowly came into focus, and he saw Blanche lying motionless, looking up at him with lifeless eyes. Kassler put his hand to his mouth. Was she dead? Dear God, what if he had killed her?

He knelt beside her and placed his head on her chest. Her heart was still beating. Thank God.

He had to get out of there. Dear Lord, he had just tried to murder his wife. What had come over him? He couldn't afford to get arrested. He had to get away, think things through. Somewhere he couldn't be found. A hotel was no good. The police would find him there. He had to isolate himself. Later, maybe he could explain to the police that this was only a heated dispute between husband and wife. But would they buy that? He couldn't afford to get dragged into a police station now if Blanche pressed charges against him. Assault. Maybe attempted murder.

Droplets of perspiration ran down the sides of his face. He went to the phone on the nightstand, found the number, and dialed it. The phone was answered on the third ring. "Marty...this is Sam Kassler." He was out of breath.

"Sam. Yeah, what can I do for you?" Martin Lang, the real estate agent, seemed surprised by the late call.

"Listen...my cabin you sold in Tioga County...do you know if it's occupied now?"

"Well, I don't think so. The buyer said he wanted to use it as a hunting cabin, and hunting isn't in season. I don't know any other reason why he'd be there now. Why do you ask?"

"I thought I'd go up there...just to get some work done without constant interruptions. I'm facing a strict deadline."

"I see. How long do you intend to be there?"

"Not very long. Maybe a couple days, at most. That should be enough time to complete my work."

"Hell, considering the long drive, that hardly seems worth the trip," Marty said, "but I think it'd be okay with Hutchinson. You want me to call him just to make sure?"

"No, I'd prefer you wouldn't."

"No problem," Marty said. "Come to think of it, Hutchinson doesn't really have ownership until the closing. That may not be for another week. I think it's fine if you want to use it. But just remember, you're not exactly in the middle of civilization out there, so be careful. Don't forget to take a cell phone with you." Marty chuckled. "And take some warm clothes, too."

"Shall do. Thanks, Marty." He hung up, looking at Blanche lying on the floor. He went to her and felt her pulse. Then he double-checked her heartbeat. He felt queasy when he thought of what might have happened. He had to steady himself.

Kassler went into the bathroom, and splashed cold water on his face. He looked in the mirror, his face dripping with water. *How quickly fortunes change,* he thought. Only a short time ago, he was on top of the world. But now the world was turning upside down. In less than forty-eight hours, he had learned that the woman he was obsessed with had been kidnapped, and discovered the possibility that his wife's lover might try to double-cross him, then lost control and almost choked Blanche to death. *Jesus, everything has gone so wrong.*

Kassler dried his face and came out of the bathroom. Where was his daughter? He would have to find Emily later. Thank God she wasn't there tonight. He stepped past his wife, lying unconscious on the floor, then ran down the stairs.

He entered the garage. He would take the Mercedes and get the hell out of that house now. Kassler still remembered the way to the cabin. Even if it did take several hours to get there, he felt he would be able to sort things out in the safety and solitude of that old, almost-forgotten shelter in the wilderness.

Dowling had been on the phone with FBI headquarters for several minutes, but he hardly spoke and his facial expression was placid, so Grant couldn't make out if the news was good or bad. When Dowling finally cradled the receiver, Grant noticed that he was frowning.

Dowling started to rub the back of his neck again, trying to relieve the tension. Merrick, Lapanski, and Santucci remained seated. "Our people ran a preliminary check on Hutchinson," Dowling said. "He's not who he says he is. That's a phony name. He also has a false Social Security number."

Grant rose from his chair. "How could he get away with such a thing for so long?"

"That's what we're trying to find out," Dowling said, "but there are ways to do it. It used to take a lot of preparation and planning, but today, you can get a false Social Security number through the Internet. And it doesn't even take very long."

Grant closed his right hand, making a fist. "I believe you, and I also believe that Hutchinson—or whoever the hell he is—is our man."

"I'll admit that it's beginning to look that way," said Dowling, "but we can't leap to that conclusion just yet. We now consider him a suspect and we have a manhunt under way for him, but this is still supposition on our part. This guy's phony identity and disappearance and Colette's kidnapping might only be two unrelated events that are coincidental."

Grant shook his head. "I don't think so, Jim."

"Tell you the truth, I don't, either, but we've got to play carefully. We don't want another incident like we had in Atlanta in '96 with Richard Jewell."

Just then the phone rang.

Dowling signaled Merrick and Lapanski, who activated the tape recorder next to the wiretapping equipment. Santucci stood next to Dowling.

Grant felt the muscles in his neck tighten as he lifted the receiver and placed it to his ear. "This is Montgomery."

"And you know who this is, don't you?" This time, the voice was unmistakable, disguised in the usual low tone like it was coming from a tunnel.

Grant stalled for time. "No, I'm afraid I don't."

Dowling signaled Grant to prolong the conversation.

The voice continued. "Oh, come now, Montgomery. I know the FBI is trying to trace this call."

"You seem to be a pretty smart fellow. How do you know the FBI is here trying to trace anything?"

"You're stalling for time, but it won't work." The line went dead.

"Hello? Hello, are you there?" Grant glanced at Dowling, who shook his head.

"He was on to you," Dowling said. "The son of a bitch knows we need sufficient time to complete the trace."

Grant hung up the phone. "You didn't expect him to fall for it, did you?"

"I'm not sure what I expected," Dowling said. "The question now is when will he call back?"

As if on cue, the phone rang again. Everyone in the room tensed at the same time, and Grant let it ring one more time. He lifted the receiver.

"Yes," Grant said.

"If you try that again, I'll kill her."

Grant's heart skipped a beat. His mouth was dry, and he ran his tongue over his lips. "You win. Let me talk to Colette."

"I'll let you hear her now," Hutchinson said. "But first, be aware that there are wonderful things you can do with a pair of pliers."

Grant heard a click and suspected that a tape player had been activated on the other end of the line. He heard Hutchinson's voice, this time undisguised, but with a faded quality in tone not present a moment ago, and Grant was sure the voice was prerecorded.

The voice became louder, indicating the volume was being turned up. "Now Colette, you tell me which toe you'd like me to crush, and I'll accommodate you."

"Oh, God. Please don't." Her voice. No mistaking it.

A moment's delay.

He heard the monster's voice again. "I see you can't make up your mind, so I'll have to make the decision for you. Let's see...this little piggy went to market ..." He could barely hear Colette sobbing.

"...and this little piggy stayed home. Well, since this little piggy is still at home, it looks like that's the one we'll go to work on."

Grant could visualize the scene and gritted his teeth. Sweet Merciful God in Heaven.

Suddenly a scream pierced Grant's ear, and everyone in the room flinched at the horrid, agonizing cry. Then silence. Ear-splitting silence. Grant pressed the receiver to his ear, straining to hear, but there was no sound. Colette must have passed out. *Dear God, don't let her be dead.*

Grant suddenly felt weak as if he had been drained of energy. "Don't hurt her anymore," he said. "Take my life. I'll give you my life in exchange for hers. Whatever I've done to you—or whatever you think I've done—I can't pay you with any more than that."

"Yes," the voice said in a soft, low tone of gratification long denied. "Yes, that's what I've been waiting to hear."

Then the line went dead.

CHAPTER SEVENTEEN

Desperation intensified pain, but fatigue could dull it. Colette learned that, and mentally surrendered to her exhaustion. Her eyes were sunken and dark from lack of sleep. Her legs were free, and although her arms were no longer behind her back, her wrists were still bound by the duct tape. She was sitting on the cot with her head bowed. Still terrified of what else Hutchinson might do to her, she nevertheless had given up any hope of escaping. He had severely bruised the little toe of her right foot with the pliers, although he hadn't broken it because her screams in panic were all he was after. She sat there still in agony, despite her fatigue, with her right foot resting on her left ankle, asking for an aspirin, any relief she could get. But her appeals were useless. Colette had just about resigned herself to dying painfully at the hands of this maniac.

"Please, my foot is throbbing," she said again. "Can't you give me something for the pain?"

Hutchinson, who was sitting at the table, smoking, cocked his head as if sympathizing with her. "I would if I could, Colette, but I haven't anything to give you." He put out the cigarette on the table, flicked the butt to the wall, then rose and walked toward her. "Here, let me take a look at that."

She cringed as he approached her.

"No, no, don't be frightened. I merely want to examine your little tootsie."

She knew that in his warped mind, every physical pain, every emotional trauma he inflicted on her, he was inflicting on Grant.

He knelt in front of her and pushed his glasses back on the rim of his nose. "My, my, that toe doesn't look good. They say if something like that is left untreated, you could end up with a serious problem, might even lose it. But then I'm not a doctor, and I can't be sure about such things." He stood and looked down at her. "Although I don't have any medicine for you, I can give you some good advice. I wouldn't try to run out of here if I were you. In fact, I wouldn't even try to stand on that foot." He started to chuckle. "That's a good one, isn't it?"

"Yes, that's just hilarious." She no longer cared if she showed sarcasm or, for that matter, any emotion that would reveal her repulsion of him. He was going to do whatever he planned to do to her, and she was powerless to prevent it.

"You know what I think will help, Colette? I think getting your mind off your little toe is the best medicine I could give you right now. So why don't I try to do that." He pulled up a chair and straddled it, sitting in front of her. "You should try to concentrate on something else. So let's work together on this." He placed a finger up to his lips as if he were deep in thought. "Let's see, what should we concentrate on. Well, we've been having good weather, but then, of course, being indoors, you wouldn't be able to appreciate it." He looked at the ceiling. "Hmmm. I read that our nation's balance of payments deficit is being reduced. That's certainly a good sign for the economy, wouldn't you say?" He paused, gazing at her, his charade a blatant mockery. "No, I can see you're not interested in that. Well, we could exchange views about the Steelers and the Pirates. But I guess you're not up to that, either." Hutchinson folded his arms. "Colette, you don't seem to be cooperating, and I'm only trying to help you take your mind off your throbbing toe." He stood and began to walk back and forth. Suddenly he stopped and snapped his fingers. "I know. Let's think about your lover. Now that's a subject I'll bet you're interested in."

Colette said nothing.

"Sure you are." He resumed his seat. "I'll tell you what. Just to show you that my heart's in the right place. I'll arrange to have Grant Montgomery pay us a little visit. Now how does that sound?"

She bowed her head again, trying to hold back the tears.

"In fact, the three of us will have a party together. Doesn't that make you feel better? Sure it does. I know you'd like to see him again. What a party this will be. Would you like me to tell you about it?"

Colette lifted her bound wrists, and wiped her tears with the back of her hand. "Yes...go ahead."

He clapped. "Now you're showing some interest. I knew you would." Hutchinson leaned forward, peering at her through his thick glasses, trying to detect any little nuance in her reaction. "Every good party has a theme. And do you know what the theme of our party is going to be?"

"No, what's the theme?"

He rubbed his hands together quickly as if he were about to treat himself to a long-awaited pleasure. "Let's kill Colette while Grant Montgomery watches. How's that for a theme? Then when you're dead, the party theme changes to—let's kill Grant Montgomery while I watch. Do you like that?"

She lowered her head again.

"No, at that point, the party's still not over. Then the theme changes to let's kill me."

Colette's head bolted upright.

"That's right. After I kill you and your lover, I'm going to kill myself."

Blanche Kassler was still unsteady when she dialed Bill Reinhardt's number, but the experience of nearly being choked to death had sobered her quickly. She knew Reinhardt didn't want her to call his office. He had always initiated the calls to her from a private phone, but this couldn't wait. She reached Reinhardt's secretary, who transferred the call to him.

"Bill, thank God I caught you in. You'll never believe what happened."

He sounded tentative. "What?"

"That son of a bitch tried to kill me." She was breathing heavily.

"What are you talking about? Who tried to kill you?"

"Sam...he tried to choke me to death." She rubbed her neck while talking. "Just moments ago."

"Why, for God's sake?"

"He went crazy. I've never seen him like that. He choked me until I lost consciousness."

"That doesn't sound like him. What made him do it?"

"I told him that he wasn't going to get away with divorcing me...that you and I were going to fight him, and that he'd never see his daughter again."

"That's when he attacked you?"

Blanche was starting to get her breath back. "Yes...no, no it was when I told him that I knew he came right back from San Francisco because he was concerned about Colette Hershfield's kidnapping. He's in love with her, you know. I called her a tramp and told him that I wished she'd get what she deserves, the same way we're going to give him what he deserves."

Reinhardt didn't respond immediately. Five or six seconds later, his voice came back on the line. "That was a mistake, Blanche. You pushed him too far. Where is he now?"

"He left the house. I was just coming to when I heard him pull out of the garage. I don't know where he went. We can press charges against him, can't we, Bill?"

Another few seconds delay before Reinhardt answered, but this time his voice sounded different, more distant and professional. "No, I don't think *we* are going to do any such thing."

"Why not? God, he tried to kill me. Don't you understand?"

"I understand perfectly, Mrs. Kassler."

"*Mrs*. Kassler? Is there someone with you?"

"Not a soul, and no one else is on the line except you and me."

She was dumbfounded. "Then why the hell are you calling me Mrs. Kassler?"

"Let me explain something. If your husband made an attempt on your life and he's running from the law, then he's lost the upper hand. He can no longer threaten to expose me without exposing himself. And even if he could, who would take the word of someone who just attempted murder? Sam is no longer a threat to me. He might even be a fugitive from justice."

Blanche didn't understand. "But what about me? Why can't we bring charges against him? And why are you being so formal?"

"Listen to me, Mrs. Kassler. There is no *we* anymore. You and I are through. I'm no longer boxed in by you or your husband. You can do whatever you want to do, and it doesn't concern me anymore."

Blanche looked at the receiver, then put it back to her ear. "You can't be serious."

"I'm afraid I am."

She began to breathe heavily again. "You double-crossing rotten bastard. I'll go to your wife and tell her everything."

"You can prove nothing without that letter. Your husband has it, and he can't use it. He's on the run. And even if he ever tries to use it, he's lost his credibility. I'll say the letter is a forgery designed to justify his attempt on your life. So you can call my wife, but your accusations will only be considered as the rambling of a hysterical shrew, whose husband tried to kill her."

"That's not true...your wife will believe me." She ran the back of her hand across her brow.

"Without proof, no one is going to believe you, not my wife, not the law, and not my business associates. I'm the quintessential conservative, remember? In fact, they might even think you're out of your head. That wouldn't be too hard to believe of a woman whose husband tried to choke her to death and then abandoned her."

Her hand holding the receiver started to shake. "You...you...you dirty bastard. You won't get away with this. Sam'll come back to me...I won't press charges against him.

We'll be together again, and then we'll take care of you. We'll figure out a way together."

"I don't know whether Sam can square it with the law or not," he said. "That's no concern of mine. But one thing I do know. He'll never come back to you. He hates your guts."

Suddenly her vindictiveness was gone, and she felt empty. Blanche began to sob. "No...please Bill, I didn't mean it. I won't go to your wife. I love you, I really do. I didn't mean anything I said. You're making me crazy. I can't be alone...you know that. How could I live it down? What would I tell people?"

"That's what's really worrying you—your social standing," he said. "Poor little rich girl who finally made it, only to discover her world is built on sand. I'm afraid you'll have to explain to your socialite friends what's gone wrong between you and Sam. Any hint of scandal—particularly attempted murder—and your social standing goes to hell, so your story is going to require a lot of creativity."

She tried to speak through her tears. "Bill, you want me...I know you do. I know how to make you happy. You told me that over and over—"

He cut her off. "Just one last piece of advice—there are several good psychiatrists in Pittsburgh. You might be needing one. Goodbye, Mrs. Kassler. I can't say that it's been fun."

Blanche heard the click and stood there, her face streaked with mascara, still holding the receiver in a white-knuckled grip.

This time they were expecting the call. In fact, they had expected it much earlier. Grant answered the phone.

The sound of the kidnapper's voice had the effect of a knife thrust into Grant's stomach. "I'd like to invite you to a party where you'll have a chance to see your girl. She misses you."

"I'll be there," Grant said. "Just tell me where and when."

"Listen carefully. I'm not going to repeat this." Grant noticed that the voice became slower, more deliberate. "Go to Route 22 East. Follow that and get on 220 North. Then get off at the first exit. You'll find an all-night diner at the end of the exit. Go in there and wait for my call. That drive normally takes one and a half hours. You've got exactly that much time from the moment I hang up. That means you have to leave now. If you're not there by then, I'll cut off one of her body parts and have it waiting for you as a present. Do you understand?"

Grant looked at Dowling and Santucci. "Yes, I'm to go to Route 22—"

"Don't repeat it. The FBI can replay the tape they're now making so you can copy the instructions. But hurry, you don't have any time to spare."

"I'll leave now," Grant said. "When will you release her?"

Hutchinson ignored the question. "We're going to have lots of fun at the party, but you better come alone. If you're followed, I'll know it. And so help me, I'll kill her."

"Wait, listen for a second—" Grant heard the click. He looked at Merrick and Lapanski. The expression on their faces told him they couldn't complete the trace.

"I've got to leave now," Grant said.

"Hold on," Dowling said. He approached Grant and grabbed his arm. "Now listen, this is no time for any hero crap. You're not going there alone."

Grant twisted his arm free. "I don't have time to argue. You heard what he'd do to Colette. I'm not going to risk that."

"Damn it, listen to me for a second," Dowling said. His face reddened. "We can follow you without being seen. We haven't been sitting on our hands all this time. We've anticipated that something like this was going to happen, so we've already equipped your car with a special transmitter. It'll give off a signal telling us exactly where you are. We'll be able to track you by computer in a van even if we're several miles away."

"So that's the reason you wanted me to use your car when I went into town. How do I activate it?"

"You don't," Dowling said. "We take care of that. Look, we don't think the kidnapper can tell if you're being followed. I'll lay odds that he's bluffing. We think he's working alone."

"But you're not sure," Grant said.

"No, I can't guarantee anything." Dowling tapped his chin with his fist. "Now here's the plan. The diner will probably be the first of several stops. He might even keep you going in circles, but we'll know exactly where you are at all times. As soon as you know where you're going to meet him, call us on your cell phone. We'll be able to hone in on your location, wherever you are. But keep in regular contact with us, just to be on the safe side. Whatever you do, don't meet him alone. Just make sure you call this number and tell us exactly where you're supposed to meet him." He handed a piece of paper to Grant.

Grant looked at it, memorized the number and put the paper in his shirt pocket. "I hear you."

"That number will reach me at all times," Dowling said. "After you've called us, your job is done. I'll have a SWAT team on hand to stake out wherever he's got her, and we'll take it from there. I promise you we'll get her out alive, if it's at all possible."

If it's at all possible. The words burned like a white-hot branding iron. And what if it wasn't possible?

"I have a feeling that he gave me directions to a place he's not too familiar with," Grant said.

Dowling looked at him. "What makes you say that?"

Grant narrowed his eyes. "Although he still disguised his voice, it slowed a bit and he was more deliberate as he was giving me the directions, like he had to think about it to make sure he was accurate. In my profession, I made a study of changes in speech patterns, voice pitch, that type of thing, and that's the impression I got."

Dowling took a sheet of paper from Dan Merrick, who had transcribed the directions from the tape recorder. He studied it for a moment. "Considering where he has you going, you might be right." He handed the paper to Grant.

Santucci grabbed Grant's arm. "I wouldn't bet against you, either. Look, why don't you let me go with you. This guy'll never be the wiser, and I'll feel better about it."

"No way, Tom," Grant said. "I know you want to be there for me, and I appreciate it. But I can't take a chance that this maniac might have an accomplice to tail me and report if I'm not following instructions." He glanced at Dowling and his two assistants, then looked at Santucci. "I know you guys think that's a very small chance, but I'm not willing to take it. I won't gamble with Colette's life."

Santucci nodded. "I understand. But Vasquez and I will follow you with Dowling."

Dowling let out a deep breath. "Okay, Grant, have it your way, but I'd still feel better if you'd let one of our men go with you."

"No, and that's final."

"All right, but remember, don't *you* take any unnecessary chances. Just follow the instructions I gave you."

Grant checked his watch. "Let's move," he said. "We're wasting time."

CHAPTER EIGHTEEN

After four and a half hours behind the wheel, Sam Kassler was becoming weary. The two-hundred-and-twenty-five-mile drive was difficult enough, but making the journey at night after an emotional episode with his wife that nearly ended in tragedy was almost more than he could bear. He felt he could sleep for days. Another twenty minutes or so and he would enter that cabin and sleep on a hardwood floor if necessary.

For the past hour, Kassler was having second thoughts about the wisdom of fleeing from his home. It seemed like the only way out at the time—to get far enough away so he couldn't be found. But he had reacted to the moment. Now, he wasn't so sure. If she called the police, would his running make him appear guilty of her accusations? And God only knew what accusations she could bring against him. Spousal abuse. Assault and battery. Even attempted murder. Kassler knew his question was rhetorical. Of course, he would appear to be guilty. He was utterly stupid to have run away. He should have stayed. Even if she did call the police, he could have explained that they had only been arguing, that she had been drinking, fell and passed out. The police didn't like to get involved in domestic disputes, anyway, and they could have corroborated his story, at least the part about Blanche drinking. But instead of thinking clearly, he panicked and ran. Strange how a few hours could change your perspective.

He wanted to turn around, go home, but he was too exhausted to face the long drive back. A night's sleep and he would return home, hopefully with a plausible story that might satisfy the police. They had a heated argument, and he decided to get out of the house for the night. That's all. If there were any bruises on her neck, he had no idea how they got there. There were no witnesses.

Kassler peered through the windshield of the Mercedes. The mountainous road at night was becoming more difficult to see. The turn should be just up ahead, then another ten or fifteen minutes and he'd be there. He saw the road, made a right-hand turn, drove another hundred yards and made another right. Only a couple of miles away now. A few minutes later, he suddenly stopped the car. The cabin was there all right, but he could see smoke coming from its chimney.

He rubbed his forehead. *For the love of God, that fellow who bought the cabin must be in there. What the hell would he be doing there now? It's not hunting season yet. Damn it.*

He put his head on the steering wheel. The nearest town was Wellsboro, and that was about a half hour or so away. He couldn't drive any further. Kassler raised his head, gave a long sigh, and decided that he would go to the cabin, tell the new owner that he thought the cabin was unoccupied, wanted to check out the place one last time before turning it over to him, and ask if he could stay the night. What the hell was that guy's name? Marty said something like Harkinson...no, Hutchinson. Surely this Hutchinson would be reasonable enough to let him stay the night. After all, as the real-estate man said, Hutchinson wasn't officially the owner until the closing.

He started the Mercedes and drove slowly toward the cabin.

Grant took the first exit off Route 220 North. Exceeding the speed limit most of the way, he had been driving for an hour and twenty minutes. He had ten minutes to get to the diner. Grant was sure this would be only the first of several stops as Dowling had predicted. He was also sure that Hutchinson was the kidnapper. If Hutchinson had every move well timed, then he was methodical, not given to taking chances.

He spotted the neon sign that read Penn's Eatery, and drove the Lamborghini into the parking lot. At that time of night, only one car and two trailer trucks were parked there. Usually, he was careful where he took the Lamborghini, because the car sometimes could attract unwanted attention, but he wasn't going to worry about that now.

Grant rushed into the diner. Two men were sitting at the counter, one in a plaid, wool three-quarter-length coat, the other in a dark leather jacket. Another man was sitting with a woman in one of the four booths at the end of the diner. Grant spotted a phone mounted on the wall. He sat at the far end of the counter, near the phone.

A middle-aged waitress wearing a pink uniform and a bored expression took Grant's order for black coffee. The diner was a typical greasy-spoon restaurant with a row of worn black swivel seats along the Formica counter. The cook could be seen through an open partition in the wall. About fifty or so, he looked like he had lived a long time on his own cooking, his soiled apron barely able to fit around his waist. His white baseball cap, worn backwards, was smudged with grease.

The waitress returned with Grant's coffee. "I saw you pull up in that fancy car out there. Boy, that's some car."

Grant feigned a smile and glanced at his watch. "Yeah."

She leaned on the counter. "What kind of a car is that?"

"A Lamborghini."

"Is that one of them foreign cars?"

Grant took a sip of his coffee. It was strong, the way he expected it. "Afraid so."

"I'll bet a car like that set you back plenty."

"You got that right."

She smiled. "Yes sir, that's some car. I sure wouldn't mind taking a ride in that."

Grant checked his watch again. Just then the phone rang. He jumped up and answered it before it could ring a second time.

"Montgomery?" the voice asked.

"Yes."

"It's a good thing you answered. If I had to ask for you by name and you weren't there to take my call, I would've known you didn't make it on time. Then I would've started working on her."

So he doesn't have an accomplice, Grant thought. "What do you want me to do?"

"Listen carefully and write this down. Are you ready?"

Grant had a pen and notebook in hand, and braced the receiver between his chin and shoulder. "I'm ready."

"Take I-80 East and get off on Exit 25. Make a right after the exit and stay on that road until you come to a roadhouse called the Lumber Mill. Go into the bar. I'll contact you there." The same, slow deliberate instructions. "You've got exactly two hours from now. No more." A short pause. "Have you got all that?"

For the first time, Grant noticed that this man was no longer trying to disguise his voice. And he wasn't rushed trying to beat a phone tap. Now there was something strangely familiar about the voice, but he couldn't pinpoint what it was. "Yes, I've got it. Listen, before you hang up—"

"Do as I tell you. If you don't, your girlfriend isn't gonna look the same when you see her. Remember, two hours."

Grant heard the click and checked his watch. 12:20 A.M. Why was he being led so far away? He had no idea where he was going, but the instructions were clear. He tossed a dollar on the counter.

The waitress picked it up. "Brother, are *you* in a hurry," she said. "You hardly touched your coffee. Important business, huh?"

"Yeah, important business."

She leaned on the counter with both elbows. "You know, I wouldn't mind taking a ride in that car of yours sometime. You coming back this way soon?"

"I wish I knew," he said and left the diner.

Jim Dowling studied the blinking light on the computer screen, which displayed a road map. The van was equipped with an array of sophisticated electronic communications and tracking equipment. Dan Merrick sat next to him, helping to work the console. Santucci squatted as he hunched over both of their chairs, while Tony Lapanski drove. Emilio Vasquez sat in a back seat; he preferred old-fashioned police work to confusing electronic equipment that he didn't understand.

Less than a quarter mile behind them, a SWAT team of eight special agents followed in an unmarked truck.

Dowling pointed to the blinking light on the screen as Tom Santucci looked over his shoulder. The computer could bring up road maps of any part of Pennsylvania while tracking the transmitter's signal, whether Grant's car traveled on main arteries or secondary roads. "He's left the diner and he's on the move again." They studied the computer screen for several more minutes. "He's made a turn," Dowling said. "He's heading east, just like he said." Grant had called a few minutes earlier and told them where he was headed. Merrick cross-referenced the coordinates on a printed map. "He's moving on I-80 East," he said.

"It takes a lot of guts to be in Grant's shoes right now," Dowling said, "not knowing where he's going or what to expect."

Merrick said, "I hope he's got more brains than guts."

Santucci changed his position and rubbed his left leg, trying to ease the pain from squatting. "No need to worry about that, Dan."

Vasquez leaned forward. "My people have a saying: to underestimate an enemy is dangerous, but to underestimate a friend is stupid." Let them have their fancy computers. He had common sense.

Merrick responded with a sharp look and a sneer. A moment later, he said, "Holy Jesus, who farted?"

Dowling brought his handkerchief to his mouth. "My God, open the window."

Santucci scowled, waving his hand in front of his face. "Goddamn it, Emilio, you've got to stop eating those Mexican beans. It's the worst thing I've ever smelled. Can't you control yourself?"

Merrick opened the window, and looked at Vasquez through the rearview mirror. "Christ man, I knew we should've left you behind."

Emilio Vasquez sat erect with his hands folded in his lap; he spoke as if making a pronouncement. "I'm concerned for Grant, not for what you smell." Then he added as an afterthought, "Angels smell fragrance, but it takes the Devil to smell shit."

The kidnapper thought he heard the sound of a car. He opened the front door a crack and peered out. He couldn't see much of anything in the dark, so he opened the door a few inches more, moved to one side and continued to survey the woods. Suddenly he spotted the Mercedes and saw a man walking toward the cabin about seventy or eighty feet away. He jumped back and closed the door. Who the hell could he be? Did Montgomery discover where he was? No, he couldn't have. He cracked open the door again, and squinted at the man approaching the cabin. He didn't look like a cop. He wasn't holding a gun and he wasn't trying to hide. If he were a cop, there'd be twenty of them out there.

He ran to Colette, who was sitting on the cot. She cringed as he approached her. He tied his handkerchief around her mouth. "Someone's out there," he whispered. "One sound out of you and you're dead. Understand?"

She nodded, wide-eyed, and started breathing heavily.

Hutchinson quickly put out the light from the kerosene lamp and took the dagger from his toolbox. No time to get the gun that was in the glove compartment of his car. He left the door unlocked and waited.

Sam Kassler knocked on the cabin door. He waited for a few seconds, then knocked again. Still no answer. That seemed strange. The smoke he saw coming from the chimney certainly indicated that someone had to be there. He tried the door handle and was surprised to find the door unlocked.

Kassler pushed the door open a few feet. The cabin was in darkness. Hutchinson might be asleep, he thought.

"Hello, anybody home?"

Kassler stepped into the cabin. He could only see the outline of a table and a stove, then he heard a grunting sound in the corner and turned to his left. "Hello, I'm sorry to disturb your sleep. I'm the—" Kassler suddenly stopped and peered into the darkness. "What the hell...Colette, Jesus—"

Just then, Kassler sensed someone was behind him, but before he could turn, an arm suddenly wrapped around his throat, taking him off balance, then a searing pain shot into his side. He tried to scream, but a powerful hand grabbed his throat, and his back exploded as something sharp and deep tore again into his flesh.

He sank to his knees, unable to get his breath, and looked up at the dark figure in front of him. All he could see was a pair of monstrous eyes behind glasses, the flash of bared teeth, and then the knife came down again, this time ripping into his neck. Kassler clutched his throat, and rolled on his side, the blood gushing from his severed jugular vein.

He lay there, looking incredulously at the dark figure standing before him, and the room seemed to get brighter. He rolled on his back, opened his mouth and tried to speak, but the words wouldn't come. The room began to blur, and the light slowly faded.

Sam Kassler died with his mouth wide open.

Blanche took another sip of the martini. If she ever needed a drink, she needed one now. Only hours ago, before Sam attacked her, she had been drunk. Now she was sober. She sat on the edge of the couch and lighted a cigarette from the half-empty pack her maid had left in the kitchen. She hadn't smoked in years. What the hell had gotten into Sam? He had never laid a hand on her, not in all their years of marriage. She knew some men were capable of violence if they discovered their spouse had been unfaithful to them, but she didn't think *he* was capable of it. She misjudged him. She misjudged a lot of things. Like Bill Reinhardt. Simpering, whining rabbit in bed, who turned into a bastard. *Men are pigs,* she thought. *Every goddamn last one of them.* But she wasn't going to press charges against Sam. She couldn't stand the publicity. Even if she didn't press charges, word might still leak. That worried her. She didn't want her friends to know. She would still take Sam back—if he came back—but she would make him pay for what he did in other ways. She would tell Emily exactly what happened when her daughter returned tomorrow morning from another pajama party. She wanted Emily to know what men were capable of doing.

More than respect, Blanche needed money and all the comforts that money could buy. She simply could not be without money. She snuffed out the cigarette. No sense in dwelling on it any more. No sense getting upset. She had to make plans. Not now. It was late. Maybe tomorrow. She finished the martini in one gulp, and went upstairs.

She entered her bedroom and suddenly fell face down on her bed and wept uncontrollably.

The killer lighted the kerosene lamp, and looked down at the figure drenched in blood. Hutchinson never saw the man before. He opened the door, and peered out into the night, but he could see no one. The police would never have sent one man alone into the cabin. If the police had staked out the place, they would have rushed him by now. He was reasonably sure the man was not a police officer, that he had come alone.

Hutchinson locked the door, and went to the body lying on the floor, a helpless figure, whose blood was running along the soles of his boots. He wiped his knife on Kassler's trousers and placed it under his belt. He checked the dead man's wallet and found his driver's license. Samuel Kassler. The name meant nothing to him. *Who was he? Why did he come here? Did he know I was here, that I had kidnapped a woman?* He looked at Colette. Even in the dark, she could see what had happened. He went to her and untied the gag. Colette was shaking. She looked at Kassler, his body covered in blood. "Oh, God...oh, God," she said. "How could you—" She turned her head and started to retch, but was unable to vomit.

"If you get sick," Hutchinson said, "you'll clean your own mess."

After a few seconds, she was no longer dry-heaving. Colette took several deep breaths, then looked up at him. Her face was drained of color. "Do you know who that was?" she asked weakly.

Hutchinson's back became rigid. "You must know him. He called you by name."

She nodded slowly. "Yes...that's Sam Kassler."

"That's the name, all right. Who the hell is he?"

Colette couldn't bring herself to look at the body. "He was a client of mine...he worked for a stock brokerage firm."

"A client? Somehow he must've found out that we were here," Hutchinson said more to himself than to Colette. Then he snapped his fingers. "No...that name, Kassler. Sam Kassler. That's the name the real estate agent gave me. He's the guy who owned this cabin."

"What? What real estate agent? What do you mean?"

"Just what I said. Kassler owned this cabin. You didn't know that?"

"No...no, I had no idea." Her head was spinning. She took another deep breath. This was a nightmare.

"Why did he come here?"

"I don't know." Colette lowered her head. "I...I can't believe what you did to him. Why? For God's sake, why?" She began to sob.

"I don't believe you." Hutchinson took two steps toward her. "You knew this man. You're holding something back from me."

Colette shook her head, still sobbing.

He took another step toward her and slapped her face with the back of his hand. "Don't lie to me."

Her head jerked back from the force of the blow, and her lower lip started to bleed. "I'm not lying...I don't even know where we are. How could I have told him or anyone else? ...He couldn't have known I was here. If he did, he would've notified the police."

Hutchinson nodded and rubbed his chin. "I don't like things to happen that I haven't planned. He came here for some reason. If he told anyone where he was going, they might come looking for him if he's gone too long. But by then, I won't care. I've got enough time to do what I have to." He glanced at his watch. "I'm overdue to contact your lover boy. He's been waiting for my call."

He went to the table, picked up his cellular phone and punched in a number. He asked the operator to dial the Lumber Mill roadhouse. After a few seconds, he said, "I want to speak to Grant Montgomery. He's somewhere in the cafe." He heard a voice call out Montgomery's name. A moment later, Montgomery was on the line.

"I see you're good at following instructions," Hutchinson said. "You just continue doing what I tell you."

"You're calling the shots," Grant said. "What do I do next?"

"Listen carefully and be ready to write this down, because I'm not going to repeat it."

"I'm ready," Grant said.

"Get on Route 220 and follow that all the way to Route 287, which will take you into Wellsboro and Route 6. You're traveling north all the way. Follow Route 6 until you come to Pine Creek Gorge. Keep bearing right and you'll come to an old log cabin about eight miles from the gorge. Go into the cabin and wait there. It'll take you exactly one hour and thirty minutes to make the rest of the drive. It's now two thirty-five. If you're not there by five after four, she's dead. You got that?"

"I've got it. Listen, before you hang up, can I at least hear Colette's voice?"

"The only thing that's keeping her alive is your following my instructions. If the police or the FBI are tailing you, I'll know it, and I'll kill her—in an instant. So just keep everything copacetic. Understand?"

Grant seemed to hesitate before answering. "I understand."

Hutchinson hung up and faced Colette, smiling. "Lover boy's cooperating because he knows you're dead if he doesn't."

Colette kept her head lowered. He knew she was afraid to look at him or the dead man.

He stared at the lifeless figure on the floor. "A former client, you say? Well, isn't this nice and cozy. We're just one big happy family, aren't we?" He asked the next question like a visitor at a funeral parlor. "Tell me, how long did you know the deceased?"

She didn't answer.

"I can see you're upset. Well, I guess I can't blame you. Life is strange, isn't it? One minute he's a client, the next minute he's dead. For him, the party's over."

He picked up Kassler's legs and dragged the body toward the door. "I'm gonna get rid of our friend, but I'll be back soon. I'd advise you to get some rest while you can, because in an hour and a half your lover boy will join us. That's when the real party starts." He dragged the body out of the cabin, leaving a trail of blood. Then he locked the door.

CHAPTER NINETEEN

The black sky was moonless. Stretched before Grant Montgomery in a never-ending series of turns, the road kept winding into higher elevations within the mountains. He felt helpless, being drawn like a magnet into a dark, unknown wilderness by a stranger who waited to complete a terrible vendetta. He gripped the wheel, his mind racing with Hutchinson's words that referred to this part of the journey as "the rest of the drive." If Hutchinson let those words slip unintentionally, that meant the log cabin he referred to was the last stop. Most likely, that's where he was keeping Colette, but Grant couldn't be sure.

Something else troubled him. The voice that this man was no longer trying to disguise seemed strangely familiar. Grant had the same feeling the last time he talked to him. Somewhere Grant had heard that voice before. But where? And this time, something more than just his voice or his eyes in the photograph lit a dim light in the recesses of his mind. Whatever it was still remained unclear, mired in the cobwebs and shadows of the past.

As he was driving, looking for the road sign, he couldn't fully concentrate on what was taunting him about his verbal exchange with the kidnapper. This was unfamiliar country, and he couldn't afford to miss a sign or make a wrong turn. That kind of mistake could mean Colette's life.

He had been driving for several minutes when he finally spotted the sign, breathed a sigh of relief, and turned onto Route 220 North, accelerating the Lamborghini. He didn't think he would have to make the next turn for a while, so he let his mind concentrate on his conversation with Hutchinson. What was nagging at him? Something was reaching out to him, but he still couldn't make contact with it.

He decided to call Dowling on his cell phone to tell him where he thought the final destination would be. He took the phone from the glove compartment. As he dialed the number, he noticed the red light on his phone, indicating a weak battery. Grant heard Dowling's phone ringing, but the line was filled with static.

"Hello, Jim, can you hear me?" He heard a weak voice answering, but he couldn't hear any words over the static, which was getting louder.

"Jim, it's Grant. Can you hear me?"

He knew Dowling or one of his men was on the other end of the line, but all he could hear was static. Damn it, he should have recharged the battery. He couldn't plug it into the cigarette lighter socket, because even though he purchased the cell phone only two weeks ago, the adapter was still on back order. The mountains didn't help his reception, either.

Grant noted the time. 2:45 A.M. He gave it a last try, shouting into the phone. "Jim, this is Grant. If you can hear me, I'm headed for a log cabin, which is about eight miles north of Pine Creek Gorge on Route 6." He glanced at his watch. "I have to be there in exactly one hour and twenty minutes. I'll try to get there sooner to give you time to catch up, if you can. Did you get that?" The static was worse. He repeated the message before the battery would die and he wouldn't be able to get through at all. He wondered if Dowling was able to hear him through the interference, thankful that the FBI team at least was still able to track him.

Jim Dowling stretched his right arm, his eyes still on the computer screen. "He's just made another turn onto Route 220, still heading north." Merrick confirmed the coordinates, while Lapanski concentrated on driving.

For the first time since they'd entered the van, Dowling took his eyes off the screen and turned, facing Santucci and Vasquez, who were sitting in the back. "Everything's going as planned. Once Grant gets his final destination, we'll be able to move in on the kidnapper and keep Grant out of harm's way. Whether our man is Hutchinson or someone else, he's not going to get away, not with the team I have ready to go." The SWAT team was less than a quarter of a mile behind them.

Santucci nodded. "I just hope Colette comes out of this unharmed."

"So do I," Dowling said. "We'll act cautiously, and we won't do anything to jeopardize her safety, but—" The phone rang. "That's Grant," Dowling said as he put on a pair of earphones with an attached speaker, and pressed a button on the console.

"Go ahead, Grant," he said. His head jolted back from the rush of static. He turned a knob, trying to adjust the volume. "What? Say again. I can't hear you." Still more static. Dowling continued to listen intently, but the interference was too much. He looked at Merrick. "He's trying to get through, but I can't make out a damn word of it. It sounds like electrical interference, but there's no storm anywhere near."

The static stopped. "Grant, can you hear me? If so, try again." No response. Then he heard more static, knowing that Grant was still trying to get through. Finally, the static stopped again. Dowling kept the line open for several more minutes, then pressed a button on the console and took the earphones off. He shook his head. "I'm afraid it's no good."

Santucci and Vasquez were leaning forward. "What do you think the trouble is?" Santucci asked.

"I'm not sure," Dowling said. "I don't think it's from our end. He might be having trouble with his phone or maybe the mountains are interfering with his transmission. If we can't make voice contact with him, our job's going to be a little tougher. Thank God we can still track him." He motioned to the computer screen. "He's still heading north into mountainous country. Once that blip remains stationary, we'll know that's where he's been instructed to stop, and we'll have a pretty good fix on his location."

Emilio Vasquez frowned. "What do you mean by 'pretty good'?"

"When he reaches his destination," Dowling said, "we may not be able to pinpoint his location exactly, but we'll be able to tell within a half mile of where he is, possibly even less than that."

Vasquez folded his arms. "With all that equipment you have, I thought you could tell the exact spot if he stopped to take a leak."

Dowling turned to Santucci and Vasquez. "Don't worry, we're only about fifteen minutes behind Grant. I just hope your friend follows my instructions and waits for us."

Grant placed the phone on the seat beside him, and pressed down on the accelerator. The trees and foliage on either side of him whizzed past in a blur of motion. The forest at night seemed as strange as a foreign land, and he hadn't seen another car on the road for miles. At this time of night and on these roads, he hadn't expected to see anyone. He seemed hopelessly alone, and if he could feel such solitude, what must Colette be feeling at that very moment, he wondered.

He tried to drive and at the same time focus on his last exchange with Hutchinson. Grant thought of Hutchinson's threat to kill Colette if he discovered that the FBI or the police were following him. Surely he must realize that the FBI would have never allowed him to make this journey alone. Of course they would be following him, and Hutchinson knew it or at least had to suspect it. So why would he threaten to kill Colette? He gripped the steering wheel harder. It's as if the kidnapper wanted to keep Grant on edge, but didn't really care about the consequences to himself, as long as he could satisfy his revenge.

Grant checked the clock on the dashboard. 3:40 A.M. He had been driving for almost an hour, and had twenty-five minutes left. He was on Route 6. He should be seeing Pine Creek Gorge soon.

He had to obey instructions to the letter for Colette's sake. How had Hutchinson put it? *Keep everything copacetic.*

Grant's back stiffened. Where had he heard that expression before? That's what seemed familiar, the something he couldn't identify.

Suddenly it flooded back like a wave of freezing water washing over him.

It had always been used by his former agent, Jack Hanlon, the man he fired for forging checks.

Hanlon always used to say, "Keep everything copacetic" when referring to Grant's bookings, travel schedule, media interviews, and whatnot. But that was more than fifteen years ago. Grant had forgotten about him. Could he have harbored a grudge all these years?

Although Grant had never considered him an enemy, Hanlon did have a motive—Grant had fired him, and when word spread throughout the industry of his dishonesty, Hanlon had been blackballed. Then Grant lost track of him. But those strange familiarities that Grant couldn't identify before now rushed through his mind like the pieces of a puzzle rapidly coming into place: the eyes in the photograph that seemed familiar; the undisguised voice he couldn't quite recognize; the phony name uncovered by the feds; the kidnapper's knowledge of Grant's interest in classical music and jazz; the often-repeated expression that just surfaced again after fifteen years. And a possible motive for revenge. It was all there, and mere coincidence couldn't explain such a unique combination of facts.

His grip tightened on the steering wheel. *The kidnapper has to be Jack Hanlon. Hanlon and Hutchinson are the same man.*

Although the person he had seen in the photograph looked like a stranger, Hanlon's appearance could have changed dramatically over fifteen years. But why would he hold Grant responsible for the death of someone?

Then he remembered that years ago Jack Hanlon's wife and a man had been found dead, brutally murdered in bed. He recalled the shock of reading the newspaper account of the double murder, which, to the best of his knowledge, had never been solved. Or, if it had been solved, he never read anything more about it. God, how many years ago had that been? And what did that tragedy have to do with him? Hanlon couldn't possibly hold Grant responsible for her death.

Or could he?

Grant picked up the phone and tried to call Dowling again, but the battery was so low that he couldn't get through. Damn, this was information that Dowling and Santucci needed to know. He tossed the phone on the passenger seat. Driving on unfamiliar roads, he was forced to keep to the speed limit; he wasn't gaining any time for Dowling and his men to catch up.

Grant saw the sign for Pine Creek Gorge, and in a flash a deer darted before his car and suddenly stopped in the glare of the headlights. The road was too narrow to swerve the car around the deer. He hit the brake so hard he almost came out of his seat as the Lamborghini spun with Grant fighting to regain control. He cut the wheel to the left, but he overcompensated, then cut it to the right, his foot still on the brake. The car spun again as it banked to the left and went off the road, smashing into a tree.

Grant was dazed, shaken, but unharmed. His seat belt had kept him from being thrown from the car. He took a deep breath. The engine was still running, and he instinctively shut it off, then immediately regretted doing so. What if it wouldn't start again? He took a few seconds to clear his head. He saw that the Lamborghini had taken most of the impact on the right side.

Grant fumbled with the door handle, relieved that the door opened. He got out slowly, and felt a sharp pain in his leg from a muscle spasm. He limped to the right side of the car and inspected the damage. The door was smashed and the right side of the hood was slightly dented and buckled. Thank God no other car was behind or in front of him, or there would have been corpses sprawled along the road. He looked at his watch. 3:57 A.M. He had to move. Would the car start? He rubbed his leg and limped to the front of the car. He released and opened the hood. Everything seemed in order. Then he noticed a flat, rectangular device about the size of a book near the battery. It was dislodged and cracked and had wires that were disconnected from a battery pack.

His heart sank. *The transmitter. Of all the rotten luck.*

Grant couldn't wait for Dowling and his men. Time had run out. He only had a few minutes to reach the cabin. He removed the smashed transmitter and battery pack and tossed them in the front seat.

He was still shaken, unsteady, but he got in the car, held his breath and turned the key in the ignition. *Please God,* he prayed, *let it start.* The Lamborghini spurted. No good. He tried again. The engine spurted a second time, then fired. Grant sighed with relief, inched the car back onto the road, and started to make a slow, but sharp U-turn. The engine sounded all right.

He backed up, completed the turn, and headed north again toward his destination. It had to be somewhere close in the black wilderness. But Grant could no longer rely on Dowling and his special team of agents to rescue Colette and to bring her captor to justice.

He was utterly alone. Grant's knuckles turned white as he gripped the wheel. Colette's fate—his own fate—now depended solely on him.

CHAPTER TWENTY

The kidnapper dragged Kassler's body to the Mercedes, parked about seventy feet in front of the cabin. He opened the door and placed the body across the front seat. The police would find Sam Kassler there eventually. He didn't want a dead body in the cabin. He didn't want anything around to remind him that his plan was not perfect, not foolproof, not without some element of surprise. He had come too far, planned too carefully, to be subjected to any more surprises.

He looked down at the slashed cadaver with its mouth open, sprawled across the front seat. *What was this son of a bitch up to? He already sold the cabin, so what brought him here at this hour?*

Time was getting short, and he knew he would never have the answer, but he didn't like loose ends. Loose ends could trip you up. He learned that many years ago from Montgomery, who was a perfectionist with his performances. Montgomery. He must not lose sight of why he was there. The hell with Kassler.

He went to his car, in back of the cabin, and retrieved the Smith and Wesson .38 caliber revolver. He would have preferred to use a knife on Montgomery, but that would only work if he took him by surprise. And he didn't intend to take Montgomery by surprise. A knife would be too risky. With a knife, he would have to get too close and risk arm-to-arm combat, and he wasn't going to take the chance that the mentalist might disarm him. The revolver was safer. He wanted to take his pleasure a little at a time, draw it out as long as possible. Wound Montgomery, disable him, force him to watch as he methodically worked on Colette. *Then* it would be time to use the knife on Montgomery—while the mentalist was helpless.

He returned to the cabin. Colette looked exhausted. She was no longer attractive with her bruised face, puffed lower lip, and her hair stringy and matted with sweat. He couldn't detect fear in her face anymore, only defeat, hopelessness. She had given up.

He sat at the table and stared at her. "Do you know what I think your problem is, Colette?"

She didn't answer.

"I think when I told you that someone was approaching the cabin, you thought it was your lover boy, who had come to rescue you. You were disappointed when it turned out to be Kassler. Isn't that right?"

She shook her head. "No, that isn't right. Please...you've already killed one person. Haven't you had enough of killing? Grant hasn't done anything to you. If you stole money from him, you brought your misfortune on yourself. Can't you see that?"

He folded his arms. "Well now, isn't this interesting. I have a philosopher on my hands. You have talents I'm not even aware of."

Colette looked at him with disgust. "You've already hurt Grant enough by taking out your revenge on me. What more do you want? Please...what good will it do you to kill again? How can you possibly find any satisfaction in that? I'm begging you to think rationally about this."

"You really haven't given up, have you? And I thought you had resigned yourself to your fate. You surprise me, Colette. You think you can talk me out of this? You think all you have to do is shed a few tears and beg for your life and your lover's life? How very foolish of you. I've been living for this day for a long time, and I don't care anymore about my own life. I thought I made that clear to you."

She fought back her tears. "You made it clear. It's just that..."

"It's just that what? It's just that you can't accept it. Is that what you were going to say?"

"Yes."

"Too bad," he said. "I want to know more about Kassler."

She lowered her gaze as a tear from her cheek struck the bare wooden floor. "I told you all I know."

"Wrong. If he was your client, you know more about him than you've told me."

She looked up and met his horrible magnified eyes peering at her behind his dark-rimmed glasses. "What more do you want to know?"

"Did he ever talk to you about this place?"

"No. I told you. I didn't know this shack belonged to him. I can't even imagine him owning such a place."

Hutchinson squinted and drummed his fingers on the table, weighing the truthfulness of her answers. "What type of a person was he? Trusting or suspicious?"

Colette coughed. "I didn't know him that well...only in business matters."

"He came here for some reason. Tell me what it is or I'll beat it out of you."

"Dear God, how many times must I tell you? I don't know. I swear I don't know."

Hutchinson stopped drumming his fingers and leaned forward in his chair. "Take a guess."

Colette was silent for a few seconds. "I don't know what you want me to tell you. I don't have the answer. I was shocked to see him come in here."

He studied her. He lighted a cigarette, held the smoke in a deep breath, and blew a thin stream at the ceiling. Finally he said, "You know, Colette, I think you're telling the truth. I really do. I just wanted to be sure."

She was still looking at him. "Why did you kill him? You didn't even know him. Why on earth did you do it?"

The kidnapper smiled. "Because he was an intruder, and I can't have anyone intrude on my plans, not at the final stage of the game. So don't be upset, little girl. It really shouldn't matter to you that he's dead. In just a short while, you and your lover boy are going to join him."

Jim Dowling and Dan Merrick studied the computer screen. "I don't know what the hell happened," Merrick said.

"Pull over on the side of the road," Dowling said to Lapanski, who steered the van to the side of a small embankment and stopped. "Damn it," Dowling said, "something's wrong."

Santucci leaned over Dowling's shoulder. "What do you mean?"

"Grant just disappeared from the screen."

"How's that possible?" Santucci asked.

Dowling rubbed his chin. "Something must've happened to the transmitter. It might've malfunctioned. Of all the goddamn times for this to happen."

Vasquez was sitting on the edge of his seat. "What can you do about it?" he asked.

"Not a damn thing," Dowling said. He looked at Merrick, who was working the console. After another minute, Merrick finally stopped and turned to Dowling. "I'm afraid it's useless. I can't make contact with him."

Dowling pulled out a map. "Our last point of contact was here." He pointed to a location. Santucci, Vasquez and Merrick were all hunched over, looking at the map as Dowling spoke. "From Route 220 North, he turned onto Route 6 and kept traveling north," Dowling said, tracing the route with his finger. "We lost contact with him about here."

"Yes," Merrick confirmed, "that's where the signal stopped."

Dowling checked his watch. "We've already lost a little time. I'd say we're now between twenty minutes and a half hour away. We've got to get to that point as soon as possible."

Santucci slapped his thigh. " I hope to hell he knows the transmitter isn't working and stays exactly where he is."

"I don't see how he could," Dowling said. He motioned to Merrick. "Call Conner, fill him in on what our situation is, and tell him to keep following us." Dan Conner was commander of the SWAT team a quarter of a mile behind them.

"Let's get going," Dowling said. Lapanski started the van, and they were on the move again.

Tom Santucci exchanged glances with Vasquez, then looked at Dowling. "I don't like this a goddamn bit," Tom said. "That transmitter shouldn't have malfunctioned. What the hell else can go wrong?"

Dowling spoke in a low voice. "I'll tell you what else can go wrong—if we get to that point where we lost Montgomery and he's not there, we're screwed and so is he. We have no other way to establish contact with him."

"We could search the area, "Vasquez said. "You have a back-up team to help."

"We might be forced to do that as a last resort," Dowling said, "but searching miles of wilderness at night to find him would take a lot of time, and time is something we don't have."

Santucci clenched his jaw. "Neither does Grant."

Grant looked in the rearview mirror. No cars behind or ahead of him. The lime glow from the lighted dashboard cast an eerie reflection on his face. He checked the odometer, inched the car to the side of the road, and stopped. He had driven exactly eight miles from Pine Creek Gorge. This is where the kidnapper told him he would find the cabin. He got out of the car and walked a short distance, surveying the area. He could only see woods filled with trees and underbrush, but no cabin.

Grant looked at his watch for the hundredth time. 4:18 A.M. He was thirteen minutes past his deadline. The accident had cost him precious time.

He won't kill Colette, Grant kept telling himself. *He's using her to torture me. He needs her. He won't kill her because I'm thirteen minutes late. I'm right. I have to be right. Please God, don't let him kill her.*

Where the hell was the cabin? Did he drive past it? Was it still up ahead somewhere? The cabin was supposed to be eight miles from the Gorge, so it must be visible from the road. But he couldn't see a cabin. He couldn't see much of anything in the dark.

Grant ran back to his car and retrieved his Beretta .32 semiautomatic pistol and a flashlight from his glove compartment. He went to the opposite side of the road, flashed the light, and spotted a pathway through the woods. He worked his way through the heavy underbrush. He had gone sixty or seventy yards into the woods when the stark realization suddenly gripped him. He was lost. There was no cabin. Time was slipping away. Would it cost Colette her life? No, he mustn't think that. But what should he do? Had he made a mistake, missed a road somewhere? He had no one to turn to. He shined the light on his watch. 4:24 A.M. Grant's forehead beaded with perspiration; fear swelled within him.

He won't kill her. Please God, he won't kill her.

Colette was lying on the cot with the blanket wrapped around her, new duct tape covering her mouth, watching the sadistic killer pace the room. She knew Grant's deadline had past. Something had gone wrong. She remembered Hutchinson's threat. If Grant didn't show by 4:05 A.M., Hutchinson would kill her. But it was almost 4:30 A.M. by her watch, and all Hutchinson did for the last twenty-five minutes was check his watch every few minutes, peer out the door, and then pace the room. Her toe was throbbing, her lower lip was throbbing, every muscle in her body was throbbing. What had happened to Grant? She was torn. She wanted Grant to save her, but she didn't want him to be in harm's way. If Grant did come to this horrible place, there was more than a good chance he would die. They all would die.

Hutchinson finally stopped pacing, and pushed his glasses up on the bridge of his nose. "Your lover has been delayed. That's not like him. Either he took a wrong road, or he and the cops are up to something." He went to the door again and opened it a crack. "They might already have this placed staked out, but I can't see anything suspicious out there." He closed the door and took several steps toward her. He took the .38 revolver from his belt and jammed the muzzle under her chin, forcing her head up.

Her eyes widened. Was this it? Was her life going to end now?

"I haven't killed you yet because I want you alive for our little party. But if the cops come and try to talk me into giving myself up or try to rush this place, you get it first. No one's going to take me alive. So if I can't take out Montgomery, I can at least take care of you. And he'll have to live with that." Then he retaped her hands behind her back.

Dowling and his crew were on Route 6, approaching the area where they'd lost contact with Montgomery. Dan Merrick was still monitoring the computer in case they would unexpectedly reestablish contact, but he and Dowling had little hope of that.

Tom Santucci and Emilio Vasquez were sitting erect in the back, looking out the front windshield, hoping to spot the Lamborghini.

"This is about it," Dowling said to Tony Lapanski. "Somewhere around here. Drive about another half mile, then pull over."

Lapanski drove slowly, while everyone in the van kept peering out the window. Santucci mumbled a few curses to himself. Finally, Lapanski slowed the van and parked it to the side of the road. "We should be close to the point where we lost him," he said. "What do you think, Jim?"

Dowling rubbed his chin, and motioned to Merrick. "Call Conner, and tell him we're waiting for him. Tell him we haven't been able to locate Montgomery, but we'll still stay on this road to see if we can spot him. Conner should start checking the secondary roads."

"Christ, that'll take forever," Santucci said.

Dowling turned to him. "You have a better idea?"

Santucci shook his head. "I'm afraid not. I'm just worried to death about Grant and Colette. He and I go back a long way."

"I understand," Dowling said, "but we have no alternative. Conner and I will divide the area up within a two-mile radius. If both of us come up empty, we might need Conner's men to fan out and start a foot search through the woods."

Merrick placed the call to Dan Conner of the SWAT team. A minute later, Merrick took the earphones off. "Conner's on his way."

Dowling glanced at him. "What did he say?"

Merrick hesitated for a few seconds. "He thinks the only thing we're going to end up finding is a corpse."

Surrounded by white pines and hemlocks, Grant kept working his way through the underbrush, fighting his fear of not finding the cabin or, if he did, finding Colette dead. No matter how he tried to convince himself that Hanlon would let her live, his nagging doubt about the unpredictable actions of the maniac still plagued him.

He came to a small clearing in the woods, and directed the flashlight beam around the area. A thick, virgin forest in the mountains that defied him to find what it kept well hidden. He heard a waterfall somewhere near. A powerful wind began to rustle the underbrush, quickly building in intensity until the forest wailed and groaned to its immense force. At night, the wind could drop the temperature thirty degrees in these mountains within minutes. Grant shivered, and turned up the collar of his jacket.

Suddenly, he thought he saw a crack of light somewhere in front of him, how far he couldn't tell. Then it was gone as quickly as it appeared. What was it? Were his eyes playing tricks on him in the dark? He aimed the flashlight in the direction of where he saw the light, but the beam was not powerful enough to illuminate anything beyond twenty or so feet.

Instinctively, Grant shut off the flashlight and stood in the dark, waiting. The wind in his face almost smothered his own breath. A minute later, he saw it again—a long sliver of faint light. It stayed a little longer this time, then it was gone. His eyes were *not* playing tricks. It was like—like a vertical ribbon of light from a door being opened just a few inches.

CHAPTER TWENTY-ONE

Jim Dowling and Dan Conner quickly mapped out the two-mile radius of roads they were to search, with Dowling staying on main arteries and Conner taking the more difficult secondary roads. They reasoned that Grant had been on main roads for the entire journey, and the kidnapper had to eventually make contact with him. If they were right, the kidnapper would plan his rendezvous with Grant in a secluded area, which meant that Grant would have to take a secondary road through the woods somewhere. If they were right, Conner's SWAT veterans would be better equipped to handle the situation should they encounter the kidnapper. And maybe Grant and Colette would have a little better chance of staying alive. If they were right.

They told Santucci and Vasquez that they were relying on their experience, but Santucci and Vasquez feared they were only guessing.

The night wind whipped through the forest with such force that Grant had to hold on to the trees as he made his way toward the light source that had now vanished. Finding his way in the dark was more difficult then he imagined, his sense of direction encumbered by fighting the wind. The gale muffled the crunch of the thick underbrush beneath his shoes. He could barely see from the continual thrust of wind in his face. The light had come from some not-too-distant point in front of him.

Grant stopped. He saw a car parked thirty feet ahead of him, almost invisible in the dark.

Then he spotted the cabin.

An old log cabin, maybe a hundred feet away, smoke coming from its chimney. His heart was racing.

This *had* to be the spot where he was to meet Hanlon. The last stop of his fated journey and his first step into hell.

He withdrew the .32 Beretta from his jacket and approached the cabin in a crouched position. As he drew closer, he noticed that the car was a Mercedes. No other sign of life in the cabin, except the chimney smoke, but he had no doubt that the light he had spotted came from this cabin.

Still crouched, Grant worked his way toward the car. He finally reached it. The Mercedes appeared to be empty. Rather than stand and peer into the window, he decided to remain crouched as he checked the door on the driver's side. It wasn't locked. He wasn't about to take any chances. He opened the door slowly, his finger on the trigger of the Beretta.

His entire body jolted back, and he almost lost his balance. In front of him, sprawled across the front seat, was the bloodstained body of a man, his mouth still open as if trying to cry out. Grant suddenly recognized him. It looked like Sam Kassler. He couldn't believe it. Was he mistaken? He leaned into the car and closely examined the man's face. It was definitely Kassler.

Good Christ, what had happened to him? What was he doing in this godforsaken place? Grant's first instinct was to get back to the road, to flag a car so he could find some help, but he knew it was useless. He hadn't seen another car for miles.

He left the car door open, not wanting to make a sound. He rose and made his way toward the cabin, careful to remain hidden by the trees. A gust of wind slapped him as it whistled through the woods with bullet speed.

The cabin was now about fifty feet ahead of him.

He kept low, slowly working his way closer. When he was no more than ten feet from the cabin, he stopped behind a tree barely wide enough to conceal him. He knew Jack Hanlon was inside, and he sensed that Colette must be inside, too. In his mind, the identity of the kidnapper was no longer in doubt.

Up to this point, he hadn't even thought about how he would confront Hanlon. His mind had been totally focused on matters that were more immediate and much more important—Colette's safety, trying to identify who the kidnapper could be and following instructions. Now, alone and with no time left, Grant had come to his own moment of truth. The kidnapper was prepared to kill, and, as much as Grant dreaded the reality of killing, he knew he had to be prepared to kill again, just as he had to kill as a soldier in Vietnam. He felt as though he were doomed by some quirk of fate to repeat a dreadful life episode without knowing if the final chapter would destroy him.

He observed the cabin. Should he shoot at the lock on the door and try to rush inside, take the kidnapper by surprise? No, he didn't have the advantage of surprise; Hanlon was waiting for him. If Grant excited Hanlon with such a move, he might kill Colette. He had to let the kidnapper know that even though he was late, he was still following instructions, that the madman was still in control.

Grant put the gun under his belt and kept his suit jacket buttoned. He would have to pretend he was unarmed, make his presence known to Hanlon, and get inside the cabin. Once inside, he would make sure Colette was all right, then, at the first opportunity, try to take him out. If Hanlon tried to search him, he would have to get close enough to do so, and that was all the opportunity Grant would need.

Suddenly the cabin door squeaked open half way, and the dim glow from the cabin bathed the entrance. Grant couldn't see anyone, but a deep chill iced his heart as he heard the familiar voice say, "Drop your gun on the ground and come inside. I've been waiting for you."

The door opened the rest of the way. Grant's heart sank. He took the pistol from his belt and threw it on the ground several feet in front of him where it was plainly visible. The wind began to cover it with fallen leaves.

He couldn't see anything inside except the dim light coming from the open door. He walked toward the cabin.

Dan Conner, the SWAT commander, called Dowling from the phone in his van. "No luck, Jim. This is like looking for a minnow in the Atlantic Ocean. We'll continue trying, if that's what you want, but I'm afraid it's useless."

Dowling heard the resignation in Conner's voice. "I guess you're right, Dan, but we just can't give up. Montgomery's out there alone. If that poor bastard's still alive, he doesn't have a chance if we give up on him. Keep the search going. That's all we can do."

Dowling feared this case would end in failure, but he vowed to himself that no matter how it ended, he would go back to his family and never leave them again. He didn't want his last case to be a failure, but he had made his decision. He would no longer be a field agent. He would parlay his experience into an administrative position within the Bureau, that desk job he often said he didn't want, which now looked just fine. As long as he could spend the precious time he needed with Susan and Linda and Billy. They were all that mattered to him now. He would call Susan the first chance he had to tell her what she had been wanting to hear for a long time.

"If that's the way you want it, okay," Conner said, "but we could be out here for a week and come up empty. At some point, we've got to call this off."

"I know," Dowling said, "but not just yet."

Santucci ran his fingers through his hair, and looked at Dowling. "Jesus, don't tell me they want to give up."

Dowling shook his head. "It's not that they want to give up...it's just that these guys are trained to do a job, and they're frustrated that they can't do it."

"That's not the way it sounded to me," Santucci said. "From what I heard you say, it sounded like they think this is a wild goose chase."

Dowling sighed. "Kidnappings are never easy, Tom, but this situation with Grant...this complicates it. If I had my way, he wouldn't be out there alone. One of our men would be with him, but he wouldn't hear of it. I should've insisted on it, but I didn't plan on losing him like this. The fact of the matter is that he's not trained for this kind of thing."

Santucci's face reddened. "Let's not blame Grant for the predicament he's in. He's just trying to save his girl."

"I know that," Dowling snapped. "You don't have to tell me that."

Santucci leaned forward in his seat. "Have you thought about getting a helicopter here to see if we can spot Grant's car?"

"I've thought about it, but I decided against it," Dowling said.

"Mind telling us why?" Vasquez asked.

Dowling observed Santucci and Vasquez. They were both searching for a miracle that their years of police experience told them would not be forthcoming. "On the positive side," Dowling said, "a chopper using infrared technology has a lot better chance of spotting Grant's car than we do. On the negative side, if the kidnapper is anywhere in this area—and there's good reason to believe he is—he could easily spot the chopper, which is a dead giveaway that Grant's being followed. We've got to be careful we don't panic this lunatic. He's liable to go off the deep end and kill Colette." Dowling paused for a few seconds. "I'd say the negative outweighs the positive, wouldn't you?"

Santucci nodded, and Vasquez grunted something, indicating that he agreed.

"What the hell happened?" Santucci said more to himself than to anyone else. "Where could Grant be?"

"I wish to God I had the answer," Dowling said, responding to what he knew was a private thought spoken almost unconsciously. "Look, I know you guys are concerned about your friend and his girl. Believe me, I'm damn concerned about them, too. This whole thing took a lousy turn, but, under the circumstances, we're doing everything we can without jeopardizing Colette's safety—and Grant's, too."

Vasquez lowered his gaze. "Maybe there's one thing we haven't thought of."

"What?" Dowling and Santucci almost asked the question in unison.

"Pray."

"I wouldn't object to that a bit," Dowling said.

They drove into the night in silence. None of them wanted to admit that the situation seemed hopeless.

Suddenly, Dowling shouted, "Look, over there." He pointed to a car barely visible in shadows about a hundred yards ahead of them on the side of the road. "It's Grant's car." Everyone peered out the front window.

"I see it," Lapanski said and accelerated the van.

Grant entered the cabin. He immediately saw Colette to his left against the wall. She was sitting on the cot covered in a blanket, her mouth sealed with duct tape, her hands tied behind her back. She looked abused, bewildered, helpless. She looked wonderful; she was alive.

Suddenly he was aware of a figure behind him. Grant turned and looked at him. "I knew it. I knew it was you, you son of a bitch. What've you done to her?"

Jack Hanlon, alias Frank Hutchinson, faced Grant as he closed the door with his back and stepped forward. The .38 revolver in his right hand was pointed at Grant. "Hello, Montgomery. I've been waiting such a long time for this."

"I'm here now, Hanlon. I've done everything you asked. Now let her go."

"How did you know it was me?"

"I figured it out."

"I should've guessed as much. Why are you late? You and the cops playing games with me?"

Grant shook his head. "No games. I was in an accident. A deer jumped in front of my car, and I hit a tree. It took a while to get the car back on the road."

The kidnapper narrowed his eyes. "I don't believe you."

"You can believe it or not. I also had trouble finding this place. Your directions made it sound like I couldn't miss it. I'm here now, so let her go."

"Not so fast." Hanlon went to the table and turned up the light of the kerosene lamp, his gun still pointed at Grant. "Let me take a good look at you. It's been a lot of years." He studied Grant for a full minute. "Yes, you haven't changed much. A little older, but the years have been good to you. The years haven't been as good to me. You can see that, can't you?"

Grant stared at him. This man who stood before him, ready to kill him, was his former agent, all right. No doubt about that, even though his appearance had changed dramatically. But now he was someone else—a stranger. The Jack Hanlon he knew was a good agent until he became a drug addict and a thief, but, even so, he wasn't a killer. He wasn't a psychotic, consumed with hatred. The man now standing before him had completely changed, and not just physically; his psyche had changed. He was driven now by a demon more powerful, more deadly than the heroin that had once surged through his veins. The demon within him was revenge; it controlled him totally. And he could never be free of it until the demon's appetite was satiated.

"I can see that you've changed," Grant said.

Hanlon smiled. "Really. And why do you think that is?"

"I don't know, Jack. I wish I did."

"Oh, now it's Jack, is it? Well, aren't we getting friendly again." He gestured his gun toward the table. "Sit down, Grant. Let's all be on a first-name basis. As long as we're going to be friendly, I might as well be hospitable. Wouldn't want you to think I've forgotten my manners."

Grant sat in one of the chairs next to the rectangular oak table. He looked at Colette. Her eyes were frozen in fear, indicating she knew what the maniac killer had planned for them.

With his revolver still trained on Grant, Hanlon went to Colette and ripped the tape off her mouth. "There, I'll bet that's more comfortable, isn't it?" He looked at her for a few seconds, then slapped her across the face with the back of his left hand. "Answer me when I talk to you."

Grant jumped up, but Hanlon put the muzzle of the gun on Colette's temple. "Sit down, hero, or she gets it now."

Grant sat down slowly.

Still looking at Colette, Hanlon turned the gun toward Grant. "I asked you if it was more comfortable without the tape."

"Yes," she said hoarsely. "It's more comfortable."

"For God's sake," Grant said, sitting on the edge of the chair, "leave her alone. Take it out on me. I'm the one you want for some crazy reason." He had to draw Hanlon's attention away from her.

Hanlon finally looked at him with oversized eyes flashing an excitement he couldn't contain. "Yes, you're the one I want. We couldn't have the party without you. Did you know we're going to have a party in your honor?"

"I'm afraid I wasn't aware of it," Grant said. He sensed that although Hanlon was exhilarated by his mastery of the situation, he was in no hurry to kill him. The monster wanted to savor the moment.

"Of course you're aware of it," Hanlon said. "You got my invitation to the party, didn't you? You're here, aren't you?"

"Okay, I'm here. But if you're going to kill me, I at least have a right to know why. It couldn't possibly be because I fired you for stealing money from me. There has to be something more to it than that."

"Oh yes," Hanlon said, his breathing more rapid. "There's much more to it than that. There's fifteen years of hell to it. Fifteen long years that you owe me. I've been living for this day, you know. Everything's copacetic now because payday is here at last." He stopped to take a deep breath. "And you're the one who's gonna pay big time for those fifteen years."

Grant knew that no matter what skill he had perfected as a mentalist, he could not penetrate this man's blind hatred. He was a madman ready to explode in a frenzy of violence, held back by a fragile thread of perverted pleasure he wanted to prolong. But the thread was about to break at any moment. "I don't know how you can blame me for whatever's happened to you over the last fifteen years. You and I parted company back then, and I haven't seen you since. We've had nothing to do with each other in all those years."

Hanlon forced a laugh. "Very good. But your acting job is no less than I expected. After all, you were once the world's leading mentalist, and you didn't get there without being a good actor. You haven't lost your touch."

"I still don't understand," Grant said. "Let's quit playing games. Why do you want—"

Hanlon interrupted. "No, not so fast. After all, what's a party without games? We can't have any fun unless we play at least one game. And I'll tell you how the three of us are going to play it. I'll ask you a question, Grant, like why do I want to kill you? And for each incorrect answer, I'll put a bullet in Colette. Maybe one in her shoulder, one in her kneecap, one in her wrist, places like that. So you can't afford too many incorrect answers, can you? How does that sound?"

Grant grimaced. "For the love of God man, take it out on me and let her go. Go ahead and put the bullets in me for every incorrect answer. That's what you really want, isn't it?"

"No, no, we play this my way," Hanlon said, relishing the moment. "My party. I make the rules. All right now, everyone get ready to play." He walked backwards toward Colette, his eyes fixed on Grant. Hanlon placed the gun on Colette's right shoulder.

The click of the hammer being cocked chilled Grant to the bone. Colette recoiled and looked at him helplessly.

"All right, Grant, first question. Why do you think I want to kill you?"

Grant raised his hand. He had to come up with something. Stall the killer. Play for time. Anything to keep him from squeezing the trigger. "Before we play your game, I have a question."

Hanlon waited for a few seconds. "Well, what is it?"

"I recognized Sam Kassler in the car. What happened?"

"Oh, so you knew Kassler, too," Hanlon said. "My, we really are just one happy family here. I'll tell you what happened. He wasn't invited to the party, but he crashed it, anyway. So I killed him."

Grant was still sitting on the edge of his chair. "What was he doing here?"

"I was hoping you might be able to tell me that. You're the mind reader."

Grant shrugged, taking a deep breath. "I don't know. I only know that he was one of Colette's clients."

Colette's voice cracked when she said, "I just found out that he owned this cabin. I have no idea why he came here tonight."

Grant gritted his teeth as he looked at the bruises on her face and lip. At that moment, he wanted to kill Hanlon. But he forced himself to speak, trying to keep the psychopath preoccupied as long as possible. "He had to have a reason for coming here. What time did he get here? Maybe that'll tell us what he was up to."

"I don't know," Colette answered. "I've lost track of time."

"That's enough," Hanlon said. "At this point, it doesn't make any difference why he was here. He was an uninvited guest who paid the price for party crashing." Still watching Grant, he nudged Colette's shoulder with the muzzle of the revolver. "You haven't answered my question, Grant. Why do you think I want to kill you? Remember, your answer better be accurate, or she gets one."

Grant knew he couldn't stall any longer. No matter what answer he would give, Hanlon was going to shoot. Begging him to let her go wouldn't help, and Hanlon was beyond reason. He took the only alternative he had.

Grant said, "Because I killed your wife, and buried her body."

Hanlon suddenly turned toward Grant. "What the..." In that one split second that his incredible answer startled Hanlon, Grant sprang from the chair. But he wasn't quick enough. Hanlon fired and the bullet smashed into Grant's left shoulder, knocking him to the floor.

Colette screamed and lunged against Hanlon, shoving him off balance as he fell. Hanlon landed on his side; his head hit one of the legs of the table as his glasses flew from his face.

Grant was on the floor, holding his bleeding shoulder. He saw Hanlon on his knees, groping for his glasses, which were only four feet from him, his gun still in his hand.

Grant suddenly realized that Hanlon was practically blind without his glasses.

Grant sprang to his feet and grabbed the kerosene lamp. He hollered, "Colette, get out of the way." She rolled on the floor, away from Hanlon, her hands still tied behind her back.

At the sound of Grant's voice, Hanlon blindly fired the revolver twice. The first bullet blasted into the wall behind Grant, missing him by inches. The second one lodged in the thick wooden table. Then Hanlon's left hand discovered the glasses.

Grant threw the kerosene lamp with all the force he could muster, and it smashed against Hanlon as flames raced across the killer's body.

Hanlon yelled, dropped the glasses and revolver, frantically slapping his body with both hands, trying to put out the flames. But the kerosene had splashed over his chest and face and the flames spread swiftly.

Screaming, he lunged at the door in panic and dashed out as if somehow he could escape the ravaging flames, but the night wind fueled the fire, and the flames instantly engulfed his entire body.

Hanlon ran blindly with his outstretched arms like a burning cross into the night, shrieking, illuminating the woods in a directionless wild run as a human inferno. Within seconds, the flaming cross folded and fell to the ground as his tortuous scream choked off to an agonizing groan, then finally ended in silence.

The stationary fire swirled into wild shapes, leaping to the snap of the wind. Then slowly, the blaze began to die out as the wind subsided, and black flecks of clothing and flesh sparked and burst from the center of the ebbing flames and fluttered to the ground.

They examined Grant's car. "He was in an accident, all right," Dowling said.

Lapanski and Merrick looked inside the hood. "Look at this," Merrick said. "Grant picked up the transmitter. It was busted. He knew he lost cost contact with us."

As they continued to inspect the car, Tom Santucci was the first to spot it. "Look, there's a fire over there, on the right."

"I see it," Dowling said. "Maybe a brushfire. Let's check it out." Dowling called Dan Conner. "Dan, we're still on the main road by Pine Creek Gorge. We just found Grant's car. He's got to be somewhere close. There's a small fire about a half mile to our right. We don't know what the hell it is. How long will it take you to get here?"

"I can be there in about ten minutes," Conner said.

Dowling hesitated for a moment. "Wait a minute...something's not right. That doesn't appear to be a brush fire...it's dying out. That might be man-made...we're not going to wait for you, Dan. We're going in now to investigate it."

"Better to wait until we get there, Jim."

"Can't," Dowling said. "We're out of time. Just get here as soon as you can."

"I'm on my way."

"What do you think it is?" Santucci asked.

"I don't know," Dowling said, "but these woods are too dense to take the van in. Whatever the hell it is, we'll have to go in on foot." Each man drew his weapon. They went to side of the road, approaching the woods. Dowling crouched and peered through high-powered binoculars. "What the hell is that burning? There's a small house or a cabin out there with the door open. It's visible by the fire. Someone has to be in there, there's smoke from the chimney...wait, I think there's a couple people inside...we might've hit pay dirt."

Dowling turned to Merrick and Lapanski. Then he looked at Santucci and Vasquez. No one said a word. "We're going in. Spread out and stay low."

The fire was almost out, leaving a small area of smoldering, scorched earth and the charred remains of Jack Hanlon.

Grant found the dagger in the toolbox, and cut the tape binding Colette's wrists. As soon as she was cut free, she turned to Grant. His left shoulder was bleeding freely, and the side of his jacket was covered in blood.

"Grant, we've got to stop the bleeding." Despite her injured toe, Colette hobbled to the cot where Hanlon had cut off her clothing, and grabbed her velvet dress from the floor. The blanket fell from her body as she rushed back to Grant and placed the rolled-up garment on his wound. "Hold it there as tightly as you can." Then suddenly Colette sank to her knees naked. She could no longer control it and began to weep, like a dam bursting in a flood of tears.

He knelt next to her, put his left hand over her dress, pressing it against his wound. With his right hand, he covered her with the blanket, and placed his arm around her. "It's over, baby. It's all over now. Go ahead and cry. Get it all out."

She managed to say it through the tears. "I never thought I'd see you again."

He heard the faint call of his name in the distance. "Listen," he said. Colette tried to stop crying as she wiped away her tears. He heard his name being called again. "It's Santucci," he said. "I'd recognize his voice anywhere. They've spotted us." He rose, went to the open door and shouted as loud as he could. "This way, over here, in the log cabin." The shout drained him of what little energy he had left, and he braced himself against the doorframe.

Seeing that he was unsteady from loss of blood, Colette rushed to him and placed her hand on top of his, covering his wound, his blood soaking through her dress and onto his fingers. Draped in the blanket, she rested her head on his chest for a moment, then looked up at him.

"You need to get to a hospital," she said.

"I guess we both could use some medical attention."

She started to look outside at the remains of the killer, but Grant turned her head away with his hand. "No, don't look at him. It's better not to see it."

The sun was just beginning to rise as the early rays of pale light splintered through the trees. The wilderness started to take shape at first blush of light with foliage and wildflowers blossoming among the white pines and hemlocks. The fragrance of mountain laurel filtered through the woods, and they could hear a mounting chorus of songbirds against the gush of a distant waterfall. Daybreak had washed away the dark hours of the past.

Grant turned and saw the five men running toward them less than a hundred yards away. He held Colette closer.

"We almost didn't make it," she said, watching the men in the distance getting closer.

"Almost doesn't count."

She touched the side of his face and held his gaze. "After this, don't ever leave my side for a second," she said.

Grant shook his head. "When I think of what you had to go through for just knowing me... I'm dangerous to your health—probably to your life."

"You're necessary to my life," she said with mist in her eyes, "and right now I need to hear you say it again."

Grant smiled through his pain, remembering another time, not so long ago. "As often as you want," he whispered.

ABOUT THE AUTHOR

Robert Aiello is a former public relations executive turned author. He completed a 30-year career with Ketchum Public Relations, taking an early retirement as senior vice president and associate director of the agency's Pittsburgh, PA office before turning to write suspense novels. He is one of several contributing authors of the book *What Happens in Public Relations*, published in 1981 by the American Management Association. During his career, Robert has written numerous business articles published by trade and professional journals. He was awarded the first annual Cornelius S. McCarthy Award from Duquesne University, Pittsburgh, for outstanding achievement in the field of journalism.

Robert has had a life-long interest in the branch of magic called mentalism, and has drawn on his knowledge of the subject in writing *The Desperate Hours, Shadow in the Mirror* and his first novel, *The Deceivers*. His novels have received praise from various publications and from several nationally acclaimed mystery authors. An active member of the Mystery Writers of America, Robert lives in Pittsburgh with his wife, Mary Beth, and their golden retriever, Bailey.

Visit the author's web site at http://RobertAiello.com and e-mail him at authorbobby@verizon.net.

Printed in the United States
26971LVS00006B/1-33

9 781587 36448